The Ghost
An Angharad Jor
By G I

theghostsofmerthyr.wordpress.com

Dedicated to Laura for being there
to Owen for all he may be.

Preface

I am Merthyr born and Merthyr bred and when I die I will be Merthyr dead.

Having said that, I no longer live in the town of my birth having moved away in 1998 in order to find work as a fresh faced young graduate. When I left I thought my future was in I.T designing and building Web sites. Time passes though and as it does you change as a person and by 2005 I was no longer building Web sites and instead working for a Police force in the South East of England. Ten years later I have moved and changed and I now have many years more experience of the world that I didn't have before. Despite the fact that it is now nearly twenty years since I left Merthyr Tydfil it is still an important part of me and influences my life every day.

For most people Merthyr is indicative of a life of poverty and of unemployment. This is a perception that is not helped by the portrayal of the place by the mainstream media. If you are from Merthyr you know that this image is wrong, that the town is so much more than that. It is a town with a proud history, a revolutionary spirit and a hard edge. When you learn the history of Merthyr you will see why, this is the town of the 1831 Merthyr Rising and its martyr Dic Penderyn and the town that elected James Keir Hardie in 1900. Today, it is still a place where the people are inspired to do things by making their own rules, finding their own way and to hell with anyone who opposes them.

For me? I can only hope that I do the place justice.

Table of Contents

Chapter 1

Thursday 8th August 1844
Translation from the original Welsh of an extract from the Diary of Sergeant Ephraim Jones

My first day as a Sergeant in Merthyr Tydfil and the Inspector was eager to explain to me the primary focus of our role during this summer. He is determined to clamp down on the den of iniquity that is called China. In particular he wants to bring the current "Emperor" to justice so that, in his words, "God can judge him and find him wanting". I'm not surprised that he has taken such a position with regard to the place. It is a hive of sin and crime that impacts greatly on the functioning of a town whose iron works are essential to the economic and military success of the country. The Emperor is at the van guard of this, ruling China with an iron fist of violence and intimidation that hurts the people who come into contact with it.

Even before my meeting with the Inspector this morning I was called to the River Taff after a runner was sent to the newly built Police Station in Graham Street to report that a body had been found in the river. I made my way to Jacksons Bridge, the nearest crossing point to where the body could be seen and there I found the lifeless corpse of a young man lying face down in the water. Two of my Constables were already present along with a growing crowd of onlookers eager to see who had succumbed to the many criminals who prayed on the innocent. Nearby, on Bethesda Street the Arches that lead through to China stand, as if the entrance to Hades, those responsible likely to be hiding in the darkened streets beyond.

My enquiries later in the day revealed that the young man was a newly qualified lawyer from a well to do English family. He had been visiting the town as part of a delegation to meet with the

Crawshays while they are in residence at Cyfarthfa Castle. It appears that the last time he was seen alive was during the late hours of yesterday when he entered China with that infamous harlot and trickster Sian Bwthyn Bach leading him by the hand. That this young man should be dead in a river only a few yards away the following day, well it is fair to say that I want to have a long chat with Sian Bwthyn Bach. Meanwhile I understand that the Crawshays have sent message to London and it is expected that the Metropolitan Police will send representatives to take control of this case within the week. The Superintendent of Police here in Merthyr would never tolerate such interference and so the pressure is on to solve this before they arrive.

I had the body taken back to the Police Station for the doctor to check over. By the time I arrived the Inspector and the Superintendent were both in attendance along with the doctor, impatient with their perceived delay in my arrival. In their presence I assisted the doctor in undressing the young man and he was found to have three large stab wounds to his chest while his purse and money were missing. Robbery and death, a typical outcome for those from out of town who meet the prostitutes of China on the wrong day.

Thursday 8th August 2013

BANG!

The sound echoed throughout the apartment and roused Angharad from her slumber with a jolt. Her senses rapidly brought everything into sharp focus, the thumping headache from the night before, the crick in the neck from sleeping half slumped on the sofa. As sensation returned to the rest of her body she realised that there was a dampness in her trousers from where the contents of a half drunk bottle of vodka had spilt out. The bottle was still to be seen in the right hand that had held it as she had finally lost her battle against sleep.

BANG!

Stretching her senses out further, Angharad could see the pictures on the wall, the diaries and book on the shelf above the desk in the corner. The large television that hung on the wall to the side of the desk and which dominated the wall opposite the sofa. In front of the television sat a coffee table a second, empty bottle sitting on it and holding down the receipt for purchase dated just the day before.

The 36 hour shift that was the culmination of a desperate three week race to catch a monster who was preying on the prostitutes of Cardiff had taken its toll. He'd been caught, the deed had been done and he would not be free to commit his crimes again but the personal cost to those involved had been massive. One member of the team had received a phone call during the investigation telling him not to bother coming home because he'd missed his tenth Wedding anniversary, his wife distraught at what she saw was his inability to prioritise the family. Angharad had seen the bodies, the mutilation, the suffering and the face of the killer, as soon as she got home she fell back on the old trick, self-medication with a vast amount of alcohol.

BANG!

This time there was a sound of splintering wood, the sound came from the front door and was echoing down the hallway and through into the living room, someone was trying to break in. Luckily the door was thick and had three locks but Angharad knew she'd made enemies in her life. Enemies that might well wish to take revenge upon her for some perceived injustice they had suffered at her hands. She jumped to her feet and fighting the feeling of nausea from her thick head moved swiftly towards the front door. As she got to the door from the living room to the hallway she stopped and looked at the collection of truncheons and batons on the wall. Her eyes took in each one and she considered their suitability, a painted Glamorgan Constabulary truncheon from the 1840's, a Merthyr Constabulary truncheon from 1910, and a pair of late 1970's truncheons; one that was issued to her father and below that, a smaller version as issued to the women at the time. The female truncheon was specifically designed to be suitable for keeping in a Police issue handbag, such had been attitudes of that era. The last one in the list was also the meanest looking. A 1980's German riot stick with side handle, a present from a long lost friend who had served in the Bundespolizei.

Angharad grabbed the riot stick from its mounting and completed the last few strides into the hallway and up to the door. It would open to her left so she took up a position to the right, taking hold of the stick by the side handle.

BANG!

More splintering of wood, there was only one lock left and Angharad could feel her pulse quickening with anticipation. The moment was coming when she would have to spring into action. She reached into her left pocket for her mobile phone, whoever it was they were determined and unlikely to be on their own. The phone wasn't there and her mind wandered back to the night before. As she had walked into the apartment she had thrown the phone onto the sofa in drunken anger. Well, it was too late now to do anything about it, all she could do was hope that she could take on the threat by herself.

BANG!

The last lock gave way and the door swung open, bouncing off the wall, a head appeared in the doorway and Angharad leapt into action. Moving her right arm in a large arc, the riot stick swung out and round, the tip rapidly gathering momentum until it connected with her attacker's nose. There was an explosion of blood and a loud scream of pain before the head disappeared from sight. Shifting her grip from the side handle to the main grip, Angharad stepped out into the doorway to confront the next attacker and froze as her mind took in the scene before her.

Lying prone on the floor was the person whose nose she had just destroyed. Aged in his forties, he was wearing the uniform of a response officer in the South Wales Constabulary. Stood over him, gripped by indecision, was a second officer who was at most 20 years old and given his reaction, a new recruit. The younger officer was clearly now battling fear and panic at what he had witnessed. Looking beyond the officers, further into the corridor Angharad could see two Welsh Ambulance paramedics rooted to the ground with fear. They were clearly shocked by the sudden and unexpected outbreak of violence that had greeted them. Angharad dropped the riot stick and stepped forward to the young officer, grabbing hold of his trembling hands as he fumbled to draw his baton and pepper spray. The situation needed to be diffused quickly, this young boy in uniform needed reassurance but it was also essential that he was prevented from arming himself. In the back of Angharad's mind was the thought that if she got this wrong there was a good chance that she would be hospitalised by an adrenaline fuelled newbie. "Stop, don't worry, I'm a Police officer as well" said Angharad before looking over at the paramedics. She nodded towards the prone body of the injured officer "are you going to see to my colleague?".

The paramedics sprang into action and Angharad returned her attention to the young officer in front of her. Speaking softly and calmly, she could tell from the vibrations of his hands that the nervous energy was already seeping away and shock was starting to kick in. It was important that this officer learned to keep in control in such circumstances. "Call in and say there has been an incident, explain what's happened and ask for a Sergeant to attend and for the Inspector to be made aware. Who is your Inspector today?". "Ah John... Inspector Tim John", "Tim John? Ask for him to call you on your mobile, I'll speak to him, I take it he knows you are here? Tell him that Angharad wants to speak with him". Nodding rapidly the officer indicated that he understood what was required.

Angharad left the probationer to do their job, she looked down at the prone figure on the floor and checked that the paramedics were dealing with the situation. Turning her back, she walked back inside the apartment, collecting the riot stick and returning it to its position on the wall as she went. Why had they been kicking her door in? Walking into the living room Angharad finally saw the clock on the wall, 1015 hours; her attention was drawn to the flashing 5 on the answer machine that sat on its own little table in the far corner. Looking at the sofa, she picked up her mobile phone and realised that the battery was dead.

"FUCK!" Angharad had been due back in work at eight o'clock that morning as the duty Sergeant and she had overslept. Nearly ten years ago, while already a serving officer she had tried to kill herself and again fearing the worst two local officers had been dispatched to investigate, Fear for Welfare they call it. Unable to raise anybody inside they had put the door in. The rest, as they say was now history, "FUCK!".

"Excuse me", the voice came from behind her and belonged to the probationer, it was sheepish and the effects of what had just happened clearly still filled the mind of the young officer. Turning round, Angharad saw the probationer stood in the doorway to the living room holding out his mobile phone, "my Inspector". Taking the phone, Angharad nodded her thanks and waved her hand at the officer to leave. The officer was torn with indecision but clearly felt it was prudent to listen to a Sergeant. Even if that Sergeant had just knocked their colleague out, turning slowly he walked back into the hallway. Angharad placed the phone to her ear, "Tim... have I just fucked up?" she asked, "You could say that Angharad, I understand you just smashed the nose on one of my best officers and knocked him out in the process. What were you thinking?" he said with a hint of exasperation in his voice. "Look I just did a 36 hour shift investigating those Bay murders, I think I'm entitled to a bit of down time and some serious drinking to get over the experience? I overslept and didn't hear the phone calls. First I knew was that some fucker was trying to smash my front fucking door in. What was I supposed to fucking do? Let the fuckers in and hope they were nice people rather than some scroat who wanted to get me for banging them up ten years ago?". Deep inside, Angharad realised that she sounded like she was ranting but on reflection, she was tired, drained and seriously hungover, right now letting off steam was an essential part of starting to feel better again.

Tim paused, waiting to see if Angharad had finished her rant completely before replying, "Hmmmm, couldn't you have called it in first? It would have saved a lot of trouble and more importantly paperwork. It'll have to go to PSD and then it's out of my hands; besides word has already got to your Superintendent and he wants to see you in his office yesterday!". Today was clearly one of those days, she reflected, where Tim was not going to be supportive towards her, given their past relationship she decided that it might be good to let off some more steam. "Screw you Tim, you have a different answer when you get to stick your cock in me, you don't worry about the occasional excessive violence then. I tell you what, don't ever try calling me up when you're desperate for a fuck buddy in the future!".

Tim went silent and Angharad hung up the phone. She was seething with anger now and paced around the living room cursing. The officer returned to the doorway and announced that his Sergeant had just pulled up in the car. Angharad returned the mobile phone and stormed off into the kitchen to swill her face with cold water. Standing upright from the sink, the smell of alcohol from her trousers caught Angharad in the nostrils and made her wretch. For a second she thought she was going to throw up but a noise to her right in the doorway between the kitchen and living room distracted her and she quickly stifled the feeling of queasiness. Turning towards the doorway she saw the response team Sergeant standing there. It was a female officer she had never met before with crew cut hair and an overly muscular frame which she carried like a body builder. Angharad reflected that this Sergeant was clearly someone who liked to challenge the idea that men were the more masculine gender.

"Angharad Jones, I never thought I'd get the chance to meet you and I certainly never thought we'd meet in this situation". Not replying, Angharad watched the Sergeant who she felt was being overly gushing towards her for reasons she could not grasp. She shrugged her shoulders to indicate a lack of understanding. "You're a hero for many of the officers in this Force, a hero for women like me and your family are le...". Angharad cut off the Sergeant, "oh that old shit? Legends? You only hear the stories and the claims of greatness, you never lived in it so don't go spouting shit about how great we are". "My father is a prick and my mother is selfish and hypocritical, going on about how society should accept people yet never being able to do that for me. As far as I am concerned the only living decent member of my family is my grandfather Thomas and he had the common sense never to rise above the rank of Superintendent".

The Sergeant was taken aback by the venom in Angharad's voice and decided not to push the point further. Wrapping up and getting out of there before she suffered more wrath from this woman who was destroying her hopes and dreams became far more important. "Look, I've had word from on high and I've been asked to get this all brushed under the carpet; it'll be written off as an injury at work but you need to cover the cost of the door yourself". Stopping to catch breath the Sergeant expected a response but there was none forthcoming, "I've also been asked to remind you that you have to go see your Superintendent". "Thanks, but do me a favour, when you get back to the station tell those on high that Tim still ain't getting any booty calls" said Angharad and she grinned evilly before another sensation of nausea swept over her. Dropping her head into the sink, Angharad fought back the urge to throw up and so didn't see the Sergeant nod quickly in understanding before making a quick exit.

Alone in the apartment and no longer feeling nauseous, Angharad returned to the living room and opened the drinks cabinet to the side of her. The idea of ignoring the demands that had been made, to act as if she had nowhere to go and simply get drunk filled her head. She picked up a full bottle of gin and opened it fighting the urge to knock the bottle back in one go. A moment passed before she finally spoke, "Fuck!".

Just over an hour later, washed and changed, Angharad waltzed into the main office of the Major Investigation Unit. Usually the room would be buzzing with detectives but at the moment it was empty except for one solitary constable who was starting their first day of detachment with the unit. That officer sat quietly in the corner, hunched over their mobile phone either texting or playing games. A duty Sergeant was always going to be needed to clear up the paperwork but also, as the Superintendent had said the night before, they needed someone to show the new guy around. Angharad stopped and watched the newly arrived constable for a few seconds, they seemed completely disinterested in the office around them and didn't even look in her direction and inside she felt a little bit of disappointment. There were too many people, in her opinion, who seemed to share the same lazy attitude in the Major Investigation Unit and as far as she was concerned that behaviour all came down from the Superintendent at the top.

A large male appeared in an open doorway at the far end of the office it was Superintendent Mike Browning, the same man who she blamed for the blasé attitude that often infected the department. "Sergeant, how good of you to bother turning up! Get yourself into my office now!". The PC still didn't react but clearly the Superintendent was not in a good mood and Angharad ensured that the walk across the rest of the open plan office was completed in double quick time. She might not like him but she also knew that he held the future of her career in his hands. As she passed through the open doorway Angharad sized up the small room. The Superintendent was stood at the window, looking out on to the car park below. Between them stood his desk, filled with paperwork, it had a monitor and keyboard squeezed into one corner and a name plate that identified the occupier sat on the very edge of the desk, threatening to jump off into the lap of anybody who sat in the visitors chair.

"Close the door, take a seat, don't say anything", the instructions from the Superintendent were clear and Angharad followed them to the letter. Sitting down, she crossed her legs and placed her hands in her lap. She realised how defensive her body posture was and that helped her relax. The Superintendent still hadn't turned around and simply stood at the window, his hands locked behind his back. For a moment Angharad wondered if he was frozen into position.

Minutes seemed to pass and eventually the Superintendent turned around. He was a tall man, a large man as well, these days more fat than muscle but once upon a time he had been a renowned rugby player, almost of international quality. At least that's what those who had seen him play said. Superintendent Browning was a friend of her father and in her opinion he was, like her the man whose genes she had inherited, a prick. Ever since he had taken over the leadership of the Major Investigation Unit, not only had the team become unfocussed but he had regularly demonstrated that he wanted her out of the team. He was a man who had clearly missed all the diversity training and modern thinking that went into creating a twenty first century Police force. For him, Angharad was the wrong gender in every sense of the word and she had a past that didn't meet with his supposedly impeccable standards. The only thing about Superintendent Browning that had caught Angharad off guard was the focus which he had applied to trying to kick her off the team.

Superintendent Browning remained standing and from his position he really dominated the room and the still seated Angharad. "Let's face it Angharad, we've never seen eye to eye, not since, well ever, really because, well, you know why", Angharad understood what he was talking about and nodded gently but made no other sound or movement. "Still, at times you've been a very competent officer, your work in catching the Bay killer was, at times, incredible but frankly, today, you screwed up big time. Actually it's not a screw up, it's a fuck up and you fucked up so badly that as far as I am concerned your career is over, history, gone. You are no longer a part of this team and if I never see your face again it'll be too soon". The Superintendent's rage was clear and simple, Angharad knew that he had always been looking forward to this moment. In fact he had spent the best part of the last four years hoping for this moment. In full flow now, the Superintendent continued. "I've arranged for you to be transferred back to uniform in Merthyr Tydfil, I know you're familiar with the place, as I understand it you grew up there?". It was a rhetorical question that required no answer and to which the Superintendent gave no space, "you'll keep your rank, sadly I can't do anything about that but you will never darken my door or the door of CID or the Major Investigation Unit again. Any questions? No, didn't think so. Get out and report for duty for the late shift tomorrow, dismissed"

Angharad stood, seething at the way she was being treated, seething at the way the Superintendent didn't even let her have a say. She turned and walked towards the door, placed her left hand on the handle and stopped. Turning to speak over her right shoulder Angharad felt that anger peak within her, "Sir, you are a bigoted cock!". Before the Superintendent could respond Angharad had opened the door, stepped out and slammed it shut. Striding across the empty office she stopped at the line of desks that the PC sat at. He finally looked up from his mobile phone and made eye contact with Angharad, "good luck, you'll need it" she said.

On reflection, Angharad could understand why the Superintendent had been angry at her about what had happened that day. However, even he had acknowledged that she had done some amazing things in the preceding few days but that was the Police for you. No matter what you did you were only as good as the last thing that happened.

Chapter 2

Friday 9ᵗʰ August 1844
Diary of Sergeant Ephraim Jones

The investigation into the body in the Taff is going well. By complete chance Sian Bwthyn Bach was seen to appear from out of the Arches just as a young PC was patrolling by. He grabbed her and brought her back to Graham Street, pursued by the "Emperor" and a number of his cronies. That young PC was lucky that the Emperor did not catch up with him for they would have thought nothing of assaulting him and taking back their own. We were able to summon enough strength in numbers to see them off, they need to remember that outside the Arches is our ground and we decide the rules. Sian Bwthyn Bach was quick to give up her accomplices once the right pressure was applied. According to her, the plan was simply to rob the young man and she was horrified to discover he had been murdered.

Given the information we were able to move quickly, by late evening each of those responsible for the murder had been arrested. I'm confident, at the moment that they will swing from the gallows by the time the courts have finished with them. Actions such as this are essential if we are to bring an end to the villainy that emanates from China.

Friday 9ᵗʰ August 2013

According to local legend, the Police Station on Swan Street in Merthyr Tydfil was built with a siege mentality in mind. This mentality, comes from a Government, still fearful of the revolutionary spirit in the town and the consequences of a possible repeat of the Merthyr Uprising of 1831. The building is 3 stories high and built in an 'L' shape with a car park making up the rest of what becomes a square foot print. The legend says that the 'L' shape allows the car park to be defended by snipers on the flat roof. The ground floor is raised above the level of the street and the windows are reinforced and do not open. Even the front door was built on top of a steep flight of steps and made of solid wood. In recent times though, the door has been replaced by a more friendly glass one, that siege mentality obviously and maybe mistakenly having eased over the years.

As she travelled to work in her Mini, along the A470 from Cardiff towards Merthyr Tydfil and her past, Angharad's mind replayed the meeting with her former boss Superintendent Browning and the realisation of what it meant. Being transferred to the valleys, to Merthyr Tydfil was a way for him to say that her career was over, finished, destroyed at the age of 35.

Given that it was her first day Angharad's tag didn't allow her through the modern electric gates and into the car park beyond so she parked in the lay-by at the front of the building, on Swan Street itself. Sensibly Angharad had dressed in civilian clothes and was carrying her uniform in a bag on her back. Climbing the steps into the empty front office Angharad rang the bell and waited for the Station Duty Officer to appear. The memories came flooding back of her childhood and being brought to the station by her parents, in a happier time when the local Police had still been respected. Merthyr had always been one of the larger urban areas in South Wales Police and in the 1960's and 1970's a career that passed through here could, if the officer was motivated, receive a boost that placed them near the top of the ranks before they retired. These days though, the old fashioned mentality of the valleys meant that Merthyr and the 'A' Division that it was the headquarters for was equally likely to see any ambition snuffed out by the stigma that the name carried with it. For that reason, Angharad, despite being raised in the town, had never worked here and had moved down to Cardiff at the first opportunity. Being on shift here, back wearing a uniform after nearly ten years out of one, was going to be a big change from Detective Sergeant in the Major Investigation Unit based in the swanky end of Cardiff Bay.

Through the small window behind which the Station Duty Officer would stand, Angharad could see a familiar face shuffle into the room. It was Helen Griffiths, big sister by 15 years of one of Angharad's friends from childhood. She had always been the gorgeous sexy role model that Angharad and her female friends had looked up to during their childhood but now, at just 50 years old she looked 60 and moved like a 70 year old. Life had clearly not been kind to Helen and Angharad was taken aback by it. The last time she had seen Helen, she had been in her early 30's and while her glamour had been fading there was still a spark in her eyes. Now she just looked, well old and there was a deadness behind the eyes that suggested that the last 20 years had been particularly hard on her.

As she spoke, Helen clearly did not recognise Angharad and at first there was a boring repetitive drone in her voice. "South Wales Police, keeping South Wales safe, how can I help you" said Helen, "Sergeant Angharad Jones, I'm reporting for duty". The deadness remained as Helen responded, "Oh yeah and you want to report an alien invasion while you're at it?". "Helen, you don't recognise me do you? I was one of Leanne's friends at school" said Angharad, hoping that she would gain a positive response, "Leanne's friends? Which one, I don't remember one who looked like you?". "Angharad, Angharad Jones?", announced Angharad slowly losing hope that Helen would recognise her. "Angharad? Hmmmm I don't remember Leanne being friends with an Angharad back then, where did you live?" asked Helen, "You must do, I was the Pol..." Angharad cut herself short, she remembered that many things had changed since she had lost contact with Leanne and it was likely easier to leave it that way especially if Helen had not immediately made the connection. "Don't worry about it Helen, anyway I've just been transferred here from Cardiff, I'm on response working for Inspector Williams?", Angharad showed her warrant card to Helen who nodded thoughtfully. "Here? Who have you annoyed to be transferred here then?" asked Helen, and the feeling of heaviness in Angharad's heart grew, even the Station

Duty Officer knew that a career in Merthyr was a curse to the modern Police officer. Helen pointed to the door opposite the small window and Angharad walked towards it. As she approached the door a buzzing sound rang out. Angharad turned the handle and walked through into another world.

A loud click echoed through the corridor as the door pulled itself shut behind her and Angharad found herself in the labyrinth that was Merthyr Police Station. There was a shuffling sound from down the corridor as Helen approached from the Duty Station Office,

"Follow me, I'll take you to the Inspectors office and he can look after you from there". Helen led and Angharad followed though at the speed Helen was moving it seemed like the shift would be over before they got there and Angharad was relieved when Helen took the lift to the first floor rather than walk up the stairs.

Eventually Helen pulled up at a doorway on the left side of a long straight corridor, even though she was on the first floor the dark, enclosed corridor made it feel like she was in the bowels of the building. The doorway was open but Helen still knocked and waited to be called into the room, "Helen, what can I help you with?". The voice sounded older and kind, Angharad had never met Inspector Williams before but was familiar with his story. A promising young officer he had managed to damage his career, through no fault of his own. While investigating a murder in the late 90's he had missed the clues that would have led to the realisation that the initial attending officers were responsible. At the time it had appeared to have been a typical crime of passion because the officers had hid their tracks well. When it all came out a few years later there was a huge corruption case and the mistakes that Inspector Williams had made were revealed. His career was ruined by that investigation, in fact it had almost cost him his job but instead of the dole queue he had found himself being transferred to Merthyr. He had been a Detective Sergeant with strong career prospects but the case ruined his life and he was forced to leave

CID.

Luckily for Inspector Williams, Merthyr actually had needed an Inspector and so he got the next promotion in his career but it was also made clear it would be his last and that he would go no further. Now, only five years from retirement, Inspector Williams was just seeing out his time. "I've got a Sergeant, oh hang on, what's your name again?", asked Helen, "Sergeant Angharad Jones", "I've got a Sergeant Angharad Jones here, says she is being transferred here to be your new skipper?" Helen announced now confident in the name of this new officer, "Angharad Jones? Oh good, send her in." the voice within said in reply.

Helen stepped back and motioned to Angharad to enter the office before turning back towards the lift and her life in the Station Duty Office and shuffling off. Angharad pulled herself upright and strode into the office, standing in front of the Inspectors desk. The room was sparse and empty except for two filing cabinets, on top of one of them sat a bottle of Penderyn Whiskey, the desk and a tall, thin man in an Inspectors uniform that sat behind it. Inspector Williams stood up and offered his hand to Angharad, she took it and noticed the firmness of his shake, "Angharad Jones, good to meet you, glad you could join us. Don't worry in this town we don't hold your past against you". "Sir, thank you for the warm welcome, I hope I can contribute to the team from day one and help make a difference" said Angharad tentatively, "Please call me George, no point standing on ceremony in this place", he said and Angharad nodded. At that, Angharad felt herself relax, she hadn't even realised how stressed she had been feeling. Inspector George Williams was doing his best to make her feel at home. "Right, I think that the best way to do things is to learn on the go, so let me give you a brief tour of the building and then we'll be ready for the shift brief, I'll lead tonight, give you a chance to find your feet. I'm thinking you haven't worked on shift for a number of years?" George had a sympathetic look on his face and Angharad could feel that she was definitely warming to him, "that's correct" she replied.

Angharad's mind raced with questions but before she could speak George Williams shot out the door, paused in the corridor before turning right while mumbling to himself. A short, sharp shout emanated from him as he disappeared off down the corridor, "You coming Jones?".

Angharad chased after her new Inspector, he was surprisingly sprightly and light on his feet and the tour was conducted at such break neck speed that she eventually lost all sense of direction. Along the way George Williams popped into the administration office so that Angharad could collect a locker key and get her fob activated for the building at the same time. Eventually Angharad was brought to the locker room, which for some reason was on the top floor of the building. The Inspector stopped outside the room and turned to her, "briefing will be in ten minutes" and he pointed in the direction of the stairs opposite in an almost absent minded way and spoke, "from here down the stairs to the ground floor, out the door, turn left and it's the 6th door on your right". At that he turned on his heels and shot through the doorway leading to the stairs, mumbling to himself yet again. Angharad just stood there feeling slightly confused by what had just happened. There was a gentle cough behind her and she turned to see a young female officer in full uniform stood in the locker room doorway. The officer offered a hand towards Angharad, "I'm Claire". Angharad smiled and looked the officer up and down and thought to herself that Claire was attractive and very new, her uniform was in perfect order. Taking the hand that had been offered, Angharad shook it firmly, noticing the daintiness of Claire's own hand shake, "Sergeant Angharad Jones".

Claire seemed to jump slightly at the announcement of the rank, which given the civilian clothing would not have been obvious and Angharad noticed that Claire pulled herself to a more upright position. Speaking formerly Claire replied, "Sergeant, welcome to Merthyr", blushing, Claire smiled again before making her excuses and rushing to the door to the stairs. Interesting, Angharad thought to herself before shaking the thought from her mind and she entered the locker room to start the process of searching for her newly allocated locker.

After a couple of minutes she finally located it, at the back of the room tucked away in a corner. Opening it, Angharad was glad to see that the locker had been properly emptied before her arrival. It was all too common for lockers to be packed full of items that the previous user had left behind on their way out the door. Unpacking her bag, Angharad hung up the items that she didn't require along with her body armour and she then pulled out the trousers and white shirt that would form the basis of her uniform. She looked around and noticed that there was a distinct lack of changing areas in this locker room, not that she was worried about changing in the aisle. Angharad pulled off her clothing and stood in the aisle in just her knickers and bra before putting on her shirt and slowly buttoning it up. Then she pulled on her trousers, doing up the button at her waist and feeding through her belt. Finally Angharad put on and did up her boots, body armour and duty belt. The uniform felt strange because it had been a number of years since Angharad had needed to wear all of it. Picking up her bonnet she closed and secured the locker before heading towards the briefing room. On the way she stopped and looked at herself in the solitary full length mirror that adorned the back of the locker room door. Despite having been in CID for a number of years the sight of the uniform always made Angharad happy and on this occasion she was even happier than normal. These days Angharad felt that she looked the part far more than she had on her first day of duty 15 years before and so Angharad smiled, a particularly broad smile.

Finding the briefing room was more straight forward than she expected but inevitably she was a couple of minutes late. This was perfect though because Inspector George Williams had settled the room down in preparation for her arrival and he was able to do a very formal introduction that looked as if it had been pre-planned. As Angharad entered the room she could see that it could have been any briefing room in any busy Police Station in South Wales. In the centre was an oval table, which the team sat around, with the

Inspector and Sergeant sitting at the end nearest the door with their backs to the wall mounted television. The room was full with 12 PC's, many of them young though with a couple of old timers who were in a race towards their full pension hiding at the back. Angharad took her seat on the far side of the table, nearest the window and with an empty seat between George Williams and herself. There should have been a second Sergeant in the briefing but the reputation of Merthyr Tydfil made it difficult to find people prepared to fill the role. Introductions around the team were made and then as he had said he would, the Inspector led the briefing, making sure it was as full as possible to give Angharad a chance to get up to speed. All eyes were glued to the wall mounted television as the Inspector guided the team through the daily briefing power point slide. Being Merthyr it was quite a lengthy briefing and there were some familiar faces and places in there which brought back memories of her childhood friends and games.

Finally, they got to a page that struck a particular chord and her brain swam with the memories of a more innocent time. Staring out of the screen at Angharad was Simon Lewis, her best friend from childhood. It had always been a natural thing for them to be best friends, they went to the same school from the age of 3 and shared the same birthday. However, things had changed on their 15th birthday when Angharad had learnt everything she felt that she needed to know for the next ten years about sexuality and gender identity. That day, Simon and Angharad had fought and Simon had won, leaving Angharad with concussion, a bloodied nose and a broken right arm. In reality it was probably the best thing that could have happened because it changed the trajectory of Angharad's life and luckily she had not been hanging about with Simon when he started getting drunk and involved in street fights. The last thing Angharad could remember of Simon was that, at some point, around their 20th birthday she had heard that he had gone to prison for a serious assault, the cause of which was rumoured to be a drug debt.

Angharad continued to stare at the photograph of Simon

as the memories flooded back into her mind until the voice of George Williams snapped her back to reality. "Sergeant Jones, this is our main target of this shift, workload permitting, you need to familiarise yourself with him. Simon Lewis is an enforcer for the Shop Boys and their drug dealing, right now CID want him for two times GBH one of which was on an elderly man who tried to stop their activities. Obviously he's on the run from us at the moment and the Superintendent has offered a large amount of alcohol to anyone who finds him, it'll be a big boost for morale if it is us". "Understood Sir, we'll give it a go", said Angharad. "Good, if that is everything then, have a good shift everyone", announced the Inspector. The briefing might have been long but George had demonstrated his experience by getting through it efficiently. As the officers started to file out George Williams pulled one of the team aside, Angharad looked at him, he looked to be the only officer from the team who wasn't in his early 20's or late 40's and if she had to guess she would have put him in his late 30's. Thinking back through the introductions Angharad recalled that his name was Rhys Evans. George Williams spoke, "Rhys I think you're the best placed person to help the Sergeant here on her first day, is that OK?". Rhys nodded and smiled at Angharad, it seemed to her there was a naughty glint in his eye and she liked it and his muscular frame.

The shift had been slow and boring even though it was a Friday night and weekend nights in Merthyr were usually an excuse for fighting. On more than one occasion Angharad had expected officers on the shift to break the Police officers superstition and declare the night as quiet so guaranteeing that all hell would break loose for the rest of the night. Rhys and Angharad were sat in a Transit van watching the pubs and clubs along Dynevor Street when the radio finally crackled into life. Two officers on patrol at the top end of the High Street had come across a fight in the car park between Pontmorlais and Tramroad Side North. The officers reported there were six people involved and they wanted support. Quickly the rest of the shift responded and Rhys started the van and turned it around while negotiating the chaos of the pub goers and clubbers who were thronging the street, the blue lights of the van helping to clear the way.

By the time Rhys was heading in the direction of the fire station and the town hall the radio was alive again, this time it was preceded by the clear, distinctive sound of an officer's emergency button being pressed followed by the cacophony of noise that showed an intense fight was taking place. Angharad looked at Rhys and despite the time of night he hit the siren, knowing that the noise would echo through the night and let those already at the fight gain comfort from the impending help. The control room operator continuously tried to raise the officers who were at scene as the lights and sound of the van bounced off the surrounding buildings as Rhys turned right into Bethesda Street and tore along the road towards the junction at the end where the car park was located. Angharad knew that she was only a matter of seconds away and she could feel a surge of adrenaline through her body.

The van slewed to a stop in the middle of the mini roundabout at the top of the High Street, looking directly into the car park, another Police car parked on the pavement directly in front of the van. As she leapt from the vehicle Angharad could see that part of the car park had been given over to some form of builder's site, the gates to which were open. Off to her left two officers, whose names she could not recall, were wrestling with two drunken men on the pavement while to her right, within the car park, Claire was standing over the fallen body of another officer, her baton drawn as she faced off three men. Angharad turned to Rhys and pointed towards the two on her left and shouted, "help those two over there, I'll help Claire!".

Turning to her right, Angharad ran and drew her baton at the same time. As she approached the four she raised the baton in her right arm and brought it down onto the back of the knees of the first man, the baton extending to its full length as she swung. A cry of pain came from between his lips and he fell to the floor as his legs went dead beneath him. The second man turned to face

Angharad and as he did so she swung the baton with all her might into his rib cage. It was not normally an area where officers were encouraged to target people with a baton but Angharad recognised it was a simple case of desperate times calling for desperate measures. As the baton made contact there was a cracking sound from the ribs and the target of her actions doubled over in pain before dropping to his hands and knees. As the second man fell from view Angharad noticed the third man move towards Claire, in his hands he held what looked like a metal pole about 5 foot in length which he swung viciously towards the younger officer. The pole caught Claire on the shoulder and she dropped her baton as the force of the blow knocked her off her feet, leaving her lying prone and motionless on the floor. There had been such force in the attack that the man's momentum caused him to spin round and Angharad found herself staring into the face of Simon Lewis.

Simon clearly worked out these days, he stood at just over six feet tall and was well muscled, on top of that he still had the pole in his hand as he moved to face Angharad. She lifted her baton up in her right hand so that it was held over her right arm ready to swing at any moment. At the same time Angharad took a step back, out of the range of the scaffolding pole. Looking around she could see that Claire and the other officer were still lying on the floor. The two men who Angharad had hit were now on their feet and limping away into the high street, already on the other side of the road. Meanwhile Rhys and the other two officers were slowly gaining the upper hand on the two men they were fighting, partly because Rhys was the Taser officer on the team. Angharad could see that he had already deployed the Taser on one of the men who was now lying face down on the floor while the other two officers were clearly gaining the upper hand on the other.

Angharad looked back towards Simon, "Long time no see" she said. Simon stared at her blankly, not recognising the voice or being able to place the face for a few seconds and then realisation dawned across his face and a big smile formed on his lips. Simon looked around and noted that his friends were still present,

"Obviously I didn't take care of you tidy before" he said and with that Simon gave the metal pole a test swing. Angharad was relieved to see that she had judged the distance well as it passed just inches from her body. Scanning around Angharad was desperate to find something that would allow her to gain the upper hand on Simon and then she noticed a Police car stop in Tramroad Side North, behind Simon. The driver got out and she could see that it was the Inspector. From where Angharad stood, she could watch Simon and also see that George had exited the car and then paused as Simon took another test swing of the metal pole. Retreating towards the car, George reached inside and immediately the siren of the Police car burst into life. It was the perfect distraction, Simon swung to his right to look behind him, the pole extended forward in preparation for the need to defend himself. As he did so, Angharad took two steps forward and brought her baton down in a wide arc over her right shoulder. The baton caught Simon across both forearms as he gripped the pole and he screamed in pain as the pole fell to the floor with a clang, the nerves caught perfectly to cause him to release his grip. Simon turned back towards Angharad, anger and hatred in his eyes but she was quicker. Dropping her own baton, Angharad had already moved forward, bending at the hips and placing her left shoulder into Simon's waist. Her arms wrapped round the top of his legs and she pulled tight, executing a tackle on Simon that an international rugby player could be proud of. Angharad drove Simon backwards into the ground, knocking the wind from his lungs as she did so and leaving him gasping for breath.

By the time Angharad had started to move into a crouched position, ready to fight Simon to get him into handcuffs, George, moving sprightly for an older officer was already alongside her, his pepper spray drawn and discharging a stream of clear liquid that hit Simon directly between the eyes and temporarily blinding him in the process. Rhys appeared by Angharad's side and together they turned Simon over before putting him into handcuffs. Looking up at Rhys, Angharad smiled her thanks before standing to survey the situation. Beneath her she could hear Rhys arresting Simon as she watched the rest of the shift finally arrive and take over the various roles in helping colleagues and dealing with the three people who had been arrested.

A Police car pulled up and an armed officer climbed out. Angharad approached him and he nodded at her as he recognised the three chevrons on her shoulder indicating her rank, "Sarge" he said. Angharad pointed in the direction of Claire who was now being tended to by colleagues but was clearly not as injured as Angharad had first feared. "Two males made away after attacking those officers, one is limping because I gave him dead legs and the other has a couple of cracked ribs, find them and bring them in, there's a beer in it if you're successful" Angharad informed the officer. "How do you know he has cracked ribs?" the officer asked and Angharad grinned back. The officer let a small smile cross his face and nodded in understanding.

The armed officer got back into the car as Angharad walked off in the direction of Claire. By the time she had got to her the first ambulance was arriving on scene. A few minutes later Claire and the other officer, who Angharad had now worked out was one of the old timers, were being taken off to hospital to be checked over. Fifteen minutes later, other than for a small pool of blood from where the old timer had found his nose spread across his face, there was no indication that any fight had ever taken place. Angharad and George stood in the car park and assessed the situation. The Inspector nodded at Angharad and spoke, "I'll take care of the officer welfare issues, I want you to keep control of the team who are still standing". Angharad nodded and turned to walk away before George spoke again, stopping her in her tracks, "Angharad, thank you, CID will love us for this". Angharad turned and faced her Inspector, "Sir... Simon Lewis is a cunt" she said and they shared a wink.

Chapter 3

Saturday 10th August 1844
Diary of Sergeant Ephraim Jones

A second body turned up today in the River Taff, this time under the Bridge of Troughs outside the Cyfarthfa Ironworks. Again it was an opportunity for the Inspector and the Superintendent to panic, especially given that the Metropolitan Police will be here within the week. I was not present when the body was recovered but I understand that it was identified as Gwilym Rees who was the head of the Town Watch Committee and heavily tipped to become the next MP for Merthyr Tydfil. The announcement of the death of Gwilym Rees will come as a big shock to those who were hoping to support his nomination as MP. He was somebody who was seen as a big player in the future of not just the town but maybe, in time, the whole of British Politics. A man who knew what it was like to live at the edge of this technological age.

On this occasion, there have been no injuries identified other than those consistent with a fall from the bridge and subsequent drowning in the river. To lose such a high profile figure, within the town, just after the murder of the young man is a great concern. However, this is Merthyr Tydfil, a place where morals seem to be non-existent whether you be at the top of society or at the bottom. While many will be worried about it and the newspapers stir up fear I am not moved. Many poor people die in this town, maybe God is just balancing up the score.

Saturday 10th August 2013

It was the early hours of Saturday morning and the shift had already been reduced to a fraction of its starting strength. There were three in custody including Simon Lewis who was now on a two person cell watch as well as two further officers to take all the clothing seizures and sort out the paperwork. Up at the hospital the fallen officer was being looked after by Claire while one of the officers who Rhys had helped was also receiving treatment for the injuries they had to their hands. George was also at the hospital taking care of the welfare of everyone while Angharad cleared things up at the Police Station. The handful of remaining officers were back in the town centre where the time of night made it impossible to remove them from such an essential role. Angharad walked into the doorway into the report writing room, a tray of drinks in her hands and she stopped to watch. Rhys and two other officers dealing with the paperwork were sat at computers furiously typing out their statements covering the events that had taken place that night. Smiling to herself, Angharad realised that although she was in Merthyr Tydfil this was a team that was dedicated to doing its job and she couldn't remember the last time that she had worked with a team like that.

Angharad walked forward, placing the tray of drinks on the desk so that Rhys could pick up his mug. "Thanks" he said, turning towards Angharad and smiling. She then picked up the tray and moved towards the other officers before stopping in her tracks as the radio burst into life. A piercing scream had been heard near the Cefn viaduct and a call had been received from a local resident that they had heard a loud thud near to their house which was under the bridge. Angharad put down the tray and looked at the three officers around her, "I'll take that" she said and let the control room know that the officers in the town centre should continue with their patrols to keep a lid on any problems there. Turning to leave the room Angharad heard Rhys speak "wait a second Sarge, I'll come with you".

The van trundled up the narrow Pontycapel Road into the looming shadow of the Cefn Viaduct, which in its heyday, had carried a railway across this part of the valley. Angharad signalled to Rhys to slow down the van to a crawl, wary that at any point they could stumble upon a body, suicide being a common problem on this bridge. They passed under the arch, slowly edging their way onto the north side when Angharad called out to Rhys "stop!". Rhys brought the van to a standstill and looked out of the windscreen into the gloom. "I can't see anything" he said and Angharad pointed out of the driver's side window and Rhys slowly turned his head. Upside down, bent backwards over a low brick wall with a heavily scratched face was the body of a man, blank lifeless eyes staring straight at the both of them. "Back the van up, slowly" said Angharad and Rhys obeyed the instruction. As he did so Angharad called up on the radio and told them what had been discovered.

Rhys brought the van to a stop again about 50 metres from where they had seen the body lying on the wall and both officers exited the vehicle. Angharad turned to Rhys, talking through the open doors of the van, "don't forget to take a torch with you and we'll move forward, inch by inch, sweeping as much of the road and bushes in front of us as possible". Rhys nodded and held out his hand towards Angharad, "can you pass me a Dragon Light from the rear of the van?". Opening the sliding side door, Angharad looked inside and in the gloomy light of the interior of the van, she could make out two dragon lights on the floor, just behind her chair. Large, powerful torches they would be perfect for the task that both officers faced. She picked both up and passed one through the van to Rhys before closing her door, the loud sound as it shut echoing from the narrow sides of the valley and followed moments later by a similar sound as Rhys shut the driver's door. Walking forward in a purposeful manner Rhys and Angharad used the extra light that they now carried in their hands to sweep the darkest recesses of the road and the bushes to either side getting right into the areas where the headlights of the van didn't reach. Glancing across at Rhys, Angharad checked that he was doing his bit as they slowly edged closer and closer towards the body.

As they drew level with the body a strange sound filled the air and caused Angharad and Rhys to turn and stare at each other, a moment of fear flickering across both their faces until they realised what was happening. Looking towards the body Angharad grinned, it was not the first time that she had heard a death rattle, where the bodies of the dead make noises as the gases within escaped via the vocal tract but then, as she shone the torch at the face, the lips moved making Angharad jump. She raced forward towards the body, telling Rhys to call for an Ambulance at the same time, "he's still alive!" she screamed.

Angharad got to the body, the crackle of the radio echoing in her ear as Rhys called up with the latest update. Putting on gloves from a pouch at the back of her utility belt, Angharad started to conduct a secondary search of the man in order to establish the level of his injuries. He continued to make sounds and now that she was up close she could tell that his chest slowly rose and fell as be breathed, a shallow, crackly sound emanating from within the chest with each breath, "what's your name? I'm Angharad, I'm a Police officer" she said.

She continued to search the body but there was no reply other than a faint moan and the slight movement of the lips. Clearly the man had broken his back, the arch was beyond what most men would be able to manage, especially when the man looked to be of large build and aged in his mid-fifties. Further, the lower part of his body was wet and a strong smell of faeces met her nose indicating that he had no control over his bodily functions. Blood slowly oozed from the inside of the ear and his pupils were unresponsive to light indicating that the man had suffered a serious head trauma and his right hand was missing, the injury at the stump of his right arm suggesting that it had been freshly ripped off. There was nothing she could do but provide an update on the injuries, keep speaking to the man and wait for an Ambulance.

As Angharad waited the man visibly weakened, his lips moved to each question but no useful sound came out, being upside down in relation to the man's face it was not possible for Angharad or Rhys to properly read his lips. A flashing blue light started to reflect from the trees around them and Angharad breathed a sigh of relief as the Ambulance crew finally arrived. Maybe it would be possible to save the man after all. The crew approached the scene and Angharad and Rhys stepped back to let them have access. Immediately they went to work but the man closed his eyes, let out one long, slow moan and then his eyes opened and his body went silent. "Fuck", Angharad swore out loud and somehow in unison with the two paramedics, the senior one turned to her, "we need to get him off of this wall, his breathing has stopped".

Stepping forward, Angharad and Rhys joined the two paramedics and together the four of them tried to lift him. The body was heavy and at an awkward height but they managed to raise it enough that it should have been possible to slide off the wall. However, there was no movement and they rocked the injured man back and fore to try and free him. One of the paramedics bent over to look underneath as the other three continued to try and move the body. When he stood back up his face was set in a grimace, "he's embedded on something sharp, based on where it has entered him it has likely split either his spleen or his stomach. Looking at the rest of the injuries and the fact that we can't get him off the wall immediately, there's nothing we can do, he'll be dead before the Fire Brigade get here to free him".

All three who were still straining to lift the body let go and fell back, the exhaustion of the moment starting to enter their muscles. "We still need to try" said Angharad who looked at Rhys and nodded. Rhys removed one of his gloves, now covered in a brown liquid and gave an update over the radio. Lifting the torch again she scanned the trees above and there, trapped amongst the branches of a large tree that spread out directly over where the body had landed was the unmistakeable outline of a freshly amputated hand, "he definitely fell from the bridge" she said.

The two paramedics and Rhys followed the beam of Angharad's torch until they could also see the severed hand trapped in the branches. Using her radio Angharad called up again, she needed someone to get up on the bridge, someone to check what was up there. While a body underneath a bridge normally indicated suicide there was no way of telling, at this stage, if something more sinister had happened. Moments into the conversation with the

Control Room she remembered that, with all the other commitments, there was nobody available. A thought flashed through her mind, shit! Angharad issued a series of quick commands to Rhys and over the radio in order to make sure the area was secure and obtain the details of the paramedics. Taking a short break to consider what to do next while waiting for a call from the night turn Detective Constable her train of thought was interrupted suddenly by the older of the two paramedics. "Shit!", he said and everyone looked at him, "he's dead and I just realised who the stiff is". The Paramedic who spoke had his hand round the throat of the newly dead body as he checked for a pulse as his statement about knowing who it was hung in the air. "Who is it?" asked Angharad and the Paramedic realising that he had not provided the answer spoke again, "I think it's Gwyn Davies, leader of the Council".

Staring at the slowly cooling corpse still lying bent over the wall in front of her Angharad considered what to do next. Potentially not only was this a murder but the murder of a significant local player on the politics scene. She vaguely recalled that Gwyn Davies had become elected a councillor when she was a child and while she could not remember what he looked like she was aware that at times he had single-handedly held the town together in a political sense. The loss of such an established town personality could be catastrophic to the immediate future of the area. It was well reported in the Welsh news that Merthyr was currently in the process of negotiating for a major electronics company to setup a European headquarters within its boundary. Negative reporting such as was likely to come from the death of Gwyn Davies could ruin everything. Angharad knew that she needed to confirm the identity of the dead man because the situation could escalate rapidly if true.

Thinking for a moment she had an inspired idea, "does anyone have a smart phone?" she asked. One of the paramedics mumbled a yes while slowly nodding his head, "I need an up to date photograph of Gwyn Davies now" she commanded. The Paramedic nodded again and slowly walked off towards the ambulance, the lack of eagerness in his movements made her take a deep breath ready to abuse him for his inaction. However, she remembered that he was not one of hers and she quickly closed her mouth and bit her bottom lip as she resisted the urge to tear into him. Eventually, after what seemed like an age, the Paramedic returned with his smart phone held in front of him. Holding it up while facing towards the body it was possible for both of them to take a look at the corpse and compare against the photograph on the phone. Reaching out Angharad traced the line of a faint scar across the face of Gwyn Davies that was just noticeable in the photograph. Then, stepping forward towards the body she raised her torch and studied the forehead intently, dirt and fresh cuts from the fall covered the face but there, just noticeable under the glare of the torch was the same scar. From behind her the Paramedic spoke, "my father came up with Gwyn from childhood, he picked up that knock when he was smashed by a milk float, split his head on the pavement he did, at least that's what my father said".

Angharad smiled at the sudden hint of local dialect that came into the paramedic's voice, the man's use of such language had been non-existent until he quoted his father. Clearly dad had been far richer in his use of Wenglish than his son would ever be. "Shit!" said Angharad realising that the situation was as bad as could be feared. Her mobile phone rang, pulling it out of her pocket she looked at who was calling, it was DC Robert Di Marco from the Major Investigation Unit and the person she trusted least on that team after Mike Browning himself, "Double Shit".

South Wales had a long history of immigration by Italians in the 19th and early 20th Century and so there were plenty of people who still held onto that heritage, especially with their surnames. In a time before, Angharad and Robert Di Marco had been friends but the world changes and now all he held for her was animosity. For Angharad this was a pity because she had once regarded him as good looking. Answering the phone, from the start the conversation was frosty, Angharad explained what was happening while listening to Di Marco sneer down the phone at her, the venom in his voice was clear for her to hear. As quickly as possible and remaining as professional as she could manage Angharad did what she needed to and ended the phone call. At least Di Marco had agreed that he would visit the scene tonight.

The paramedics cleared off minutes later, no longer needed now that they had confirmed that Gwyn Davies was dead. Angharad turned to Rhys and checked with him that he was happy to look after the scene on his own. She needed to get to the top of the bridge and the sooner she got there the better. Unfortunately there was no way to get there by foot. Pontycapel Road was a small lane at the bottom of a narrow, steep sided valley which was covered in thick vegetation. Even with a torch it was guaranteed that at this time of night Angharad would get lost and need rescuing herself, or even worse, fall in the river that flowed quietly in the darkness to her left. She looked up at the bridge again as if studying the underneath of its dark shadow

Her mind made up, Angharad took the keys to the van from Rhys and jumped into the driver's seat. Slowly and carefully, Angharad edged the van along the dark and narrow lane until she reached the junction with Job's Lane. Finding first gear, the van lurched forward at an angle onto another narrow road that led up into a small housing estate at the back of the High Street. Following the road round to the right Angharad found herself in the car park of Cefn Coed Rugby Club. Parking up, Angharad grabbed the dragon light that she had deposited into the front passenger seat. She walked out onto the path that ran passed the rear of the club and looked to her left where the white walls of the Station Hotel stood out against the night. Having confirmed that she was on the correct path Angharad turned to her right and started walking, following the bright beam of her torch as she did.

Progressing slowly, Angharad studied every inch of the path as it became more enclosed with trees and the buildings of Cefn Coed were left behind her. The trees moved in around her and this made the walk feel oppressive and threatening and Angharad felt the hairs on the back of her neck stand up. She felt on edge and alone, there was no way of telling if someone was hiding in the bushes that surrounded her. Casting the light forward Angharad realised that the trees suddenly stopped and gave way to the bridge itself as it stretched out over the valley below. She stopped and studied this change, noting the old stone sides of the bridge. From an initial sweep of the beam the bridge appeared to be empty and Angharad found confidence in this. She started forward, fighting the urge to run for the freedom and space that the bridge seemed to promise in that moment.

Reaching the feeling of safety that the bridge provided, Angharad forced herself to slow right down until she was almost creeping along what had once been the track bed of a railway. Suddenly, the beam of her torch caught on something sitting about 40 metres ahead of her and she stopped to take the scene in. From her position Angharad was able to make out that there was a briefcase leaning against the brickwork of the north side of the viaduct. Without moving she cast the torch around the area and then paced forward twenty five metres before stopping again. From the closer distance Angharad could see that it was a black briefcase and that on top of it was what looked like a small white envelope, balanced between the briefcase and the brick wall. Her gaze cast upwards and she was relieved to see that while small clouds crossed the night sky there was no real risk of it raining anytime soon.

Angharad moved her position on the bridge to the south side until her arm brushed against the wall and then she again edged forward towards the location of the briefcase, as she did so it became possible to make out that there was writing on the front of the envelope. Flashing the torch up the wall again, to the area above the briefcase, she noticed that there was a gap in the wall where a small stone should have sat. The wound in the stonework looked fresh to Angharad's eyes but there was no way of telling for certain without a forensic examination. Drawing level with the briefcase she studied the wall on the south side before scaling it and looking over the top. Below she could see the trees and the faint line of a road below. Shining her torch over the top and down onto the road she shouted at the top of her voice "Rhys!"; below she detected movement as Rhys stepped out from the dark form of a tree and looked upwards. Rhys waved upwards, the white of his hand reflecting off the strong torch light, sure that she was in the right place and the briefcase was relevant she dropped down off the wall and back onto the floor of the bridge. Turning, Angharad shone the torch directly at the envelope and briefcase and studied them intently. Losing herself in thoughts about what the briefcase and envelope meant the sound of a door slamming reached her from the valley below. Looking back over the wall she could see a small car parked in Pontycapel Road and walking in front of it, towards Rhys was the unmistakeable shape of Di Marco. This should be interesting she thought to herself.

Turning back around and crouching down on her haunches Angharad settled in to await the arrival of Di Marco at her location. It didn't take long for him to appear, in fact it was such a short period of time that it made her worry about what thought processes were going through his head; it struck her as possible that Di Marco had already made his decision about what had happened. Di Marco approached her, walking along the span of the bridge at a quick pace and not paying any attention to the scene around them; clearly he didn't want to be here. When he pulled level with her he looked at the briefcase and envelope. As he spoke Di Marco sounded disinterested, "have you looked in the envelope yet?", "of course not, I've been waiting for you to come and assess the situation" Angharad replied. "Well you should have, obviously this is a suicide, that envelope will confirm it and then we can scoop up the body and get out of here" said Di Marco flatly while his face indicated displeasure at having to work with Angharad.

Looking at Di Marco, Angharad did not speak and kept her face completely free of emotion but inside she was boiling with anger. She knew that Superintendent Browning's team had become a bunch of idiots, but now, standing outside of the team she realised that the situation was even worse than she had thought. Casting the torch to a spot in the wall that was directly above the briefcase she pointed while keeping her voice completely level, "what about the missing stone?" she asked. Di Marco followed her gaze and the torchlight, "how is that relevant? That could have happened at any time, after all if it had happened when the guy climbed the wall it would be resting on top of the briefcase". Angharad couldn't help herself this time and she exploded, "Constable we are directly above the spot where Gwyn Davies has fallen to his death and you think it irrelevant that there is a stone missing from the wall while failing to ask why it is that he has climbed the wall at the spot directly above where he has rested his briefcase and the envelope. Don't you think he might have knocked them while he climbed?"

Di Marco bristled at the onslaught from Angharad. She had clearly wrong footed him, anyone who thought that her transfer to uniform in Merthyr would take the wind out of her sails was wrong. Taking a deep breath he moved onto the offensive, picking up the envelope with his bare hands, he read the words written on the front aloud, "my dearest wife", then he ripped open the envelope and pulled out the letter that it contained. Opening the letter he read out its contents so that Angharad could hear, "my dearest Betty", Di Marco looked at Angharad a question etched on his face and she slowly nodded in reply. "There we go, the name is correct, my dearest Betty. Life has been hard for me for a number of years. The stress of being a Councillor and the Leader of Merthyr County Borough Council has taken its toll on me. I have consistently failed the people of Merthyr and I was again going to, during the latest round of negotiations that was supposed to help the people of this town. You know that I have always been a student of the history of this town and I cannot live with the fact that we, the modern people of Merthyr do not live up to the expectations of those who came before us. It is not your fault and I hope that I have done this at a time that allows you to move on with your life. Know that I will always love you. Gwyn."

Di Marco again turned his gaze on Angharad and spoke quietly. "Suicide", he declared, "seize this letter and the briefcase and get the body collected by the undertakers, then we can get the road reopened, not that anyone will use such a country lane at this time of night and by the morning, nobody will be any the wiser". At that Di Marco turned and walked away, dropping the letter and envelope onto the floor as he went. Angharad watched him walk away and then stepped forward, taking another pair of rubber gloves from the small pouch on the back of her utility belt, the previous pair having been discarded when she moved the van. Moving the letter and envelope out of the way Angharad then approached the briefcase. Picking up the briefcase she looked behind it and found a stone, perfect in size and shape to have filled the hole that was still in the wall above. It was enough to make Angharad pause, why was the stone still here? In exactly the spot you would expect if it had been knocked out when Gwyn Davies had fallen to his death. Inspecting the wall she noticed small scratch marks in the stones and concrete, as if someone or something had been pushed over the wall rather than having jumped. Scaling the wall on the north side of the bridge, Angharad was able, with the use of a torch, to make out the hand resting in the tree directly beneath her.

Climbing back down she placed the briefcase on the floor and fiddling with the catches she popped it open. Inside was empty except for a pen, a notepad and a small pack of ten envelopes. Counting the pack she saw that there were only nine left and comparing the notepad with the letter it was possible to see that they were also the same. Angharad scribbled with the pen onto the pad and compared the ink marks that it left behind with the words in the letter and again there was a clear match. Yes, this looked just like a suicide but a small number of things didn't add up and Angharad was convinced that Di Marco had overlooked something important but there was nothing she could do about it right now, there was just nowhere near enough evidence to challenge him.

Half an hour later, Angharad was back down in Pontycapel

Road with Rhys, the briefcase and letter sealed in exhibit bags in the back of the van. As she approached him Rhys looked at her with a quizzical face, "what's the matter? It's a simple suicide isn't it?". Angharad looked Rhys directly in the eye and smiled, "If you say so" she said. Rhys opened his mouth, ready to speak but the look from Angharad would have killed most people and he quickly shut it again, afraid to speak and leaving him look offended. "Rhys, I don't know you that well yet, yes I have my doubts but we're not in a position to discuss it" Angharad said.

Rhys nodded and turned away to go and study the silhouettes of the trees. The noise of a car coming down the road attracted Angharad's attention and she turned to see a panda car driving towards her. It stopped short of the van and George Williams climbed out and walked towards them, "hello sir, I didn't expect you to be free yet?" she said. "I've still got paperwork to do but I wanted to come and pay my respects, Gwyn Davies was a good man and I've sunk many a shot of whiskey with him over the years, in fact that bottle of Penderyn that you might have noticed in my office was a gift from him". Angharad nodded, and indicated for the Inspector to follow her as she turned and walked off down the road. At the right moment she turned to her right and pointed up onto the wall where the body of Gwyn Davies lay, the Inspector stopped and followed her gaze. The Inspector spoke, sounding incredulous as he did, "suicide they said?". Angharad nodded, choosing to keep silent out of respect to the Inspector. He walked forward and looked in on the body until his face was literally only one or two inches from that of the deceased. "I understand there was a letter?" he said, "yes sir" came the reply, "what was in it?", "he apologised Sir, apologised for failing the people of Merthyr, said that he was going to fail in the latest negotiations yet again and that he couldn't bear it". The Inspector looked at Angharad, a moment of anger crossing his face before he could bury it deeply. "There is one thing that Gwyn Davies would never have described himself as and that was a failure! Are you sure that is what the letter said?"

Angharad paused for a moment, she wanted to tell George

her doubts, that she felt that CID had jumped to their conclusions and that there were alarm bells ringing at the back of her head but then she remembered. She still had nothing; no evidence, no credible proof to back up her doubts and besides she didn't know this man, if she gave the impression that she thought CID was incompetent this man could be a danger to her as much as he might be an ally. "I saw the letter with my own eyes, it's in the van as my exhibit I can show it to you if you want" offered Angharad. George Williams watched Angharad, looking for what, she did not know but she suspected that he might be equally judging her trustworthiness given that they had met only a few hours before. He snapped out a short and curt reply before turning and walking away, "fine".

Chapter 4

Sunday 11th August 1844
Diary of Sergeant Ephraim Jones

Suicide they reckon, Gwilym Rees jumped from the bridge and due to his injuries he would have been unable to regain his footing in the river and so drowned. That is presuming, of course, that he would have wanted to regain his footing in the circumstances. Personally I am not convinced, why would a man of his position want to end it all when he was so successful and influential and was potentially about to become even more so. However, I have been told by the Inspector that a letter was found in the inside coat pocket of Gwilym Rees, water damaged but still readable. The contents of the letter declare that he was unable to act in the best interests of the town and his belief that this truth would soon be exposed. The Superintendent seems to be particularly touched by this death declaring that he counted Gwilym Rees amongst his personal friends.

Things have taken an even stranger turn for the worse though. On the night of Saturday 10th August I was the cover Sergeant, working with a small team of officers to keep the streets safe. About one in the morning a runner found me on the outskirts of town near to Pontmorlais, a body had been found in the doorway of a house on the edge of China. It was not a particularly long run for the time of night and by the time I got there a small gathering of officers were stood in the street. Approaching I could see that a couple of them were carrying pistols, something that is not a standard part of the equipment that my officers would normally carry. That such equipment was present concerned me. Hoping to impress one of the officers, a PC Davies, was quick to inform me that there had been a shooting and that the victim looked like James Smith. The fast response from PC Davies threw me for a second and I looked into his eyes. "James Smith", I queried, "the

James Smith, the English man, the Emperor?". I was then informed by PC Davies that the Emperor had been at the house in relation to a debt owed. The occupants of the house claimed not to be involved but in the circumstances it was appropriate to have them arrested anyway.

Shootings are a rare thing in Merthyr but attempts to kill the Emperor are not unusual, still this particular one seemed to be invincible up until now having survived numerous previous attempts on his life. The death of the Emperor is as good a reason as any to send a runner to the Inspector even in the early hours of the morning. A battle for control of the town's crime may be on the cards and such an event will possibly stretch our resources beyond its limits.

Sunday 11th August 2013

A second night shift in Merthyr was progressing along typical lines by the time Angharad managed to get a breather at about 3am. While she had hoped the night would not be as eventful as the previous shift the reality was that busy town centre pubs and clubs had filled the cells yet again. Further, she had also had to send a couple of officers over to Aberdare to assist them after a fight had broken out between two groups of locals from the outlying villages, an event that had completely swamped the local resources. George Williams had tried to make light of the situation, "it could be worse, it could have been Aberdare against Merthyr". Knowing the valleys all too well, Angharad could only agree with the sentiment. The outcome of such an event would have united the two groups who had fought and probably doubled or even tripled the numbers involved.

Thinking the night could not get much worse, Angharad's blood froze as the radio sparked into life with details of another serious incident. There had been a report of gun shots at number 13 Gwern Llwyn in the Gurnos, an area reputed for its crime but a long way from where Angharad stood in the town centre. She looked at the last of the nights revellers as they left the kebab houses and other late night takeaways on the upper High Street and then at the two officers who stood with her. Angharad found herself in a Catch 22 situation, there was nobody else left to deploy except for herself and the two officers. Balancing the situation in her mind she realised that she would have to take a risk that the handful of people left in the street would behave themselves. Turning to the officers stood next to her, Angharad spoke quickly, "Rhys, we need to deploy to this, go get the van and bring it round. You!", she said, pointing to the second officer his name escaping her mind for a second, "have you ever dealt with a shooting before?". The officer shook his head, "no Sergeant", he replied. "Not a problem, just stick with me and you will be fine". At that, the van appeared and they both climbed aboard.

For the second shift running, the van sped through the night, the blues lights bouncing off the buildings around as Angharad's mind worked quickly. Being unarmed it was essential to set up a location for other resources to attend and there was an obvious spot, the car park to the rear of Gurnos shops. The sound of the Inspector over the radio indicated that he would also be on his way once he had gone round the station and kicked out all the officers who were not tied up with anything but the most essential of Police procedure. Given the developing circumstances everything locally was progressing as it should and another four officers would soon be deployed to help at the scene. However, the radio also informed Angharad that there was an ongoing siege in Cardiff and so finding armed officers was proving to be a little more difficult.

The van pulled into the car park at the rear of the shops and Angharad assigned the second officer to control the flow of vehicles in and out from the junction with the main road. She still couldn't recall his name but the situation was such that asking the question was not really appropriate, Angharad needed to remain focused on the task at hand. An ambulance was already at the scene having only had to travel from the nearby Prince Charles

Hospital. From memory, Angharad recalled that the shops were only 300 metres or so from the scene of the shooting and yet the location seemed eerily quiet even for this time of night. Pulling out a map, Angharad studied it to work out which of the houses the shooting had been in. "Does anyone have any idea of how this looks on the ground?" asked Angharad as a car containing Claire Doyle arrived, "I do Sarge" said Claire, "I had family who lived in the street a couple of years ago". Angharad looked at her and nodded, "go on then". "The street actually backs onto itself, it's essentially a square with the houses looking forwards onto the neighbouring streets across pedestrian walk ways and the rear of the houses looking into the street and a concrete car park".

Nodding carefully Angharad called up on the radio and was informed that a number of people had reported the sound of gun shots and that two men had been seen to run away down the path in the direction of Clos Ywen. Studying the map Angharad identified the location and confirmed that there was still no firearms support available. Looking up at Rhys she smiled, her eyes set hard as she mentally confirmed the decision in her own mind. "I can't order you Rhys", she said, "but fancy joining me?". Rhys met her eyes and fixed his face into a grim smile, "we've only worked together for one and a half shifts" he said "but let's face it, where you go I go". Nodding slowly, Angharad looked around and met the eyes of Inspector Williams who was quietly overseeing from the side, "it needs to be done" he said before motioning towards the Police car that was pulling into the car park. "That's the Aberdare Sergeant, he can oversee this side of things while you are gone".

Moving quickly, Angharad and Rhys headed for the pathway at the rear of the car park that led through into the streets beyond. Sticking to the shadows as much as possible it became clear that the streets beyond were as silent as those they had already passed through. Working by looks, hand signals and whispered commands Angharad and Rhys moved along a path between houses on their right and a single storey building covered in graffiti on their left. As they reached the end of this building they stopped and scanned the surroundings. Ahead was a one hundred metre open space which they needed to cross before they would be safe in the shadow of Gwern Llwyn itself. Angharad looked at Rhys and nodded towards the space which formed the entrance to a car park at the rear of the shops. "We need to run" she whispered and he nodded, checking one more time that they could not see anyone else, Angharad rose up and moved forward.

Moments later Angharad and Rhys found themselves in the shadows of the terraced houses of Gwern Llwyn. They stopped and caught their breath before making their way along the grass verges that bordered the pedestrianised walkway. It was not ideal as it limited their view of the houses in Gwern Llwyn but the houses on the other side, that formed part of a different street, were bathed in the amber glow of street lights. Door by door, they moved up the street until a corner came into view. At that corner the houses and the street turned to the right so that they could look at the whole row. However, there in the apex, on the ground floor was a dim light shining through an open door. Stopping both of them, Angharad checked around her and provided a quietly spoken update to the control room. Turning to Rhys she looked at his kit belt and body armour and then motioned towards the Taser that was still holstered. It didn't take any words for Rhys to understand and he slowly and quietly drew it out, keeping it pointed at the ground. Leaning in close, Angharad whispered her next instruction, "I will stay in front but I want that on my shoulder the entire time, any movement from that doorway and we stop and reassess". She could sense Rhys nodding in the darkness, their heads close enough to each other that they were almost touching.

Turning again so that she was looking towards their target, Angharad and Rhys moved forward towards the open door. Slowly and carefully they approached until it became clear that there was a silhouette of something large lying across the sill. Angharad paused, reaching out with her hand, backwards to block Rhys and ensure that he did not push her over. "I can see it", he whispered into her ear, his hot breath making her ear wet as it met the coolness of her skin. For a moment, Angharad thought about smiling, in another situation the closeness of their bodies and the tension in the air would make for a build up to a very erotic finale. However, the danger, the working relationship and the need to work quickly, safely and effectively meant that such thoughts were completely inappropriate. Rhys and Angharad rechecked their situation but there was still no movement from the address and so they moved forward again until they were just one house away from the open door.

Now, the light was enough that it was possible to clearly make out what they were looking at, the silhouette lying across the door sill had resolved itself into the shape of a male body. Studying it for just a moment from their position in the darkness Angharad and Rhys looked for signs of movement but there was none. Looking at Rhys, Angharad used her hands to signal her intentions and Rhys nodded. Then, moving her lips and fingers she gave a noiseless count down, 3 2 1, throwing her hand forward they both moved at speed towards the body. As they got to the door Rhys used his Taser to check inside the corridor beyond to make sure that nobody lurked inside. Angharad grabbed the body with both hands while Rhys used his free left hand to do the same. The body lay face down in the doorway and they threw it over onto its back to reveal the face of an old, overweight man with a thick beard.

Pulling with all their might the two of them dragged the body as quick as they could manage back down the path in the direction from which they had approached. As they reached the end of Gwern Llwyn Angharad felt safe enough to call up on the radio, her breath already coming in short, sharp gasps. By the time they had crossed the road to the safety of the low building the sound of others running through from the car park reached her ears. Then she became aware of shapes surrounding the three of them, the shapes of uniformed Police officers. The first two made no effort to help though, they stepped beyond Rhys and Angharad, beyond the body that they were pulling. In the amber light from the street lamps she heard the sounds and saw the movement of large firearms being raised, they were safe. More people appeared and they took hold of the body and started to pull it, pushing Angharad and Rhys out of the way the officers who joined them spoke quickly, "we'll take it from here, you two concentrate on getting back and recovering". Angharad watched as a stretcher and two paramedics appeared and the body was quickly lifted onto it before being run back in the direction from which it had come.

Sitting on the floor Angharad and Rhys looked at each other gasping for breath, a smile creeping across both their faces as the adrenaline of the previous fifteen minutes escaped from them. A voice from Angharad's left sparked her back into life, "when you are ready Sarge, shall we get you back to safety?". Rhys pulled himself upright and then offered a hand to Angharad which she accepted. Rising to her feet with his help the pair of them walked slowly back towards the car park and the growing team of Police officers who were gathered there. As they walked the shuffling sound of the feet of the retreating firearms team followed them.

As they entered back the car park the paramedics could be seen working frantically on the body that they had brought with them. Over to the right the Inspector was in deep conversation with the firearms team and Angharad made straight for them still walking arm in arm with Rhys. George Williams turned towards them, "well done Sergeant Jones and PC Evans, now before you get a rest, the firearms team need a debrief as to what you saw so that they can plan their tactics". Drawing herself free of Rhys, Angharad brought herself fully upright and looked directly into the eyes of George, "yes sir", she said and then turned to the firearms team, "where would you like me to begin?".

Four hours later the debrief and the paperwork had been completed, the Major Investigation Unit had taken over the investigation and Merthyr Police Station was already crawling with the officers who would be taking the lead. Luckily for Angharad neither Robert Di Marco nor Mike Browning were amongst them. She had also managed to establish that the man that they had pulled from the house was alive when they had rescued him but that he had subsequently died. Unfortunately he had never regained consciousness and so had been unable to reveal any more information about what had happened to him. It would be later in the day before it was announced who it was who had been murdered but within the station it was already well known, his name was Stephen Thomas and rumour was that no crime took place in the town without his say.

As Angharad walked out of Merthyr Police station, her uniform stored in a rucksack on her back she found Rhys, Claire and some of the other officers waiting for her. While for Angharad it had only been her second shift, for the rest of the team it was the end of 6 long days and nights. The team had four whole days of freedom to look forward to, days in which they would avoid being anywhere near a Police Station as much as possible. "I bet you need a drink after that?" asked Claire with a big smile on her face and Angharad nodded, "those of us who don't have anywhere to rush to after work often go for a drink after the last shift", Claire raised her eyebrows making it clear that it was an open offer. Angharad smiled at the thought, "I'd forgotten this was the last shift of the run for you guys", she said, "having said that, after two shifts like that I need a really big drink". Looking at her watch, Angharad noticed the time, "where do we get a drink though at 8am on a Sunday morning?" she asked and Claire grinned, "you've just got to know the right people".

Following everyone else onto the High Street the crew walked towards a well-known haunt from Angharad's younger days, The Eagle. Rhys guided everyone round to the back door and knocked gently in a repetitive three knocks and two knocks rhythm. Moments later the door swung open to reveal a rather busty 25 year old woman on the inside. "Hello all", she said with a big grin on her face and Rhys smiled back, "hi Rachel" but before he could say anything else Rachel laughed. "Finished your shifts and you could do with getting a few drinks down your necks?", said Rachel as she stepped out of the way, holding the door open in a clear invite to the group. Rhys stepped in through the door and walked passed

Rachel before stopping next to her in the corridor. Everyone else filtered in and headed straight down towards the bar. Following last, Angharad stepped into the door and Rhys immediately introduced her to Rachel, landlady of the Eagle. "Rachel Morgan" she said shaking hands with Angharad who smiled back, "any relation to Colin Morgan?" she asked and Rachel smiled, "he was my father, God rest his soul". A memory popped into the mind of Angharad, "little Rachel?" she said inquisitively, "are you little Rachel, you must have been 8 or maybe 10 when I last saw you". Rachel smiled, "that'll be me but I don't remember you" she said, "what was your name again?". Angharad smiled, "Angharad Jones but don't worry, you wouldn't remember me" she said and quickly walked off inside as the sound of Rachel closing the door followed behind her.

Chapter 5

Monday 12th August 1844
Diary of Sergeant Ephraim Jones

This is starting to annoy me now, I have had to cover another night shift and as if the last two days haven't been bad enough, the third day was even worse. There was a large fire on the High Street, naturally I made my way there and found that the men of the fire watch were already doing all they could to contain it. It was a fire that had consumed two shops, the occupants of the houses above and the lives of countless cellar dwellers who lived beneath. After the fire was put out and a count of the bodies was completed there were twenty two dead in total with eight cellar dwellers homeless. Another three people lost their home in the fire but were able to find others who would take them in, cellar dwellers have no such advantage as they are the lowest of the low. Two of the cellar dwellers were injured during the fire such that they will be left having to beg on the streets for the rest of their miserable lives.

As if the fire itself and the deaths that came from it were not bad enough, one of the shops was the home of Samuel Powell who was head of the local business community. Along with Gwilym Rees, he was seen as an essential stalwart of the administration of the town, indeed Samuel Powell also sat on the local watch committee. For me the death of Samuel Powell was particularly touching as this was a man who was known to me, a man who I might even have called a friend. It looks like the fire started in his premises as well, though we have not been able to get inside at this stage to work out what happened. The death of Samuel Powell has not been confirmed at this time as his body has not been found but it is certain to be the case. He regularly used to work late in his shop on a Sunday night, was seen there only an hour or so before the fire started and he now cannot be located.

The town as a whole has been devastated by this cycle of events, over three days we have lost Gwilym Rees the Town Councillor and chair of the local watch committee, and Samuel Powell the head of the local business community. I can only hope that strong leaders will come through to take control because without them the future of the town could be in trouble. On top of that, James Smith has also been murdered, it is true that many will view his death as a good thing but it needs to be viewed in conjunction with what else has also been lost. Three lynch pins of local society have died in such a short space of time and that does make me wonder. Is there more than just a coincidence to this? If there is then, first, I need to answer another question, why would someone want to get rid of all three at the same time?

Monday 12th August 2013

A phone rang out, echoing in the distance but Angharad didn't react. Her eyes were closed and the bed was way too comfortable for her to want to move. The phone rang again, she was aware it was the second time she had heard it but could not tell whether one minute or one hour had passed since the last time it had rung. Keeping her eyes closed she moved her left arm out to the side and her little finger made contact with the warm skin of another. She tensed and kept her arm there, not moving, not reacting to the sensation of touching another person. Lying still and keeping her eyes closed she reached out with her other senses, the sheets felt like hers and the room smelt like hers but there was definitely a sound of someone else, a gentle snoring that filled the room. Maybe she was still fast asleep and dreaming she thought so moving her right arm and hand she gently pinched herself and the sensation of it was definitely real.

Her mind raced as she attempted to recall what had happened the night before but without success. Clearly, she had been very drunk and a dull thud that was growing across the front of her forehead and was slowly reaching towards the rear of her skull confirmed that the day before she had been drinking excessively. The phone rang out again, a third time, this time the sound not just echoing through what she presumed was her apartment but also echoing through her hangover causing even more pain. What to do, she thought as she became aware of the body lying next to her moving, turning over in the bed. She took the opportunity to snatch her hand back and then slowly, unconsciously stroked it as if she could gain knowledge of who the other person was. It was as if her right hand could gain information that her left hand had kept from her in an act of betrayal.

Slowly, painfully, opening her eyes the light of the day streamed in to overwhelm her sense of vision. The light curtains that Angharad used were no good in protecting the room from being immersed in the bright sunlight of the late morning. Angharad smiled, at least it confirmed one thing, she was still at home but that still left the question of who was lying next to her. For the fourth time the phone rang out and now that she was certain that she was home she also became aware that it was her home phone that was ringing. Reaching out with her right hand, to the edge of the bed, to the bottom of the mattress Angharad felt the cold steel of the knife that she always kept hidden there. It was a Khukri, a Nepalese knife that one of her ancestors had acquired while serving in the army during the 19th Century and which had found its way into her possession. Knowing it was near gave her confidence and as her fingers slowly closed round the handle ready to pull it out in defence she turned her head to the left to look upon the person who was lying next to her. Lying on his right, looking back at her was a man, a man she immediately recognised, her on again, off again boyfriend Tim John. "Are you going to answer the phone?" he asked quietly, keeping his eyes closed. "I thought we had broken up?" asked Angharad, "I distinctly recall telling you it was over last week", Tim smiled, "you told me we were back on again last night", he said with a grin, "around the time you begged me to come back to your place".

Finally a memory from the night before triggered in

Angharad's mind and she recalled the drunken conversation that had taken place towards the end of the night, the décor looking like one of the private booths at Madame Mimi's in the centre of Cardiff. "You do realise that I had been out drinking for about 17 hours at that point?". "Yes and you also told me that you were probably still drunk when you dumped me". More memories of the conversation flooded her mind and Angharad had to admit that Tim was right about what she had said and probably right about how she had felt as well. Tim moved in looking to kiss Angharad and the phone rang out for a fifth time, putting her hands up against his chest to stop him Angharad met his eyes, raising her eyebrows in the process before slipping out of his grasp, "I thought you wanted me to answer the phone?".

Standing naked but with her back to Tim she caught her balance as the world briefly spun around her and then headed for the door, though not before Tim could plant a firm hand on the left cheek of her backside, "I love that ass" he said as she disappeared from his view. The phone was still ringing as she entered the living room but it rang off just before she could pick it up, "Damo" she screamed out loud. "Missed it again?" came the voice of Tim from the bedroom "yes" she replied and then realised that the phone was showing that a voicemail had been left. Picking up the phone Angharad pressed a few buttons quickly and then held it to her ear. "Angharad, this is Gramps, I've been trying to call you all morning but either you're not there or are too hungover to care", said the distinctive voice of Thomas Jones, her grandfather. Hanging up the phone on hearing that last comment and cutting off the rest of the message in the process, Angharad cursed herself, I can never do anything without my Gramps knowing she thought.

Tim appeared in the room, he was also completely naked and she looked at his toned body remembering one of the big reasons why she kept going back to him, "who was it?" he asked, "nobody", replied Angharad. She had a tendency not to admit contact with her grandfather to Tim as he would always complain about why she was spending so much time with an "old fart". For

Angharad though there was something important in Thomas, he was like her protector and the only part of her family that she still had contact with. He had been a Superintendent in South Wales Police and acted as the guardian of her family's history.

"It can't be nobody" said Tim, "it has to be somebody otherwise the phone wouldn't ring". Angharad knew that it would be best if Tim was not here so that she could phone Thomas, "I don't recognise the number so it can't be someone important" she said and Tim shrugged, "are you sure?" he asked and she smiled. "Why don't you go start the shower and I'll join you in a minute", said Angharad, "I just want to get myself a drink first". Tim grinned and headed for the bathroom while Angharad moved into the kitchen, the phone discretely held in her hand. The sound of the shower reached her ears and she replayed the voicemail, this time listening to the whole thing. "There was a fire in Merthyr overnight, that's a bit of a coincidence don't you think, August 1844 and all that, give me a call when you get this, love Gramps". Angharad cleared the voicemail and rushed into the living room looking at the book shelf that sat over her desk she searched desperately for the right book until her eyes fell upon it. "Edited extracts of the diaries of the Jones Family 1840 to 1960". Putting down the phone, she pulled the book out and flicked through the pages to the right date, it was only half a page in length but contained enough to attract her interest.

"August 1844: During this time Constable Jones was promoted to Sergeant Jones and he wrote a number of entries regarding cases that he was involved in while he served in central Merthyr Tydfil. Of particular interest is the events of the 10th August to the 21st August 1844. During this time there are four deaths recorded by Sergeant Jones, two murders, one suicide, and one accident. One of the murders appears to be unrelated but Sergeant Jones refers to the other deaths as the Llofruddiaeth Triwriaeth or Triumvirate Murders. According to Sergeant Jones there is no coincidence to the fact that the three people died and he indicates that they were all killed for a very specific purpose. However, the

Inspector and Superintendent refused to investigate them as such and in the end he had no evidence to build a case".

Angharad lifted the phone up off of the desk again and rang Thomas who answered instantly, "are you serious" she asked and without introduction but he did not reply, "OK, we need to meet", she said and finally her grandfather spoke "we need to get our hands on the original diaries, we need to get them translated word for word as opposed to just having access to edited highlights". Murmuring her approval, Angharad waited for Thomas to finish telling her the plan that he clearly had already put together in his head, "Merthyr Library, 4pm today" he said and Angharad agreed. A voice called out from the shower, "come on Angharad, what's taking you so long?". "I need to go" she said, "love you Gramps" and hung up the phone. Walking through the living room Angharad caught sight of the clock on the wall both hands pointing directly upwards, it was midday. Not much time Angharad thought to herself but then she heard Tim call out again, his voice more demanding this time. Taking a breath she realised that he would not be happy if she made excuses now. Angharad found herself caught, she didn't want to risk letting Thomas down but to let Tim down would definitely cause an argument. She walked to the bathroom door and entered, pulling back the shower curtain as she approached the bath itself. Stood in the bath under the warm spray of the shower was Tim and it was clear he was very eager to see her. Forcing a smile onto her face Angharad climbed into the shower and allowed Tim to paw at her body.

The bedroom clock showed 14:00 as Angharad pulled a light jumper over her head and checked her hair in the mirror. She was already alone, Tim had made excuses for leaving the second that he had spilled his seed. If she took the time to think about it Angharad might have accepted that her relationship with Tim was too toxic to tolerate. That maybe, if she had met herself in the course of her job she would be full of advice to leave him and offering all the support that she could manage. Things weren't helped by the fact that Tim was married with children and so spent most of his time not being around and when he was around he could be incredibly argumentative and controlling. However, Angharad didn't have the time to consider such things and made a mental promise to herself to stop and deal with it at some point in the future. At some point when she would have to deal with the fact that she loved him and not loving him might leave her very much alone in the world.

Grabbing her house and car keys she rushed out the door of her apartment, just in time to see the lift doors closing on an inside that was already crammed with people. Turning to the stairs Angharad found herself starting to jog, a jog that quickly turned into a sprint. Taking the stairs two and three steps at a time she made it to the underground car park just as the doors to the lift opened in the same place and the last two occupants spilled out into the same space. She recognised them as residents from the same floor as her and she nodded towards them, keeping eye contact to a minimum. Despite living in the same apartment for two years Angharad had never associated with the other residents, she valued her privacy when she was at home. Besides, given the events that had taken place at her door just the week before and the noisy sex she had been involved in just an hour or so before, now was not the time to start befriending them. Angharad checked her watch without actually taking in the time that it showed her, she needed to get a move on or she would not be in Merthyr by 4pm. Walking through the car park she got to her space and noticed that there was a rather significant absence, there was no car. Pausing, fear filled her as she considered the possibility that her car had been stolen but then a memory returned from the night before. She hadn't brought her car home in the first place, the drinking had started in Merthyr and that is where her car had remained, in Merthyr, at the Police Station, she had got back to Cardiff by train.

The shutters to the underground car park started to open and the other people from her floor drove out of the door as Angharad ran after them, climbing the short ramp before coming to a dead stop. Outside was bright, warm sunshine which contrasted heavily with the dark coolness of the car park. A contrast which the mild headache in Angharad's head couldn't fully cope with given the speed of the change. Stopping at the top of the ramp, Angharad closed her eyes before forcing them into a squint and looking around her. By chance, a short distance away, a taxi was parked at the side of the road, the driver's window open and from her position she could see the occupant sitting in the seat with his head down as if reading the newspaper. Making her way across the road Angharad approached the open window.

"Alright drive?" she asked and the taxi driver jerked his head up in surprise, pulling his head back from the window and further into the car as if he was expecting some kind of attack. Angharad crouched down, keeping her distance from the window and smiled gently, "how much for a fare to Merthyr Tydfil?" she asked and the driver relaxed slightly. She smiled more deeply as she recognised the taxi driver, Ibrahim was the son of a prominent leader in the local Somali community and had transported Angharad to and from her home on a number of occasions. "Angharad", Ibrahim said, an equally broad smile spreading across his face as he recognised her back and visibly relaxed. "Angharad, I would normally refuse such a fare but for you, I will make a special exception", he said. "Thank you Ibrahim", said Angharad and she walked round onto the pavement before climbing into the back seat of the taxi. Ibrahim watched her in the rear view mirror of his car and they made eye contact through that mirror. "It's OK", said Ibrahim, "I can see you need time to think, so I will leave you in peace". Ibrahim smiled again and Angharad smiled gently back, "thank you" she said.

As the taxi pulled out and moved off into the main street and joined the flow of traffic Angharad closed her eyes. Memories from the night before started to fill her head. Drinking in The Eagle, what should have been a couple of drinks before a longed for bed and sleep had been anything but. The experiences of the night before had turned things into a session, a session that had gone on long into the afternoon before the lightweights had started to drop with exhaustion. There had only been five of them but Angharad had felt by the end that after just two days she was really starting to become part of a team. A team where, for once in her life she was being accepted as an equal. In particular, Rhys and Claire were people who Angharad felt she would be able to rely on. Rhys, was not just a mid-career Constable but also the muscle bound hard man of the team with a caring, sensitive side. Meanwhile, Claire was young, sometimes naïve and inexperienced but the way she spoke, the way she saw the world, Angharad felt sure that one day she would make a great detective.

By late afternoon Angharad had left The Eagle and realising she had drunk way too much to drive, she had got the train to Cardiff. The plan had been to get back to her apartment, get some sleep and return to Merthyr the following morning to collect the car. On reaching Cardiff, Angharad realised as her memories returned, things began to go seriously wrong. As she had walked through the station she had bumped into a couple of friends, Glyn and Stephanie who were renowned party goers and always up for a drink or ten. When Glyn's parents had died while he was in his early 20s due to a car accident they had left him a large sum of money, enough that he could live off it. Unfortunately, or at least, unfortunately in the eyes of his parents prior to his death, Glyn was gay. They had never approved of Stephanie or Stephen to give him his legal name, who was Glyn's cross dressing boyfriend. Seeing that Angharad had already been drinking Glyn and Stephanie didn't need to twist her arm too much to encourage her to join them in another session of around the bars, pubs and clubs of St Mary's Street. Amongst the groups they associated with all three of them had a reputation for being able to handle their drink and so it was not surprising to find them in the queue for Madame Mimi's at a quarter to eleven on that warm summers evening.

Thinking back on it she knew that she shouldn't have gone there, she always had a good time but she also knew that Tim haunted that place like a ghost and that he had that hold over her. Tim also worked the same shift pattern that Angharad had been moved to, so with three more days to kill he was bound to be there. This time she really thought that after he had sent people to kick down her door that she had made the break, that she would never forgive him for not just coming round himself as a loving boyfriend but how wrong she was. Going there meant that she had seen him, spoken to him and inevitably kissed him. The events of that night had put her back under his spell and instead of ending it forever she was now hopelessly in love with him again. In reality, she suspected that she would have taken him back eventually anyway, but going to Madame Mimi's when that tired and drunk meant that she never gave herself a chance. Angharad's mind started to spin with thoughts about what had happened and what it all meant and soon she fell into a fitful sleep filled with strange dreams.

There was a sudden and sharp jerk from the taxi and her eyes shot open. It took a moment to focus but looking to her right she could see the outline of Rhydycar Leisure Centre and she realised that her sleep must have been deeper than it felt. "Are you OK?" asked Ibrahim and Angharad nodded slowly before murmuring a reply, "yes" she said, finding her voice raspy. Realising that Ibrahim had clearly not heard her, she cleared her throat and raised her voice before replying again "yes, sorry, I must have fallen asleep", "that's OK", said Ibrahim, "I didn't talk in my sleep did I?" she asked and Ibrahim smiled, "nothing that I could make sense of" he said.

Under Angharad's guidance, Ibrahim found his way to the library on the High Street in Merthyr Tydfil. She looked at her watch, just in time as well she thought to herself as she registered that the time was quarter to four. Exiting the taxi, Angharad paid the fare, amazed herself that she had £70 in her purse to pay the full cost without having to pop to a cash machine. Then she took a seat on a bench outside and watched Ibrahim and the taxi pull away as she waited for Thomas. Angharad knew that she would not have to wait long as Thomas was the most organised person in the world and as far as she could tell he had never, in his entire life, been late for anything. A voice called out behind her "Angharad!" and she turned her head to see Thomas standing at the top of the steps in the doorway to the library. On seeing him, Angharad instantly smiled, a very warm loving smile that was immediately returned by Thomas. Standing she ran up the steps to him and they hugged, Angharad nestled into Thomas's arms. He was a giant of a man, incredibly tall and now, despite the fact that he had turned eighty in June he was still very much a bull of a man, full of muscle and strength that had served him well over the years. Being held in his arms had always made Angharad feel safe and secure even when the rest of the family had turned their back on her and today was no exception.

"First we will pop upstairs and look at the original diaries" said Thomas as he released her from what felt like a massive, life squeezing hug, "then we will discuss what we do next". "Gramps, you already know what you want to do next", said Angharad and they both broke into wide grins. "True", he said, "but you need to buy into it and besides, you are a good Police officer, you may have an alternative plan". He guided Angharad in through the doors and they climbed the wooden steps to their right up into the reference library. Thomas opened the small wooden door into the room beyond and stepped through followed by Angharad who found memories of childhood flooding back as she saw and smelt the wooden interior. Stood at the other side of the room, near to a caged off area was a middle aged woman who Angharad did not know. Wearing a light summer dress, she stood and waited patiently though Angharad could detect a distinct happiness in her face on seeing Thomas, a happiness that was more than just a sign of patience having paid off, it was a happiness of desire, of love and of trust. A happiness that seemed to fade slightly on seeing Angharad following behind.

As they approached Thomas was quick to introduce the pair of them, "Angharad, this is Julie Williams the head librarian. Angharad shook hands with her, "you might know my cousin?" Julie offered and Angharad frowned, "George Williams, the Inspector in Merthyr?" she said by way of further explanation. The handshake became firmer as Angharad responded to the name, "yes, I've just been transferred to Merthyr and he is my boss" replied Angharad. "You won't want for anything then", said Julie, "just like with your Thomas here". There was a distinct grin from Julie as she said that last bit and she looked at Thomas, making eye contact and Angharad could have sworn that there was a hint of love and lust in them, "isn't that right Thomas?", said Julie. "OK!" said Angharad making it as clear as she could without stating so that she didn't want to stand there and discuss her grandfather's love life. "Shall we check out these diaries then?" she continued and luckily Julie and Thomas both acknowledged her, the moment between them being broken and seeming to disappear beneath the surface as if it had never been there.

Julie opened the door to the secure area and led both of them in. She spoke quickly and quietly though clearly was aiming her conversation at Angharad. "As I am sure you know, Thomas, your Grandfather, is currently guardian of your family diaries and in his wisdom, knowing that many of the older manuscripts are very fragile, he has entrusted their care to us at the library". Angharad nodded thoughtfully, "yes and he also had someone produce an abridged version of each diary which each member of the family has a copy of", said Angharad, "unfortunately, the abridged version contains very little information regarding the incidents we're interested in". Julie stopped and turned to Angharad and nodded while putting on white gloves, "well we have the diary you're after" said Julie before turning to a book case and selecting one of the oldest looking volumes. "That was an odd way of putting things" thought Angharad noting the condescending voice that Julie spoke with, "I know you would have the volumes, Gramps would be tamping otherwise".

"You need to be aware, the original text is written entirely in Welsh, so unless you can read Welsh then it is not exactly going to help you!", Julie emphasised the last part of her sentence, aiming it at Angharad while a look of malice flashed across her face. In that moment, Angharad formed the opinion that she did not like Julie, it seemed that Julie saw Angharad as a challenger for the affections of Thomas and so was determined to show her up. Luckily for Angharad, she was able to be one step ahead of Julie on this point, "I know the original version is in Welsh", said Angharad, "and you are right I can't speak or read Welsh". The look of malice in Julie's face started to change and Angharad was sure that she could detect a look of triumph. "I am sure that Gramps isn't knowledgeable enough on the subject either" Angharad continued and while Thomas ignored the comment it was possible to see that the barb had stung Julie. "However, I intimately know the senior lecturer in the Welsh language at Cardiff University" said Angharad and as she finished her sentence she could see Julie's ego deflate with her seemingly strange hope of making things uncomfortable for Angharad evaporating before her.

Despite seeming to have ignored it, Thomas had picked up on everything and his face filled with a wicked grin, "two women fighting for my affections?" he said sarcastically, "well that has never happened before". "There is no battle for the two of you to fight, never mind for one of you to win" he continued, "my love for each of you comes from very different places and there is no clash". His interlude seemed to relax the situation but Angharad continued to eye Julie with suspicion.

Placing the book onto the desk in front of all three of them, Julie slowly turned the pages until she found the right area and Angharad's eyes fell upon the original diaries of her family. While she had been in the library in the past and seen the books sitting on the shelf she had never seen the actual words written within before. Even though it was written in Welsh she gazed with admiration on each page as Julie searched out the relevant section. Although none of them spoke it all three of them had been taught Welsh in school and their knowledge was enough that they could understand the words written at the top of the page "Dydd Iau, 8 Awst 1844". Julie slowly turned the pages further and it was clear that Angharad's ancestor had said a lot on the matter of the Llofruddiaeth Triwriaeth, after all not only was it mentioned on multiple pages but there was also an entire section specifically titled as such. "We need all of this", said Angharad, "can you photocopy all of it?" she asked and Julie smiled before looking towards Thomas, "is that what you require Thomas?" she asked and he nodded, "yes". Picking up the book Julie took it out of the secure room and she walked across the reference library disappearing through the door which Angharad and Thomas had used to enter.

Half an hour later they left the library and on stepping outside Angharad took a deep breath of air. The tension between Julie and herself had been stifling at times but even stranger, she didn't understand exactly why it was there. Yes, Julie might be interested in Thomas and maybe Thomas was interested in Julie but at the end of the day that was their business and Angharad had no desire to interfere in it. "Drink?" asked Thomas, breaking into Angharad's thoughts and she brightened up at the distraction, "I'm not sure I should have any alcohol after yesterday and besides, I need to drive home later". Thomas nodded in understanding, "well I was only going to have a glass of pop and maybe some food in Lewsyn yr Heliwr" he said, "and we haven't had that discussion about what happens next yet". "Lead the way", said Angharad and they crossed the road to the local chain pub. As they entered Thomas leaned in close, "I still laugh at the fact that they had to change the name of this pub after public outcry, Lewsyn yr Heliwr would have been proud", Angharad patted him on the back, "I'll pay" she said and she stepped in front of Thomas and lead the way to the bar. Moments later both were seated in the quieter area of the pub hidden to the right side of the bar and overlooking Castle Street. Angharad looked at Thomas, his eyes were alive, clearly he felt that he was back on the job, catching the criminals of South Wales. "How certain are you that this is another series of murders as mentioned in the diaries, after all we don't even know for certain that the story they contain is accurate anyway?" asked Angharad and Thomas sat there quietly, contemplating the question and his answer before he spoke.

"We have three deaths, on the same dates as three deaths

that took place 169 years earlier", Angharad nodded at the obvious coincidence, "and the three deaths are similar, if not identical in nature and order", Thomas continued. "So we have a major coincidence", said Angharad, "that doesn't mean there are three murders". Thomas nodded thoughtfully, "it doesn't but it is interesting that two of the victims have the surname of Davies and while I cannot speak Welsh I did notice that there are Davies' in the diary, with several of these mentions giving a first name of Abraham". Angharad nodded but then stopped short, "what do you mean, two of the victims have the surname of Davies?" she asked, "I wasn't even aware that there had been a fire until you called, never mind that they had announced the name of the victim". Thomas grimaced, "they don't need to, it is the accountancy office at the bottom of the High Street", Angharad shook her head, not understanding the point Thomas was trying to make, "the owner was Marion Davies who was in school with your father and the only people who worked there were her family, on top of which I was good friends with her father". Now, Angharad finally understood, "you contacted the family?" she asked and Thomas sighed, "yes, her father is stricken with grief". For a moment, the conversation fell to silence and Angharad and Thomas stared at each other, unsure as to what to say.

The silence was broken by Angharad, "hang on", she said, "you are saying that the fact that the Davies surname is involved is relevant, so there must be a familial relationship there...", Thomas broke into her question, already knowing the answer, "I've been assured that Gwyn Davies and Marion Davies are related he said, they have a common ancestor called Abraham Davies". He left what he had just said hanging in the air and Angharad stared at him, not sure what to say or how to word the thoughts running through her head. "So is that the...", she cut herself off, "Do we know that it is...", she cut herself off again, "is it the same Abraham Davies?" asked Thomas rhetorically, "I don't know, what I do know is that Marion's father has done some of the family history and traced the Davies family back to an Abraham Davies who was living around the same time. He was strongly involved in the local churches but he couldn't find out the detail of how, anyway they had a huge family get together last year for all of those people who he managed to trace in the family tree and guess who was there?", "Gwyn Davies", replied Angharad the realisation of the situation dawning on her.

"Right, we need to see if they declare the death of Marion as a murder", said Angharad, "they won't though will they, whoever, is behind this knows what they are doing" came the reply. "We don't know that though, we don't know what is going to happen, if they declare it a murder then we can raise the issue of Gwyn Davies with them", Angharad sounded confident, despite the issues she had with the Major Investigation Unit herself she was still hopeful that they wouldn't be as blind as the officers had been all those years ago. "They are not going to declare it a murder", said Thomas, "you forget, I have contacts throughout the Police and I have been assured that they are looking at an accident, a blanket left on a fire". The flatness of his tone made Angharad's shoulders sink, "you really have been busy today then?" she asked and Thomas nodded.

Angharad looked Thomas in the eyes, "right", she said, "in that case we need to start with the obvious, we need to see inside that shop, we need to get the diary translated and we need support from other officers". Thomas nodded, "and we keep everyone else out of it on the grounds that they are incompetent and on top of that, Mike Browning is a complete cunt". The use of that final word by Thomas made Angharad jump, that her grandfather used the word and also that he seemed to know the man. She looked at him startled, "didn't you know?" he asked, "from the day he was allowed to complete his probation I told everyone what I thought and yet, here I am 28 years later and your father managed to promote him to Superintendent". "Well we are agreed on one thing as always then", said Angharad and Thomas looked at her questioningly, "my father has no ability to make decisions". This time, they both laughed out loud. They parted, both knowing what needed to be done, "send my love to them" said Thomas without saying who them were. After all, he didn't need to say, they both knew exactly who he was talking about and they both knew that sometimes it was best not to rake over the past too much.

It was 10pm before Angharad pulled up on Queen's Road near to the villas that overlooked Thomastown Park on the eastern side of Merthyr. The warmth of the day had given way to heavy rain and thunderstorms and sitting inside her car she stared up at the houses, making note of which lights were switched on and which windows were in darkness. Rain fell heavily onto the roof of the car giving out a constant drumming sound as another flash of lightening lit up the park and the valley beyond. Originally, Angharad was supposed to make this trip after she had left Thomas three hours before but nerves about the visit and the request had caused her to drive around aimlessly, never quite making the turn towards the spot where she was now parked. Then, as if being guided by someone else she found that her aimless driving brought her to a parking space directly outside the houses that she now looked upon. Angharad didn't believe in a higher power but she had not consciously driven to this location, if anything, she had tried to do the exact opposite. Yet here she was, parked up outside the houses and in between the flashes of lightening she looked to the heavens and wondered whether Ephraim Jones was looking down and willing her on.

Even now though, she still couldn't bring herself to get out of the car, she used the rain as an excuse but deep down she knew that it was just that, an excuse. Reaching into the central console of her car she picked up the mobile phone that she had stowed there and cycled through the numbers in her contact list until she saw the name she needed, Susan Rogers and then her thumb hovered over the green button to start the call. Something still pulled her back, a nagging fear of how she would be received made even worse by the time of night. Angharad found herself quickly pressing the red button before throwing the phone across the car in frustration. "Why is it always like this?" she muttered to herself before answering her own question, "you know why, because you broke her trust, because you ruined everything and threw her into a world that she did not want".

By the time Angharad finally got out of the car it was approaching 11pm, the rain had eased off and re-intensified in that time and as she ran towards the front door of the house she needed she knew that her lack of a coat would cost her. Luckily she had found a carrier bag in the car which she had placed the photocopied manuscript inside of to protect the paper from the downpour. When she got to the door Angharad was soaked to the skin and the only positives she could find from the situation was that her short hair meant that it would dry quickly and she didn't have any long strands of hair helping to make her back even wetter than it already was. Standing in the small amount of shelter provided by a small porch that hung over the front door Angharad rang the bell. There was already a light on in an upstairs front bedroom but otherwise the house seemed silent and she found herself having to ring the bell another three times before a separate beam appeared through the glass of the door. The glass was opaque but it allowed enough brightness to shine through for Angharad to see that it was coming down the stairs from a source at the top of the landing. A shadow crossed in front of the light and Angharad braced herself in preparation for the door to be opened. All the nerves had been about being face to face with Susan but now a more horrifying thought filled her mind, what if the person coming to the door was Susan's husband, Marc Rogers.

Angharad steeled herself for the worst possible result until a voice called out from the other side of the door, a female voice, "who is it?". Letting out a loud gasp, Angharad realised that she had been holding her breath, "it's me", she said before realising that it was possible that Susan wouldn't even recognise her voice, "it's Angharad". A faint, "what the fuck" came back through the door followed by the sounds of locks being turned and the gentle creak as the door was opened. "What are you doing here?" asked Susan, it was clear that she was not happy at the presence of Angharad on her door step but at the same time the opening of the door made it clear that she knew Angharad did not pose any physical threat to her. Looking Susan up and down, Angharad thought that she was more beautiful than ever, despite being the mother of two children in their early to mid-teens, Susan had a slight figure that would have fooled many into thinking that she had never had any children. Since Angharad had last seen her she had grown her hair. When they had first got together Susan had worn a very short, very boyish cut; they had been in university after all but now Susan had long, flowing, blonde locks. Maybe she wants to reinforce her femininity, her gentleness, thought Angharad and who can blame her.

"Well?" asked Susan and Angharad found her voice, "I really need some documents translated from Welsh into English", she said and Susan looked at her disappointed, "you, being here now, I thought that the world must have ended", Susan said and her face took on a sterner look, "couldn't this have waited for some other time?". Angharad shook her head, "if I didn't come now, then I would never have come" she stated, her face hardening as the importance of her task came back to the forefront of her mind.

Susan sighed deeply and stepped out of the doorway, indicating with her free hand for Angharad to pass in. As she entered she heard Susan whispering to her, "you are lucky that Marc is away on business, he might have just thumped you one irrespective of how you look now", the door was closed by Susan who then shooed Angharad down the hallway and into the kitchen. "Don't get any ideas either about seeing the kids", Susan growled, "you are here for the reason you gave and nothing else". Nodding, Angharad whispered "I understand" in reply. It was clear to her that after 10 years none of the anger at the betrayal that Susan felt had subsided and yet she could sense that still, deep inside, trying to break out was a feeling of love.

On entering the kitchen, Angharad was amazed at what she saw in front of her. When she had been here last, when it had been her home, the kitchen had been small, nothing special or exciting. Now though, with the construction of an extension and knocking the kitchen through into the dining room the kitchen was something spectacular with a range cooker and a marbled top island in the middle of the room. Placing the wet bag onto the island Angharad looked around for a towel to dry things off. Susan, understanding immediately what Angharad wanted pulled one off of the radiator and handed it to her. Wiping herself down Angharad looked into Susan's eyes and the mixture of betrayal and love that Susan clearly felt seemed to shine out of them like torch light. "I know you don't want me to see the kids but how are they?" Angharad tentatively asked and she saw that Susan's face softened slightly, "they are good, not that you ever see them" replied Susan. A sudden spike of anger filled inside Angharad, the main reason she never saw them was because of the way Susan and Marc responded to her and her attempts at a relationship with the children. In the end, she had found it easier on herself and the kids if she never saw them and generally stayed away. "So what is this document of such importance?" demanded Susan, interrupting Angharad's thoughts and she realised that she had fallen silent for an uncomfortably long time.

"You know about the three deaths that have taken place over the weekend?" asked Angharad and Susan nodded slowly, "I do keep up with the news in my home town" she ventured. Smiling at Susan's sarcastic reply, Angharad continued, "so Gwyn Davies was the leader of the council and appears to have killed himself in the early hours of Saturday morning, Stephen Thomas, was the de facto head of the local criminal fraternity and was murdered in the early hours of Sunday morning and Marion Davies who is head of the local business community died in a fire at her offices late on Sunday evening". Angharad paused and it was clear that what she had said so far was not enough for Susan who stood there, watching, still expecting the great revelation. "So Gwyn Davies and Marion Davies were related, they have a common ancestor called Abraham Davies who was some sort of Church minister" continued Angharad hoping that she had already said enough to spark Susan's imagination but instead there seemed to be an almost bored look falling over her face. Susan cut off Angharad preventing her from speaking any further. Pointing at the bag on the island she spoke "all this is very nice but the thing in there requires urgent translation because?", Angharad could detect a tinge of seething anger lying underneath it.

Reaching inside the bag on the island in the middle of the kitchen Angharad pulled out the pages of photocopy and put them down directly in front of Susan. "My ancestor was involved in three identical incidents in 1844 in which an Abraham Davies is mentioned repeatedly but his diaries are in Welsh". This time Angharad knew she had delivered information that would grab the attention of Susan who was clearly already scanning the pages of text, "Sergeant Ephraim Jones referred to them as the Llofruddiaeth Triwriaeth" said Angharad hoping to add that final piece of spice to the work that she was asking of Susan, "the triumvirate murders" murmured Susan in reply.

Susan looked up at Angharad and there was a clear glint of intrigue and excitement in her face, "either your ancestor was a genius or a mad man. He suspected Abraham Davies of being involved in the murders but that is all I can tell you immediately, to translate everything, properly will take time" said Susan, "time I don't have right now". Angharad's face fell, this was her one chance at getting to the bottom of what happened in 1844, "however", interjected Susan, "I will do it anyway because if your ancestor is right and if your instincts are right, which they normally are, then I want to stop the monster who is responsible for these crimes". Relief flowed over Angharad, "thank you", she said, "if there is anything that I can do to help?" she offered, realising that she might regret that statement as it left her lips. "Marc is away all week, I might need help with child care at some point", said Susan, "otherwise this should take me about a week, there are a number of bits of old fashioned language and incorrect grammar which will need unpicking". Angharad nodded and realised that as far as Susan was concerned this conversation and visit was over. "I'll see myself out, thank you again", said Angharad and she walked towards the front door. "Goodbye" said Susan tersely.

Chapter 6

Today it was possible to get into the shells of the buildings that burnt down on the High Street over the weekend. My visit confirmed what I already believed, that the fire started in the shop of Samuel Powell. The damage inside was extensive but it was possible to trace the source. There was a large fireplace in the shop itself within which there had clearly been a lit fire on the night in question. How this sparked a larger fire is anybody's guess, I only wish I knew because given the time of night nobody stood a chance. Many of the victims would have died in their sleep and those that didn't would have been consumed by the fire as they tried to escape.

What I don't understand is why Samuel Powell would have lit such a fire? Given the location of the fire it would not have been used for cooking, its sole purpose would have been for heating the large room within which it stood. However, it was a very warm night, hot even and he was known to be a relatively fit man, someone who would complain that he found it too warm even when others were complaining of the cold. From my inspection of the property there was no fire guard in place, which seems strange. The alarm was not raised until the fire was well alight and no body was found within that room so my conclusion would be that the room was empty when the fire started.

Others disagree with me, my Inspector insists that this must have been an accident, how else would the fire have started he asks. In his opinion, Samuel must have been trying to dry something, a rug maybe and had left the room unattended. I knew Samuel Powell personally though and he was an intelligent and cautious man, I cannot see him making such a simple mistake. His sister had died in a fire when he was young, a fire which almost took his own life and so he always put suitable precautions in place when dealing with it. The thought of a man like Samuel Powell walking out of a room and leaving an unguarded and unprotected fire without someone to watch over it does not sit well with me.

Tuesday 13th August 2013

By the time Angharad had got home from visiting Susan it was gone midnight. She was completely drained from the night shifts and the lack of sleep since but that did not stop her from waking before 7am the following morning. Lying in bed and alone Angharad was glad to have the silence and freedom from the rest of the world as her mind raced trying to make sense of the case that was taking shape before her. At present there was, officially, one suicide, one murder and one accident that had taken place in her home town and yet, along with Thomas, she was convinced that someone had conducted a series of well disguised murders. For what purpose though? Who or what could benefit from these crimes? Yes, it was true that they were all important figure heads in their respective fields but one person could not hope to gain from the death of all three. Unless of course, it was more than one person? A conspiracy maybe? Angharad's head hurt at the thought, why would there be a conspiracy to remove these individuals? Angharad could not see how any conspiracy, which would have to act to a common goal, would benefit from the death of three people with such disparate interests, even if two of them were related. It was too much for Angharad, she needed to clear her head and so ten minutes later she found herself starting a long run from her apartment, around Cardiff Bay to Penarth Pier and back via the barrage.

Just 40 minutes after Angharad had started her run she staggered back into her apartment to find that her home phone was ringing. She picked it up, still panting heavily from the exertion of the run, "Angharad, is everything alright?" came the worried voice of Thomas over the phone, "yes Gramps", she replied, "I just came back from a run". "Oh good", said Thomas, "when do you think you can get to Merthyr?" he asked his voice sparkling with excitement and expectation. "What's the time now?" asked Angharad before realising that from her position she could see the clock on the cooker, a clock on the living room wall and her watch which she had left sitting on the coffee table the night before. "0805 hours exactly came the reply" and Angharad smiled at the fact that even after 20 years of retirement Thomas still functioned as if he was on duty. "Well?" pressed Thomas as Angharad counted out the time in her head. "How about 10am?" she offered finally, allowing herself a bit of extra time for delays and traffic, after all he was a stickler for being on time. "Perfect", came the reply, "park in the small car park opposite the fountain shop and walk up the path between Caedraw school and St Tydfil's church, you'll soon find me, ta-ra", said Thomas. The conversation was ended by Thomas and before Angharad could reply he had hung up the phone. Angharad couldn't help but laugh. She didn't know what had Thomas so excited but she did know that at such times his ability to interact with others sometimes went out the window.

Luckily the journey was quick and efficient and Angharad found herself pulling into the car park that Thomas had mentioned at a quarter to 10. There was only one space and conveniently it was right next to a green Gilbern Invader Mark III, Thomas' car. It was now over 40 years old and he could have easily afforded a replacement and at various points it had been one of two or three cars he had owned but this car he loved and he had bought it from new on his promotion to Inspector in 1972. Parking her Mini carefully alongside, Angharad got out and spent a few minutes admiring the Gilbern, something she couldn't help but do every time she saw it. She knew it was a temperamental old thing but she also knew that she probably loved it almost as much as Thomas did. Thinking back to her childhood her mind filled with memories of trips out in the car or Thomas tinkering underneath it or around it. On Sundays when he was not working, he would spend a couple of hours in the morning just cleaning and waxing it.

Pulling herself away from her reminiscence, Angharad followed Thomas' instructions and walked up the path between the school and the old Parish Church, the Church of St Tydfil, the female saint who was martyred and after whom the town was named. Angharad found that whenever she walked passed this old building she wondered if the story about Harry Half a Man from the book Off to Philadelphia in the Morning was true. That he was buried in the churchyard in the middle of the night by his friend. Harry Half a Man, so called because he had no legs had died from Cholera, a cause of death that meant you were banned from being buried on sacred ground. However, in the book Harry made the request and his friend obliged. A little bit of Angharad smiled at the thought that it was true, she saw it as more proof that the people of Merthyr Tydfil couldn't help but stick two fingers up to authority at every opportunity.

Continuing the walk up the path, Angharad approached a bend, just passed the junction with Three Salmon Street and she knew that around that corner the Police Station on Swan Street would come into view. Prior to that, stood on the path directly next to the junction itself she could see Thomas patiently waiting but he was not alone. Stood next to him were two other men but the distance was such that she could not make out either of them other than to say that one was old and one was young. As she got closer Angharad realised the tang of burnt wood hung lightly in the air and on scanning around she was able to put everything into context, Thomas and the other two men were stood at the back entrance to the shop that Marion Davies had died in.

Finally Angharad was close enough to see the two other men clearly, the older one she had a vague recollection of meeting in the past; a similar age to Thomas his physique was almost exactly the opposite. In every way that Thomas looked young for his age, his powerful build, his energetic walk and the spark of life in his eyes, this man was bent over and frail looking as he leaned heavily on a walking stick. His face was one of a man who was awaiting death and Angharad guessed that from what she had previously discussed with Thomas that this must be Marion Davies' father. She wondered how much the man before her was frail because of his own general health and how much was the impact of the death of his daughter. The younger man was clearly a relative, the nose and chin were similar but here was a person who was angry at the world. He stood tall and strong but his fists were clenching and he looked to be ready to lash out at anybody who challenged him, a man who seemed desperate for a fight.

"Angharad", called Thomas as she got close enough, "thank you for coming". "Gramps" said Angharad, happiness in her voice as she embraced him quickly, realising he was carrying a ruck sack as she did so. As she released the embrace she raced to beat Thomas to the introductions, "I take it you are Marion's father?" she asked while offering her hand which he shook gently, "Berwyn" said the man quietly, "and this is my..." he indicated the younger man but Angharad was feeling a need to impress this family who appeared to be looking to her and Thomas for answers. "This is your grandson and Marion's son" she said, again offering her hand to the man who refused to shake it as his anger continued to course through his veins. She could sense Berwyn looking at the man with a hint of disappointment, "Jack", said Berwyn, "this is Jack and he was Marion's only child". Angharad nodded slowly, "my sympathies to both of you" she offered and Berwyn nodded in understanding. Looking back to Thomas, Angharad waited for him to continue the discussion, she knew that he would be on the ball and he did not fail. "At 0700 hours this morning the decision was made to lift the scene watch on the shop after it was concluded that Marion's death was an unfortunate accident", said Thomas, "the property has been returned to Berwyn and Jack and they have been very kind to have granted us a chance to look inside before they start cleaning up". Nodding in understanding Angharad acknowledged Berwyn and Jack and the painful decision that they had taken, "thank you" she said quietly and while Berwyn just looked pained she noticed that Jack looked at her and nodded quickly.

Thomas took a deep breath, allowing a moment to pass

quietly but ensuring that it did not linger too long, "shall we?" he offered and indicated towards the rear of the shop with his hand. Turning in the direction indicated Angharad noticed that a large roller shutter, built into a brick wall with a concrete face marked the rear boundary of the property. Small traces of Police tape could be seen on either side where the scene watch had been. Beyond the roller shutter was a tarmac area which clearly was now a small car park having, presumably once been a garden at the rear of the premises. Looking further, was a rear entrance into the shop itself the door of which was showing the signs of damage having been caused by the fire crews as they had entered the building. Leading the way Angharad walked towards this open door followed by Thomas while Berwyn and Jack walked slowly behind. As they entered the ground floor Angharad could see that the damage to the downstairs was not complete, all of the surfaces were smeared black more through the effects of smoke than the fire itself, the smell of which hung thick in the air. To her left Angharad could see a stair case that lead upstairs, while a large pool of congealed blood lay in front of the bottom step. Turning to Berwyn, Angharad pointed up the stairs, "what's up there?" she asked and Berwyn followed the direction of Angharad's hand. "That would be her private office, it's where she would normally sit when working" said Simon, "and downstairs?" asked Angharad, "she had a small team of three staff who were based down here" added Berwyn and Angharad nodded.

Turning to face back into the ground floor and then looking back up the stairs at the first floor Angharad considered her options. Then, her mind made up, Angharad faced Thomas and she discreetly pointed to the pool of blood at the bottom of the stairs, Thomas nodded in understanding without saying anything. "Gramps, will you take the upstairs?" asked Angharad and he nodded again before stepping carefully over the blood and climbing the steps two at a time. "Berwyn, why would Marion have been working on a Sunday night?" asked Angharad, "was such a thing normal?". Thinking carefully, Berwyn replied, "Marion never liked

Sunday nights, I don't know why, even in childhood she would save up all her homework and spend hours working into the night on a Sunday and then on Monday she would be up like a lark, however, late she had worked. It was just her thing". Angharad nodded, "so Marion being here on her own, so late on a Sunday night was not unusual?" and Berwyn confirmed Angharad's thoughts, "no" he replied, "she was well known for it". Berwyn lapsed into reminiscence about his daughter, "normally she would cook a big Sunday dinner for everyone and then go to work until the early hours".

Angharad walked further into the ground floor passing by the stair case and entering into the open planned space where the staff were clearly based. Once, this area would have been a shop but Marion was a trained accountant and had turned the building into her own office serving the local business community. The floor was wooden, clearly by design rather than the product of the fire having burned away the carpet. As Angharad walked forward she heard the floorboards squeak and could feel them give way slightly. Looking down Angharad noticed that she was standing on a trap door in the floor. Angharad looked up at Berwyn a quizzical look on her face and realising what she wanted to ask he answered without the question being set, "this is one of the buildings with the old cellars that aren't used anymore, where the cellar dwellers used to be" he said, "normally it is hidden under a rug as Marion never used the cellar". "Where is the rug?" asked Angharad and Berwyn shrugged, clearly lost for an answer. She then turned her attention to Jack who shook his head, "I don't know but it was in place when I visited mother on Friday" he said. Angharad continued with the questions, "when was it last used?". Berwyn shrugged, "Marion was very safety conscious and would have the building inspected annually by a surveyor but other than that they went down there, who knows, maybe 40 or 50 years ago, when my father ran his shop from here". "So you worked here?" asked Angharad, "no, I never worked here, Marion inherited the premises directly from my father. My business supplied services to the local factories but I sold that off 25 years ago when my health started to suffer". Angharad nodded and returned to her search of the ground floor.

In the middle of the room, amongst the desks stood an old fashioned portable electric fire that was heavily fire damaged. There was a small piece of woven material hanging off the one side of it. Angharad looked at the small piece of fibre carefully, taking care not to touch it at the moment. "That's the rug!" offered Jack unprompted, "are you sure?" asked Angharad and Jack was quick to confirm. "Definitely, it is a very distinctive pattern with those feathery, crest things on them and it is the only thing with that pattern in the whole building" he said, "Fleur de Lys?" Angharad offered and Jack replied, "yeah, them" he said. Studying the piece of material carefully Angharad could see that it wasn't a cheap rug, "what would Marion do if she wanted it cleaned?" asked Angharad. "She was very particular" said Jack, "I remember her buying it, it wasn't cheap and she would get it sent out for professional cleaning even if all that was dropped on it was a small amount of water" he continued. "Why leave it on the floor of a busy office?" asked Angharad, "if it was such a valuable and treasured item?" but neither Berwyn nor Jack could offer and answer other than, "that's Marion for you".

A shout from upstairs attracted the attention of all three. "Angharad, you need to come see this" called Thomas. Standing, Angharad turned to Berwyn and Jack and indicated for them to wait where they were and she headed off back to the stairs. Climbing them she could see Thomas stood at the top his face full of excitement as she got to him. "What's the matter Gramps?" she asked and he smiled and pointed towards the door hinges. Angharad followed Thomas' gaze and saw that the hinges were damaged, the door had clearly been pushed open too far. It had happened recently as the wood under where the hinges had held the door was far cleaner, even with the smoke damage, than the wood around it. "Someone has knocked into the door" said Angharad "knocked into it with enough force to stress the hinges". Thomas nodded "and that isn't the only damage up here" he said, turning into the office and pointing out the indentation in the carpet which indicated that the desk had moved slightly before further pointing to a smashed mug on the floor. Angharad looked back down the stairs, "Marion was found dead at the bottom of the stairs, a mixture of injuries from a fall and smoke inhalation having killed her, correct?" she asked and Thomas nodded, "well deduced" he said and Angharad pondered in silence for a moment. "Gramps, do you have a torch in that bag?" Angharad asked and Thomas smiled, "of course", he said, "what are you thinking of?".

Turning to Thomas, Angharad grinned this time, "so we are supposed to believe that Marion was upstairs, there was a fire, she went to investigate in a panic, bashed her desk knocking the mug over, bashing into the door and then falling down the stairs knocking herself out before being overcome by the smoke and dying of that and the injuries from the fall?". Angharad posed it as a question but it was as much rhetorical for herself as it was a question to Thomas. "I think that is an accurate assessment of the situation" Thomas replied. "Except, a fastidious, safety orientated, hard-working woman who had an expensive rug which she always had professionally cleaned and which covered a trap door that was never used decided to hang it over an electric fire, presumably to dry it, in the middle of summer when we have had a series of hot days and warm nights thus, by accident, causing the fire that subsequently killed her" said Angharad. Thomas immediately understood what she was thinking, "we need to look under the trap door" he said and Angharad nodded, "exactly Gramps".

A few moments later all four were reunited on the ground floor, Angharad and Thomas looking at the trap door while Berwyn and Jack stared at them, confusion on their faces. Thomas put the bag on the floor and opened it up, searching for the torch he had stowed in there, "what's going on Thomas?" asked Berwyn and Angharad replied for the both of them. "We need to see inside the cellar" she said, "we're not sure what we are looking for but we are convinced that there are answers inside". The answer from Angharad didn't seem to help the situation, if anything it left

Berwyn and Jack even more perplexed. Finding the torch, Thomas handed it to her, "it's your idea" he said, "you should get the honour". Nodding grimly Angharad took possession of the torch and reached down to lift up the trap door. It was heavy but not impossible to move, the fire damage not being such that it had left the hinges seized up. Turning on the torch, Angharad shone it into the dark and the light flashed over a set of wooden steps that led down to a concrete floor. Placing one foot slowly onto the top step, Angharad tested its strength and found it to be in good condition. Moving carefully she climbed down into the cellar while Thomas stood in the opening at the top and watched. After just six, steep, awkward steps Angharad found herself stood on the floor of the cellar and she started to move the light of the torch around absorbing everything that she could see in its narrow beam.

The cellar was empty and was only about six foot in height and surrounded on all four sides by stone bricks that were clearly at least as old as the building that stood over her head. As Angharad scanned the room she could feel a nagging sense that she was missing something obvious, something that answered the questions of how Marion was killed, not by accident but at the hands of a killer. The torch light flashed against the side of the cellar, the side that bordered the next building further up the High Street and then onto the floor before illuminating the same bit of wall again. Then Angharad saw it, the clue she was looking for, chips of stone on the floor. She flashed the light towards the other areas of the cellar and confirmed in her mind what she had seen, clearly the rest of the cellar had been swept clean and unused for a period of time but there on that one side were small chips of stones which seemed to scatter away from the base of the wall. Looking up at the brick work above her, she found the second clue staring her in the face. A four foot wide section of wall had clearly been rebuilt, very recently. The cement holding the stone bricks together was so much cleaner and newer looking than the cement to either side or on any of the other walls. Angharad leaned back over the steps and looked up towards Thomas, "Gramps, do Berwyn and Jack know the last time any repair work was required down here?" she called up and the sound of Berwyn's reply echoed back down into the cellar, "at least 15 years ago". "What work was done?" she asked but this time she could not hear the answer until Thomas conveyed it, "some of the wooden beams were replaced in the floor". Angharad glanced back into the cellar and could see which wooden beams had been replaced; they were at the other end of the room from where she had been looking.

Angharad climbed back up the stairs so that she could look at Berwyn and Jack directly. Standing in the trap door she looked around it, just her head showing up above the level of the floor. "What building is that way?" she asked, pointing further up the High Street. "It belongs to my third cousin" came the reply, "but it's been empty for the last couple of years as the business went bust" said Berwyn. Looking up at Thomas Angharad nodded with her head for him to follow her and she disappeared back inside the cellar. Shining the torch onto the steps Angharad provided Thomas with enough light so that he could find his way down the stairs until he was stood next to her.

"Look", said Angharad as she shone the torch light around the cellar capturing the floor and the walls as she went, "what do you see?". At first Thomas stared unseeing into the gloomy room not understanding what Angharad had observed but then he realised what he was looking at and gave a sharp intake of breath. "Stones... cement", he mumbled before racing forward towards the far wall where Angharad had previously seen the same issues. Tracing the stones with his fingers Thomas finally found what he was looking for, then glancing down he spotted a suitable piece of rock on the floor of the cellar and picked it up. He beckoned Angharad forward and she quickly joined him at his side, "look", he said, "there is freshly exposed stone here and this piece fits the break perfectly". As Angharad watched Thomas gently put the piece that he had collected from the floor into place on the wall, the fit was exact. "Gramps, any idea how long since this wall was put up" asked Angharad and he turned to face her, "there's no way of telling for certain" came the reply, "but it was recently". Reaching out with his hand he pushed on the stone wall and gasped as the stone moved under the pressure he exerted. "Shit!" exclaimed Angharad, "the cement is still wet" and Thomas simply nodded in reply. "What do we do?" she asked and for a moment, in the torch lit cellar all they could do was look at each other, speechless.

As if working through some psychic connection they both nodded and almost raced each other to get back out of the cellar. Back on the ground floor of the offices Thomas reached for his bag and searching it he pulled out a small lump hammer and a second torch before disappearing from view back through the trap door. Meanwhile Angharad raced out of the back door and climbed over the wall into the rear of the next door business. Berwyn and Jack could only look at each other in shock and surprise as Angharad and Thomas raced around completing their individual tasks until curiosity was too much for them and together they ventured down into the cellar. "Thomas? What's going on Thomas?" asked Berwyn as he got down into the cellar and found Thomas pushing with his fingers against different parts of the wall. Before any answer was given Angharad reappeared, "there is nobody there, it is all locked" she said, "but let me take a photograph first". Pulling out her mobile phone Angharad took three photographs from the far side of the cellar before walking over and taking a few more close up. Then she looked at Thomas, "right Gramps, do it", she said and he swung the lump hammer against a stone he had specifically chosen.

It didn't take much effort to push the stone through and it fell with an echo into the cellar next door. "Thomas!", screamed Berwyn, "please tell me what you are doing!" he demanded. This time Thomas reached into the gap where the stone had once been and scraped his finger through the cement picking up a small amount on his finger tip. Then he walked up to Berwyn, "wet cement" he said, holding his hand out with his finger tip extended, "this wall has been rebuilt very recently". Berwyn and Jack stared at the fingertip and in unison their mouths fell open, Jack was the first to recover his senses, "what does this mean?" he asked. Angharad stepped forward and shrugged her shoulders, "specifically?, we don't know", she said, "however, it does indicate that either Marion was not alone when she died or someone visited immediately before or after the event, either way whoever it was didn't want anyone to know they had been here". Berwyn finally regained his senses and was the first to mention the word, "murder?". Thomas was the first to reply, "we have no way of knowing, what we do know is that the Major Investigation Unit are not interested". He looked at Angharad and she nodded in agreement, "that's correct", she said, "it is down to us to investigate".

Angharad and Thomas started to remove more of the stones that formed the cellar wall until there was a gap big enough for one of them to look through. Lifting her torch Angharad pointed it through the hole and pushed her head into the gap. Beyond was just another empty cellar much as the one they were currently in. Moving the light around, her eyes fell upon a large wooden board on the floor that showed the remains of cement on it. She withdrew her head from the gap, "the only thing in there is the wooden board they used to mix the cement" she said and she looked at Thomas, "we need to go through then?" he asked rhetorically and Angharad nodded in agreement anyway.

To clear all of the stones so that there was a gap big enough for Thomas took the best part of an hour but eventually they were both stood in the cellar of the building next to Marion's office. Looking back into the room from which they had come Thomas asked if Berwyn or Jack wanted to join them. Jack was eager, an adventure for a man of his age but Berwyn declined and returned up to the ground floor rather than stand in the total darkness. Together, the three of them slowly climbed the steps, Angharad in the lead until she was directly below the trap door of the adjoining building. Putting pressure against it with her shoulder she found that it gave way surprisingly easily and Angharad opened it enough to be able to look out through the gap into the room beyond. It was dark, cold and silent and Angharad looked at Thomas for reassurance before pushing on the hatch again and soon after it made a loud crash as it rose passed the point of being vertical and fell open onto the ground floor of the building.

All three climbed up into the silence and looked around to get their bearings. In many ways this building was much the same as the one next door in terms of design except it contained the old fixtures of a shop rather than the fire damaged office furniture they had come from. Moving out into the room it could be seen that a layer of dust had slowly built up over everything and that in places this fragile surface had clearly been disturbed in the recent past by one or more persons. Finding that the downstairs held no information of benefit Angharad moved towards the back of the building in search of the stair case. This part of the ground floor was in darkness except for a dull light that streamed down from the upstairs. The windows at the rear had been boarded up and the door was made of solid wood, Angharad checked the door and found it to be securely locked. Standing at the bottom of the stairs and looking up towards the open door through which the light streamed she felt a moment of anxiety. While the shop had appeared empty up until now there was always the possibility that someone was lurking at the top of those stairs, waiting in silence for her to approach. Slowly, step by step Angharad climbed towards the door her ears and eyes straining for any sign of movement beyond the threshold.

Reaching the door, Angharad stared inside and found herself letting out a big breath of air and she then realised that throughout the climb she must have been holding her breath. The room beyond was clearly as abandoned as the downstairs except for in one corner where there were the signs of recent habitation. "Gramps!", Angharad called back down the stairs, "I've found something up here". Moving forward Angharad approached the area of disturbance that she could see and as she did so the outline of an oblong object made itself clear in the dust and dim light. An oblong space the perfect size and shape for some form of camping mattress or blow up bed. Next to this were a number of discarded items including a small camping stove and a couple of empty food tins. Angharad pulled out her phone and photographed the room and the items as Thomas joined her. "What do you think?" asked Thomas and she stared at him, "what do you mean, what do I think? I suspect I am thinking exactly the same as you" she said. Thomas looked at her a grin on his face before the sound of Jack interrupted both of them, "I'd like to know what either of you think", he said and Angharad and Thomas shared a discrete smile at the situation.

Keeping her eyes on Thomas's face, Angharad nodded slightly towards Jack and Thomas took the hint, "clearly, someone has been living here recently, not for long but long enough that they could stay here without being seen" he said. Not quite understanding Jack simply watched both of them with a vacant stare. Picking up on this Angharad spoke, "OK, someone has been into your mother's office, either when she died or around the time she died", Jack nodded and she continued, "the Fire Brigade and the Police have turned up and then kept the place under watch for the next 36 hours or so". Angharad waited to see if Jack was keeping up with this bit and a nod from him indicated that he was, "in that time, whoever it was needed to brick up the wall in the cellar and then wait for the Police to bugger off". Finally, thought Angharad as she saw Jack mouth an "Ah" and then he spoke, "so they needed to camp here?". A faint smile flickered across Angharad's face, "exactly", she said as if Jack had solved some complex mathematical problem. "So what do we do now?" asked Jack.

Not knowing where she was going or why she was going there, Angharad had not brought anything with her that might be of help for the gathering of evidence, however, Thomas was far more prepared. Returning to his rucksack that he had left in Marion's office he came back to Angharad bearing gifts in the form of evidence bags, "these should do nicely" he said with a smile on his face. "Should you even have those Gramps?", asked Angharad and Thomas smiled, "I don't, you do" he said and she grinned back. A short while later the three of them returned to the cellar under

Marion's office. In agreement with Thomas the decision was made to not rebuild the cellar wall but to make it look like it had fallen down naturally as if the repair job that had previously been done was of poor quality. "There will have to be a full structural investigation anyway" reasoned Thomas, "they can claim the repairs on the insurance, if that is what they wish to do". There was no argument from Angharad, after all it was unlikely that they had the skills, equipment or time to properly repair the wall themselves. Leaving the office by the route that they had come in they found Berwyn stood out on the path at the back. Angharad and Thomas both shook hands with him, "we'll solve this for you and for Marion" said Thomas as they bid him farewell knowing that they had no way of providing support to Berwyn or his family through the hard decisions that lay ahead.

Forty minutes later Angharad pulled her car up behind Thomas' car at the gates to his house. As a child Angharad had always loved coming to visit the house, positioned as it was in the woods and overlooking the reservoir at Pontsticill. It was a dream place to play on warm summer days such as this day was proving to be. In fact it was getting hot enough that Angharad thought about whether she could get away with sneaking down to the reservoir for a swim. At the very least, she thought, it would be nice to stand on the banks and feel the cooling breeze blowing off the water as she watched the steam train moving up the other side of the valley. The whistle of the narrow gauge engine echoing off the sides of the mountain as it went. After parking her car she walked out on to Thomas' patio while he disappeared inside the house to get a drink for both of them. Nervously, Angharad looked back at her car and used the remote control to ensure it was locked with the exhibits that she had collected secure in the boot. Even though Angharad had full view of them she had a nagging feeling that she had to really protect the items that she had collected.

Thomas strode out onto the patio a decanter of port in one hand and two small glasses in the other. Angharad smiled, she knew that whatever was in the decanter would not have been cheap, her grandfather always whinged about the idea that people would drink cheap or low quality alcohol. In some ways, Angharad had the same opinion but for her there were times when needs must and she didn't care what she was drinking or how much she had paid for it. As he took his seat in the sun Thomas looked at Angharad. "Who do you trust at the station?" he asked and Angharad shrugged her shoulders. "Nobody yet" she replied, "I've only just got there, a couple of the PC's seem like stand up people and so does the Inspector but other than that", she shook her head to indicate reinforce her point. "I was thinking specifically about getting those exhibits tested" Thomas prompted, and Angharad shrugged her shoulders again, "in terms of that, at this stage, I'm fresh out of answers Gramps", she said. They both fell to silence as Thomas pondered the situation, "I know just the person", he said and got up and walked into the house.

A few moments later Angharad could hear the sound of talking coming from the other side of the patio doors but it was too distant and quiet for her to fully make out what was being said. There was only one voice though, Thomas' and on looking into the house she could see he was on the telephone as a big smile grew across his face. "Perfect!" he suddenly said very loudly before mumbling what appeared to be some form of goodbye and hanging up the phone. As she watched, Thomas walked back onto the patio, "I've found someone who can help with our little predicament" he said and Angharad nodded, "we are, as in all three of us, are going to meet tomorrow at the The Recreation Ground in Brecon, somewhere out of the way for us". "Are you going to tell me who it is?" asked Angharad but Thomas shook his head, "no, it can be a surprise for you tomorrow, I don't want you getting all worried about it". Deep down Angharad thought that not knowing might make her worry more but she decided to not argue with her grandfather on this occasion.

Hours later, as the heat of the middle of the day started to wear off, Angharad returned home to her apartment. As she walked in she realised how stuffy it had become having been locked up all day and in direct line with the sun. She opened the patio doors and was just about to collapse onto the sofa, the exhaustion of the last few days catching up with her when the phone rang. Picking it up she mumbled "hello" into the receiver only to be met with the voice of an angry Susan, "do you want my help or not?" she asked. Angharad found herself off guard for a second but recovered, "yes, of course I do, what's the problem?" she asked and Susan went into a rant, "I've been ringing your mobile and your home phone for the last two hours, I need you to look after the kids tomorrow". Taking a moment to gather her thoughts, Angharad pulled out her mobile phone to see that the battery was dead. As she did so she replayed what Susan had said in her head, "you want me to look after the kids tomorrow?", she asked, "you never want me to look after the kids?". Susan grunted before explaining the situation, "well this time is different, I've been at home, looking after the kids and trying to do this translation for you while Marc is off on business", she said. "Because of you I need to go into the office, because your long dead whatever he is speaks some strange colloquial Welsh and the only way I am going to decipher it is if I go to work tomorrow". That last bit was delivered as if Angharad should be eternally grateful and prepared to do anything in order to please Susan. "OK", said Angharad, "I take it you want me early?" she asked and Susan grunted again, "yes, the earlier the better". "Is there anything you can tell me so far?" asked Angharad and she could hear a deep sigh from Susan, "yes, there is something I can tell you", she said without elaborating, "OK, do I need to beg?" asked Angharad and as she did so she realised that she had fallen into some form of trap that Susan had set for her.

A note of triumph sounded in Susan's voice as she replied, "what are the four pillars of 19th Century Merthyr? Or at least, what would be the four pillars in the mind of a power hungry Welsh Rector with a large family?". There was no answer from Angharad, she was completely lost as to what Susan was getting at, "I don't understand" she said and there was a distinct snort down the phone, "It's all about control of the four pillars" Susan said,

"Abraham Davies had one but how would he get the other three?".
At that, Susan put the phone down leaving Angharad listening to
the dead tone. Since when had Susan taken to setting riddles
thought Angharad as she realised that she probably needed to sleep
on the matter.

Putting the phone down, Angharad stepped back towards
the sofa with the intention to slump on it again but just like before
she was prevented from doing so, this time by the sound of a knock
at the door. It was rare for someone to knock at the door as she had
very little to do with her neighbours and at this time of the evening
it was necessary to use the door entry system to get into the
building. Walking slowly, Angharad reached the door and without
checking through the spy hole opened it. Stood outside was Tim, a
large and heavy looking bag slung over his shoulder. "Hey sexy",
said Tim, "I've got some good news for you!". Angharad looked at
him not being able to comprehend what was happening, in fact, she
realised that she hadn't even listened to him. "What?" asked
Angharad, confusion spreading across her face, "I've got good
news", said Tim, he seemed to be in a joyous mood and Angharad
was too tired to work out whether he was being honest or forcing a
big smile onto his face.

Angharad again failed to respond, or at least respond in the
way that Tim was hoping for and so he forced the situation, "I've
always said I would leave that bitch of a wife of mine", he said, "I've
always said I would leave her and we could be together always and
now I have". An even bigger smile crossed his face and he pushed
his way into the apartment passed Angharad who finally started to
catch up with what was going on. "You've left your wife?" she asked
in clarification and Tim smiled, "yes and so here I am to live with
you!". He did seem very pleased with this turn of events, a change
in fortune which, when it had been discussed in the past had been
met with anger and threats. "So you're going to live here?" asked
Angharad, "of course", said Tim, "or at least until we can get
somewhere more suitable for me and my gorgeous girlfriend". Tim
dropped the bag and scooped Angharad up in his arms, "so are you

going to tell me how happy you are with this situation?". Angharad smiled but in reality she did not know what to make of the situation, "it's wonderful news" she lied not knowing whether Tim had picked up on her falseness.

"So what are we going to do tomorrow?" asked Tim as he let go of Angharad and went to pick up his bag to take further into the apartment. "We've both got tomorrow off so let's do something fun" he called as he disappeared from view into the bedroom. "I can't", replied Angharad, "I have things I need to do tomorrow and I can't change them". There was a moment of silence and then Tim appeared in the bedroom doorway anger etched across his face, "what do you mean "you can't"", he said, "I've moved in with you, we can live together as a happy couple and you haven't got time for me?". Angharad flinched slightly, she had seen this anger from Tim in the past and knew that she needed to stop it now, "it's family things", she partly lied, knowing that she was also meeting with Thomas regarding the case. "If I had known you were coming early I could have refused" she said but Tim was clearly not calming down and was not happy about the situation. Stepping towards Tim, Angharad acted as seductively as possible, a difficult task when dressed in a pair of trainers and dirt covered t-shirt and jeans, she lowered her face and wrapped herself up in his arms again. "Why don't I make it up to you right now?" she asked, slowly lifting her head until their faces were millimetres apart, "we can have lots of fun tonight and then tomorrow, I'll come home as soon as possible so we can do it again" she said. The tension that she could feel in Tim's body started to subside and he kissed her, "good girl" he murmured as he pulled her into the bedroom.

Chapter 7

Wednesday 14th August 1844
Diary of Sergeant Ephraim Jones

I think the Inspector is starting to doubt whether it was a good idea to make me a Sergeant. He found out I had been into the shop of Samuel Powell and asked me what was going on as it was not my investigation. Faced with such a challenge I had no choice but to tell him the truth; that something doesn't make sense to me and I think that the events of the last few days are more sinister than he believes. His response was to put me behind a desk for the day taking statements and reports from the people who come into the station. According to the Inspector I need to remember that while I am a Sergeant it is he who is in charge. He said that if I wish to investigate murders and crazy ideas of conspiracy then maybe I would be better off moving to the Metropolitan Police in London.

He seems to be hoping that a day or two of distractions will cause me to forget about the case. However, I am not sure his resolve will last, one of the reasons I was made a Sergeant is because of my particular skills out on the streets and if I am right then the next few days will see some very interesting developments. The rumours coming out of China is that there have been a number of violent incidents as people and gangs vie for control of the empire and that things are getting rapidly worse.

War is breaking out in China and if things don't calm down soon then we will need to restore order in that cesspit by force. If that happens then the Inspector will be desperate to get me back on the streets. For now we will just have to see what tomorrow brings.

Wednesday 14th August 2013

It was difficult, Angharad was really feeling drained but she made sure that Tim had a night to remember so that when she woke early the following morning he didn't stir. As she slid gently out of the bed the sound of him snoring gently reached her ears. She gathered up her clothes quietly and left the room, heading for the bathroom to get showered and changed. Freshly washed, she skipped breakfast and sneaked out of the house before eight leaving Tim fast asleep.

Getting across Cardiff was a pain, it always was on a Wednesday morning but the trip up the A470 was better and so she got to Susan's house just before nine. Even then Angharad was clearly not early enough for Susan who answered the door with a scowl on her face before refusing to acknowledge or engage in any conversation. A moment later Sion and Sioned, Susan and Angharad's twelve year old twins appeared behind their mother. Susan remained in the doorway like a sentry guarding the entrance to the inner sanctum and the two children had to squeeze passed her. They were a strong reminder that once upon a time the relationship between Angharad and Susan had been very different, that where there was now anger and mistrust there had once been love and belief. Angharad had not seen either of them for three months and she looked on Sion and Sioned with pride in her eyes before she felt tears welling up from within. Since her last meeting with the twins they had clearly both grown quickly though they had retained the slenderness of their mother. It was also possible to see that they were starting to show the height and toughness of her own family so causing them to look more lithe than simply thin. For a moment, Angharad continued to just stare at the pair of them letting their features sink in, noting to herself how Sion reminded her so much of the child she had been and how Sioned looked so much like the child she had wanted to be.

"Come here, both of you" said Angharad enthusiastically as she returned to the present. She held out her arms for a big hug and for second she feared the worst as Sion and Sioned looked at her, unmoving. Sion was the first to break, his face creasing with emotion and he dived into Angharad's arms before being followed by Sioned and she embraced them both desperately, holding onto them as if she would never let go. Angharad kissed both of them on the top of their head and then finally released her grip, "say goodbye to your mother" she said and they both turned and waved to a still silent Susan who was stood in the doorway, her face passive and unflinching.

Angharad drove the three of them to Dowlais Top, to the large supermarket where the three of them selected food for a picnic lunch and then they made their way to Brecon to meet with Thomas. Sioned sat in the front as they drove with Sion hiding in the back, "still in charge of your brother?" Angharad asked as they travelled and Sioned laughed, "he spends too much time reading and being all soft" came the reply. "Sion may love you but he doesn't see you as a role model whereas I do, he still follows Mam far more" said Sioned. The comment sounded almost throw away in the way it was delivered but it surprised Angharad and for a moment she was lost in a sea of wild emotions. Susan had been in a relationship with Marc for a number of years but for some reason neither Sion nor Sioned had ever linked to him as an inspiration for their lives. Angharad had always hoped that Marc, despite her personal differences with him, would be a more masculine influence on the children, especially on Sion. Deep inside, Angharad had a deep fear that Sion would turn out like her and that was not something she wanted. Not because she hated herself but because she did not want one of her own to go through the same pain that had engulfed her. The reality though was that from a young age Sion had gravitated towards his mother, gentle, calm and openly emotional yet tough inside. On the other hand Sioned had always been like Angharad, always hard on the outside even when inside she just wanted to curl up in a ball and cry.

"Cariad?" a voice spoke from the back seat of the car, technically it was not an appropriate word for Sion to use towards Angharad. It was more of a name used between lovers but as a family it had been agreed that Mam had already been taken as Susan had given birth to them and Dad was not suitable especially as it was now a term used to refer to Marc. "Cariad?" Sion said again, a bit louder now and with a bit more urgency in his voice. "Yes?" said Angharad, finally replying, "are you happy?" asked Sion and Angharad smiled into the rear view mirror before giving the answer that she knew Sion would want, "of course I'm happy Sion". As she said it Angharad thought about the fact that there were many words, "tired", "stressed" and "angry" being just three, that would describe how she felt right now but for the children she would do her best to make sure that she was happy.

The three of them arrived at The Recreation Ground and Angharad was surprised to see the car park empty despite it being already mid-morning on a warm summer's day. Looking around there was no sign of Thomas and she let Sion and Sioned out of the car to run down by the river and over to the arcade while she waited for him to arrive. They hadn't agreed a specific time but still, she was surprised that he hadn't been here at 9am just in case. A few moments later the distinctive sound of Thomas' Gilbern reached her ears as it raced down Fenni-Fach Road at a speed she knew would be completely unsuitable for the narrow width of the lane. As the car appeared around the junction, the sound of Sion and Sioned running back to be with Angharad and greet their great grandfather reached her ears. Angharad smiled at the thought that they were so happy to see Gramps and in that moment she knew that she had at least, despite being a largely absent parent, done something right in the raising of her children. The Gilbern came to a stop in the space directly next to Angharad's car and a moment later the big, grinning frame of Thomas appeared from the driver's seat. Sion and Sioned couldn't wait and they raced round to see him, his arms easily enclosing both of them in a large hug. Looking at Angharad he continued to smile, "at least some of my family love me" he said before letting out a throaty laugh as Sion and Sioned attempted to tickle him. "Don't you two think you're a bit old for such games?" he asked and Sioned stepped away for a moment before meeting Thomas' gaze directly, "never" she said with a note of defiance in her voice before shouting instructions to Sion, "get him!".

A few minutes later Thomas opened the boot of his car and pulled out a traditional wicker picnic basket filled with food. Together the four of them carried their lunch down to the river, Sion and Sioned struggling with the hamper between them as Angharad and Thomas walked arm in arm. When they got to the river, the party turned right towards the field where Angharad recalled spending hours playing on the swings and slides that had once marked this as her favourite park. Laying down a blanket, Angharad and Thomas sat down while Sion produced a Frisbee from the rucksack he had been carrying and raced off with Sioned in hot pursuit. "They cope well with everything that has happened" said Thomas as he watched the two of them playing together, "they love you very much". Angharad, who was finding a simple pleasure in watching her two children play happily in her presence did not respond. Thomas realised that she was lost in thought and left her alone for a while to think about things. Standing he followed after Sion and Sioned, calling out to them and challenging them to throw the Frisbee towards him, in the process revealing the big kid that still hid within. Meanwhile Angharad remained seated, silently watching the three of them play together as their laughter carried across the field.

Rising to her feet, Angharad walked over to where Thomas was stood as if at the pinnacle of a large triangle with Sion and Sioned making up the two points at the base. The three of them were passing the Frisbee back and fore and trying to trick each other into dropping it. "Did Susan say how she was getting on?" Thomas asked and Angharad shook her head as she replied, "I've heard very little, all she has said so far is a riddle". Thomas turned towards Angharad just as the Frisbee got to him and it bounced off of his right arm causing Sion and Sioned to break out into a peal of mock laughter. "A riddle?" he asked, his face full of question and query. Angharad nodded before bending over, picking up the Frisbee and making to throw it towards Sioned before changing direction at the last minute and sending it sailing through the air towards Sion. "Come on, what's the riddle?" asked Thomas who was clearly impatient to find out more and so she told him, "what would be the four pillars in the mind of a power hungry Welsh rector with a large family?". Thomas thought for a second before replying, "four pillars?" he asked and Angharad nodded again, "yes, the four pillars of 19th Century Merthyr".

Letting out a gasp the face of Thomas changed from one of a perplexed man into one who fully understood what was in front of him. "It's easy" he said, "well easy if you think about the history of the town, the murders we know of and what our ancestor has already told us. "Easy?" said Angharad, "go on then, fill me in with your expertise" she continued while struggling to keep the sound of cynicism from her voice. Smiling, Thomas grabbed Angharad in a hug, "give me a cwtch", he said reassuringly, "I am sure you can make sense of it as well". Being held safe, Angharad felt a wave of tiredness and stress wash over her before seeming to evaporate just as quickly leaving her mind clear and calm. In that moment, Angharad had the clarity of vision which she needed to resolve the question that Susan had posed.

Pushing away from Thomas, Angharad looked him straight in the eye, a new determination spreading across her face. "Pillar one, religion", she said, "Abraham Davies, the 19th Century one, was a Rector so he already controls that pillar". Thomas smiled at Angharad, "go on", he encouraged her. "Pillar two, politics", she said and Thomas nodded again, "pillar three, business and pillar four, crime!". Angharad almost shouted the last one and Thomas grinned, "so now we just have to work out who benefits now" he said. "I can't help but think that the Davies family are still the key to all of this" she said and Thomas nodded, "it is looking that way". Angharad thought again, "well we have the exhibits that we got yesterday, let's hope they can tell us something of use", Thomas nodded and then looked at his watch "soon we'll have someone who can help us answer that question" he said.

Sion and Sioned tucked into their food greedily, it wasn't quite lunch time but they had been nagging that they were hungry for the last half hour and eventually Angharad relented. As they ate on the blanket Angharad sat next to them and watched feeling content that, if even for a couple of hours, she was able to pretend that she had a happy and close family. Nearby Thomas stood by the river, looking out over it and watching the first customers for the hire boats as they struggled upstream against what was, in reality, a very gently flowing river current. A movement caught the corner of Angharad's eye as someone entered the field from the direction of the car park but she paid no attention to it. In the time since they had arrived a number of other families had followed the same route and the field was slowly filling with people taking a chance to enjoy a summers day by the river. There was no reason for Angharad to think that this person was any different, however, instead of walking passed Angharad and her family they stopped and called out to Thomas. Angharad turned towards the voice, surprised at hearing the name of her grandfather, just in time to see Thomas respond to the person who had called to him. "George!" replied Thomas as the two of them met in front of her and clasped hands in an affectionate manner.

Staring at Thomas and the interloper, Angharad's mouth hung open as she recognised the face of her Inspector, George Williams. George and Thomas turned towards Angharad and started to walk over the grass as she scrambled to her feet to greet them. "Fuck", she thought to herself, "that wasn't what I was expecting". George approached with a big smile across his face, "Angharad!" he said, offering his hand, "and who are these lucky two?", he motioned towards Sion and Sioned with his free hand. Finding herself thrown at suddenly having to reveal the inner workings of her family to her boss Angharad stumbled over her welcome, "Sir, um, George" she said, "I didn't expect to see you here, at this time". Worried about how George would react Angharad looked to Thomas for advice as she spoke and found his face blank. Sioned got to her feet and took the initiative, "hi", she said, "we're Sion and Sioned and Angharad is our...", she thought for the best word to use in the circumstances, "Mam" she said, settling on its simplicity. George turned to Sioned and smiled and Sion stood up quickly and offered his hand which George took in a firm grasp, "I'm Sion, Sioned's twin brother" he said. "Good to meet both of you" said George before turning his attention back towards Angharad, "I understand but you don't need to explain" he said. On hearing the reassurance Angharad felt the sudden tension that had built in her body release.

"Angharad", said Thomas, "why are you so worried, why would George not be the person we were waiting for?" he asked. "Because..." said Angharad, not sure what to say, "because..." she said again and then gave up, "because" she said one last time and George struggled to suppress a laugh, "Thomas and I have crossed paths a number of times over the years" said George, "he was my first Inspector in 1986 before he was forced to go for promotion and he gave me a commendation when he was my station commander. It's because of him that I got promoted to Detective Sergeant and he was the there to protect me when I fell out of favour and found my way to Merthyr, I owe him a lot" he concluded. "I never doubted your integrity" said Angharad by way of apology. George raised his hand to silence her, "it doesn't matter, I didn't think you did", said George before turning towards Thomas again, "why don't you tell me what you need?", Thomas smiled, "shall we sit" he said, indicating the blanket. George and Thomas moved to sit on the blanket leaving Angharad standing next to Sion and Sioned. "We're going off to explore the river bank further up" said Sion. Angharad grabbed Sion and Sioned and pulled them close, "thank you" she whispered before releasing them to run off up the river. As Angharad finally took her seat she noticed that George and Thomas were already tucking into the food that Sion and Sioned had left behind as if they had not eaten for a week.

"Mm" said George, clearly deep in thought as Angharad and Thomas finished explaining the situation. "So we have three copycat murders that were committed over the weekend and they all match three murders that took place in 1844?" said George. Angharad couldn't work out if his question was rhetorical and simply him processing the information that he had been presented with or whether he was seeking clarification. "As far as we can tell", said Thomas, "that is the correct assessment of the situation". "Mm", said George again, "so the death of Stephen Thomas was murder, everyone agrees with that while the death of Marion Davies, while not declared a murder, clearly has some very worrying elements to it". Angharad and Thomas nodded again, "so what makes you think that Gwyn Davies was murdered? From what you have told me the only suggestion is this 169 year old diary?". Holding his hands out, palms up, Thomas made it clear that he didn't have any other information he could offer to explain the situation and George turned to Angharad, "you were there", he said, "do you recall anything that makes you suspicious of what happened?". Angharad replayed the events of that night in her head, telling George and Thomas everything that she could see as she recalled that first night she had spent in Merthyr as a shift Sergeant. As she told the story George suddenly interrupted, "he what!" he shouted, "he opened the letter there and then?" he asked and Angharad nodded, "was he wearing gloves?" he probed further and she shook her head. "I always knew that Di Marco was a prick" said George, "getting forensics from paper is hard enough, never mind when it has been tampered with by a bumbling buffoon" he was clearly seething and his interruption had brought the story to a sudden and unexpected conclusion.

Realising that he had completely interrupted Angharad's train of thought, George apologised and indicated that she should continue. The delay had worked in Angharad's favour though, waiting for George to calm back down she had played the next few moments through her head repeatedly and in that moment she had realised the mistake that the killer had made. "The stone", said Angharad and Thomas and George looked at her, "what?" they said in unison and Angharad grinned. "The stone", she said again, "the stone was under the briefcase and it can't be unless someone else was there". They both continued to look at her, "you're not making much sense", said Thomas and Angharad looked at him, "but it does make sense", she said. "When I arrived there was a hole in the wall of the bridge, a stone had been knocked down", Angharad paused to let that piece of information sink in, "the stone from that hole was under the briefcase". "So?" asked George, "maybe he had tried climbing the wall, dislodged the stone and then moved his briefcase out of the way and climbed a different part of the wall?". Shaking her head, Angharad made it clear she disagreed, "it all lined up, the point where he went over was directly above the point where he was found, the briefcase was put in place after he fell".

George looked at Thomas, "it works for me Thomas", he said, "you've got an accident and a suicide which both have things to indicate possible murder", Thomas nodded, "good". "So what do you want from me?" asked George and Angharad spoke before Thomas could answer, "we have exhibits that need to be examined" she said, "exhibits that need to be examined without the Major Investigation Unit finding out what we are up to". It was George's turn to grin, "that's easy" he said, I know just the people who can do the work for me". Thomas and Angharad nodded, "but why don't you take this case to the Major Investigation Unit?" asked George meeting the gaze of each of them in turn. "You know how I got here", said Angharad, "they are not interested, it's in Merthyr and anything to make the case go away is good for them". "Besides", offered Thomas, "you know how well they respond to Angharad, they'll use it to get her sacked". George nodded in understanding as Angharad looked at her grandfather, yet again his access to information within the Police astounded her.

It was late afternoon when Angharad got home and even though she was feeling tired again there was a bounce in her step as George now had possession of the exhibits. Further, George had agreed to get the briefcase out of property the following day and put that forward for analysis as well. As the lift doors to her floor opened Angharad became aware of the sounds of noisy sex coming from her apartment. She approached the door carefully and listened, on the other side the sound of a woman's voice reached her ears, a voice she did not know but there was no mistaking the fact that the voice was begging to be taken by a man who remained silent. Putting a key in the door, Angharad turned the lock and as slowly and as quietly as possible she opened the door. She knew from the past that Tim had not been faithful to either her or his wife but what was making her blood boil, what was making her feel angry is the thought that he had turned up on her doorstep one day and the following day he was screwing someone in her bed. As she stepped into the hallway she realised that the sound was coming from the living room. Silently closing the door, Angharad crept forward towards the opening into the living room. Stopping just short of the door frame she steeled herself for what she was about to find and then stepped forward. Her eyes settled on Tim and her body relaxed rapidly at the sight that greeted her. He was sitting on the sofa, trousers round his ankle as he beat his erect penis while on the television screen a woman lay naked on a bed. In the foreground of the picture a man approached this woman while his ridiculously large weapon bounced in time with his walk the woman giving out an "ah" sound as he finally got to her.

Angharad edged into the room, moving around from behind Tim and towards the television until she was in his view. The sound had been loud enough that Tim had not heard her enter the apartment. On seeing Angharad he visibly jumped. "Turn that down" demanded Angharad as Tim tried to pull his trousers back up but it was clear he could not hear her properly as the sound was so loud. Reaching down onto the coffee table, Angharad picked up the remote control and turned down the volume on the television. When she looked back up Tim was stood upright, his trousers having fallen down round his ankles again, "you fucking bitch, how dare you go out without letting me know, where have you been?" he demanded a sudden anger replacing his rapidly cooling ardour. Angharad looked at him, "I told you I had to go out today" she said but that seemed to just make Tim angrier, "and who did you fuck today then?" he asked, "I bet you are covered in the love bites of others!". "The only person who gives me love bites is you" shouted Angharad, "you're the one who likes to kiss like a teenager, nobody else". Clearly her response to Tim was not having any effect and he tried to pull his trousers back up again as his anger continued to boil over, "who have you fucked?" he asked again.

Grabbing the front of her blouse, Angharad ripped at the buttons opening the top up and exposing her bra, pulling the blouse from her shoulders and rapidly unclasping her bra which she let fall to the floor Angharad stood exposed before him. "See, the only love bites are yours" she said and she noticed Tim glance at her breasts with a look of lust in his eyes. Stepping forward, Angharad reached Tim and dropped to her knees. She was not a fan of having sex while he watched pornography, in fact she wasn't a fan of having sex right now but she also knew that keeping Tim sweet was more important.

Chapter 8

Thursday 15th August 1844
Diary of Sergeant Ephraim Jones

The deteriorating situation in China has forced the Inspector to revise his plans and I have been put back on the streets. I was given three officers and a runner and asked to go and take a position opposite the arch next to the Pontstorehouse Shop. This is the main entrance to China and while there I was to keep an eye on who was coming and going from within the narrow streets and dark alleyways beyond. From my position I could see nothing for the first couple of hours, in fact it was too quiet, normally there are people coming and going to take advantage of the services offered by the ladies contained within if nothing else. That there was no movement suggests that the fear that must be filling the occupants of that slum had spread to those who would choose to visit as well.

While I watched a familiar face appeared, Abraham Davies the Parish Rector had walked up from St Tydfil's Parish Church. On seeing me he approached with a determined look on his face. We spoke briefly and he informed me that he had come to help, come to preach the word of Jesus and try and bring peace to China. I, like any decent man, am a God fearing man but I am also a realist having worked the streets of this town since the introduction of the Police. I didn't hold back and I told Mr Davies that he stood no chance of bringing peace to that hell hole, especially given that he is High Church, that is to say, a member of the Church of England. It is common knowledge round here that God, if he exists in any form within China would almost definitely be nonconformist. His followers belonging to any one of the countless Independent Chapels that have been springing up in the area. I could not persuade him otherwise and Abraham Davies walked under those arches on his own, with nobody to protect him and in that moment

I thought it would be the last time that I would ever see him.

It was gone four in the afternoon when I had to rub my eyes with shock on seeing Mr Davies return from within the walls of China looking unharmed and in that moment, surprisingly chirpy. He took great pleasure in telling me that the word of God had been spread within and that everyone had agreed to put aside their differences and seek a better life than the one they already followed. Sometimes, I am left amazed at the power that God seems to hold in the hands of the right people.

Thursday 15th August 2013

Angharad returned to work on an early shift at Merthyr Police Station, picking up from the chaos of the night before. It may have only been a Thursday but she was gleefully informed by the night shift Sergeant that the cells were full and there were two scene watches in the town, one for the murder that had taken place in the Gurnos where Stephen Thomas had been shot and one from a fight that had taken place the night before involving Simon Lewis. Angharad was surprised to hear the name of Simon again, she had managed to get him arrested and was disappointed to find that the CID had not been able to get him off the streets. Luckily, the officers who had attended had managed to arrest Simon Lewis though it did mean that two of them would be off work for a protracted length of time due to the injuries they had received.

After the briefing and the duties for the day had been handed out, duties that had already tied half her shift up with the various prisoners, Angharad went to seek out her Inspector. George Williams was sitting in his office with the door open while he stared out the window lost in thought. Knocking on the door she waited for him to return to the land of the living and acknowledge her before entering. "I have good news Angharad", he said as he motioned for her to take a seat, "I've had a chat with my friend in forensics and the various bits of evidence have been taken away for analysis. Be careful though, the Station is crawling with Detectives from the Major Investigation Unit today, I've already seen Mr Grumpy himself". The use of the term threw Angharad and she looked at her Inspector while hoping he would clarify himself, he seemed to get the hint, "Superintendent Browning". "Ah", said Angharad in understanding as to what George was getting at.

"Did I hear my name being mentioned?", boomed a voice which made Angharad look back over her shoulder towards the still open door. As she looked, Mike Browning stepped into the doorway. "I hope it is not being used in vain?", he said as he looked at Angharad and George while giving out the air of a man who had full confidence in his own importance. George stuttered in response, catching Angharad off guard and she turned to watch him. "J J J J Just... um, just telling my Sergeant that you were taking the Stephen Thomas murder very seriously and that she should ensure you get full support in the matter", said George in a way that Angharad could only interpret as fear. Mike looked at Angharad, that disdain he had for her still in his eyes, "as long as the scene watch is maintained I see no reason to call on your people!" he said as he made a point of spitting out the last word, "just don't interfere in my investigation". At that, Mike Browning was gone from the doorway and Angharad noticed that George visibly relaxed at his disappearance. Angharad looked at George, catching his eye and questioning him without saying anything but he just shrugged and waved a hand making it clear he wanted to be left alone. Standing, Angharad nodded and pushed her chair back into place as she walked out the door she closed it and headed down the corridor towards the stairs to the ground floor.

Turning a corner she found Mike Browning stood in her way, an eager Robert Di Marco standing just behind him. "Freaks better know their place" said Mike, stepping towards Angharad until his physical frame dominated her. For a woman, Angharad wasn't short but she had not gained the height that most of her family had, mainly due to illness when she had been very young. Normally this was not a problem as it meant that she didn't look too out of place in a town where so many women were short but sometimes, times like this, that lack of height could appear to be a disadvantage. Angharad raised her head until she could look Mike in the eyes, "I don't know what you have done to the Inspector", she said, "but you do not scare me, Sir!". Mike bristled at the way she spat out the word "Sir" and he stepped towards her again forcing her to take a step back. The presence of Di Marco made sure that anything the Superintendent did would be brushed over but even the smallest action from her could be blown out of proportion and cost her dearly. Mike placed a hand on Angharad's neck, he didn't take a strong grip, just touched the skin but the threat was obvious and the message was clear. "Admit it, you want me", said Mike with an evil grin but Angharad refused to bow to the situation and braced herself. She did not know what would happen next but she tried to make herself ready for it all the same. Along the corridor a loud ping sound echoed and Robert spoke, "sir, the lift, we best not be here". Mike grinned again and leaned in close to Angharad's ear, "you were lucky this time, freak" and with that he released his grip and walked away.

Letting out a breath, Angharad visibly relaxed and leaned against the wall, "now I understand what happened to George" she thought to herself as Claire appeared in the corridor from the lift. "Sarge", said Claire a hint of worry in her voice on seeing that Angharad was leaning against the wall as if using it for support. Angharad looked towards her, "PC Doyle, did you really just use the lift to get between floors?" she asked and Claire blushed at the mention, "yes Sarge" she replied quietly, almost under her breath. Angharad shook her head playfully, "what do you want Claire?" she asked. "I need to talk to you about my prisoner" said Claire and she smiled back, glad that the subject was returning to simple day to day policing, "what do you need Claire?".

By early afternoon Angharad was fed up of being trapped inside the station and looked across the shift office to see Rhys typing away on a computer. "Rhys, what are you up to?" she asked and he turned to face her with a bored look on his face, "just updating one of my investigations and then I will be heading back out" he said. "Do you fancy some company?" asked Angharad and Rhys's face lit up at the suggestion, "sure Sarge", he said, whatever you need.

Ten minutes later Rhys and Angharad drove out of the gate and headed up towards the Gurnos, "I just want to check on the officers on the scene watch" she said almost absent-mindedly as Rhys drove. While they travelled up through the town Angharad's mobile phone rang and she answered it, it was Susan, "I've got some of the translation done for you, can you come pick it up? Marc isn't here and so now is a good time to get it". Redirecting Rhys, Angharad reflected on the fact that they had not gone by a direct route to the Gurnos and so the detour was not a massive one. As they pulled up outside the house Angharad realised that she felt abnormally trusting of Rhys and so she invited him to join her. She rang the doorbell and they waited together for someone to answer.

Susan's voice could be heard from inside the house, calling out for one of the children to answer the door and a moment later Sioned appeared in the doorway. On seeing Sioned, Angharad introduced her to Rhys and noticed that a large smile quickly spread across the face of her twelve year old daughter. Clearly, Sioned was already discovering boys thought Angharad before looking at Rhys herself briefly and reflecting that her daughter had good taste. In a different world Angharad felt that she would have been tempted herself, in fact very tempted. Letting Angharad and Rhys into the house Sioned almost threw herself at the new love of her life as they entered the hallway, "come see what me and my brother have been doing" she said. Rhys looked to Angharad, his face giving away that he had picked up on the interest from Sioned and indicated that he would prefer to be somewhere else. However, this situation would naturally work well for Angharad, the alternative being that Sioned would follow them both into the kitchen. Nodding her approval, Angharad gave Rhys a look that made it clear that he needed to entertain Sioned even if it did leave him feeling uncomfortable. "I'm sure he can cope", she thought to herself, "and besides, it is one thing to introduce him to my family and another to introduce him to this case right now".

As Rhys peeled off with Sioned into the living room Angharad continued down to the kitchen where she found Susan elbow deep in flour at the far side of the island. "So you still love baking then?" asked Angharad and Susan nodded, "yep, the stuff you need is there" she said motioning with her head to a folder that was on the side of the island nearest to Angharad. "Will I find anything of particular interest?" she asked and Susan looked her in the face, "you need to read it", she said, "you need to read it carefully, that is everything up to Saturday 17th August 1844, which is about two thirds of the entries, I'm still working on the rest but you will definitely find it of interest". Angharad nodded, "thanks" she said and Susan gave her a withering look and she realised that her welcome was over. "I'll wait for your next call", said Angharad, "take care" and with that she turned and walked back to the patrol car making sure to rescue Rhys as she went.

A few hours later Angharad made it home, her mind still racing with the information that she had gleaned from the diary entries Susan had given her. She was feeling exhausted and was glad to find that Tim was not yet home, despite him being the shift Inspector for her local area. It was the perfect moment to take some time out and get peace and quiet so she jumped in the shower. The warm water washed over her skin and seemed to cleanse her inside so that by the time Angharad stepped out of the shower she felt completely refreshed. Wandering through into the living room in just a towel, Angharad found that she was no longer alone as Tim had returned. "Fancy a meal out?" she asked Tim, "my treat". Tim nodded, "now that is more like the Angharad I love" he said, a comment that made no sense to her but she let it go anyway. Luckily, living in Cardiff Bay meant that there was no need to go far in search of a nice restaurant and within a few minutes they were sat in Tim's favourite Chinese restaurant looking out over the waters of the bay. It gave Angharad a chance to finally broach a subject that had been playing on her mind, how was it that he had left his wife without warning?

Tim smiled at the question, "you know I have always wanted to leave her" he said, "ever since I met you". Angharad was not convinced by the answer, Tim had promised to leave his wife countless times in the last two years but he had never followed through. In fact, Angharad had stopped believing it would ever happen and she had even stopped listening when he did talk about it. This negativity had infected her view of the situation so much that when he had appeared on Tuesday it had come like a bolt from the blue. "I ended our relationship last week when you had two of your boys kick my front door in" she said, a hint of anger in her voice, "then we meet up in Madame Mimi's and we end up spending the night together but when we parted that morning there was no mention from you that a split with your wife was on the cards this time".

Smiling awkwardly he spoke again, "I didn't know, I left you, went home and spent the next couple of days with my wife but she is such a pain, she told me that I need to do more around the house, that I need to spend more time with the kids and that I need to be more attentive to her every need". His face fell and his shoulders with it and for a moment Tim looked like he was a broken man, "what about my needs?" he said as if he expected his plea to fall on deaf ears. "I already do most of the house work, I spend every moment I can with the kids and give her everything while she swans around spending my money on lunches and clothes", he said, "anyway, I was missing you more than ever the thought of not being with you was playing on my mind". Angharad stared at her boyfriend who was looking forlorn, his head bowed low before her, "and?" she asked. Tim raised his face to meet Angharad's hard eyes "and?" said Tim but Angharad stayed quiet, "that's it, there is nothing else, I realised it was time to leave her and move in with you".

Angharad suspected that Tim was lying about something. In fact, she was convinced that he was hiding something from her but she didn't know what part of his story he was being untruthful about and so wouldn't be able to prove it anyway. "You could have given me some warning" she said optimistically. She wondered if her questioning would push him too far and make him snap. If Tim was being untruthful about why he had left his wife he was sure to give everything away in the heat of anger. However, his tone did not change, he continued to play the part of a hard pressed man who had run away to be with the love of his life. "I didn't have time, I just couldn't cope and I walked out the door" he said. "So you want me to believe that cock and bull story you just gave me?" challenged Angharad but Tim did not bite, "Angharad I love you" he said his eyes full of pain and hurt, "what I tell you now is the truth". In that moment Angharad doubted her own instincts, it was a weakness she had with Tim. He would make promises and she would blindly follow even when part of her was screaming that she shouldn't trust him. Maybe Tim was telling the truth and that what she thought she had detected was not lies but simply the pain of the man she loved. "What about the kids?" asked Angharad and Tim's face fell, "I'll work something out, but I'm not going to force you to be a mother to them". Angharad felt relief at that last bit, she struggled to be a parent to her own children never mind someone else's.

Chapter 9

Friday 16th August 1844
Diary of Sergeant Ephraim Jones

     In the day since the visit of the Rector Abraham Davies to China things seem to be on the up, maybe he has found a way to make his brand of God appeal to the lost souls that it holds. As the threat of war among the criminal classes has eased so the Inspector appears to have stopped stressing about it. In the process I am also thankful that he appears to have forgotten about his plan to keep me in the station until I had learned to keep my nose out of the business of others.

     In relation to that matter things took an interesting turn today. I was on patrol in the High Street during the early morning when I was approached by a woman. She was young and clearly impoverished, so much so that I am sure I could detect the smell of China on her clothes. Despite the grime and dirt it was clear that she had been very lucky, her skin and teeth had somehow survived the worst of the horrors that growing up in poverty can bring. I thought I could detect a natural beauty underneath her outer layer, a layer which also bore the hardness of someone who had been raised in the most awful of conditions. From the way she carried herself it was clear that this woman, whose name was Delyth, had done many things to survive in the underworld that she occupied. Throughout it all though she had maintained a lightness of spirit and a kind heart that shone through in everything that she did.

     As I spoke to Delyth she revealed to me another fact, she was the only surviving daughter of Sian Bwthyn Bach who was now languishing in prison for her involvement in the robbery of that young English lawyer. I had not even known that Sian had had a daughter never mind one who was as beautiful as this girl. One who came across as someone with a good soul despite the things she had seen. In that moment I changed my opinion of Sian Bwthyn

Bach. Until meeting Delyth I had seen Sian as someone without morals who had sold her body for money and sold out her accomplices in a murder to protect her own skin. Now I realised that Sian was as much a victim herself, a woman trying to provide for herself and her family in the most horrendous of conditions, how else could she have raised such a daughter as Delyth?

So how does this impact upon my investigation? Well it is in the information that Delyth imparted to me on behalf of Sian. Due to her involvement in the murder, even though she was not personally responsible, Sian was being held in prison in Cardiff. Delyth had just returned from a four day walk to and from the prison to visit her mother. During that visit Sian had instructed Delyth to speak to me and only me about the things that she knew. According to Delyth she was to speak to me as I, more than anyone had treated Sian with kindness.

At first I was suspicious of what information Sian could provide to me, after all neither she nor Delyth would have known about my investigation. Though of course they did not know that the information they were providing was of benefit to any investigation I was involved in. It turned out that Delyth was the only surviving daughter of Sian but she was not the only surviving child as there was a son, a man of nearly twenty five years of age called Iolo Thomas. Sadly Iolo and his mother had fallen out and had gone their different ways a number of years before. In fact, Sian had thrown her lot in with James Smith in order to try and protect herself from Iolo who himself was building a reputation as a China had man. Now, with James Smith gone and Sian in prison awaiting her trial Delyth was alone and scared.

I asked Delyth why she did not approach the new Emperor for protection, if one had been appointed or maybe even ask Abraham Davies for help while he had visited China the day before. In reaction her face fell for I had stumbled upon the biggest part of the story that she wished to share, the new Emperor had been proclaimed as Iolo himself and his father was Abraham Davies.

The idea that Abraham Davies had a bastard son who was

now the Emperor of China shocked me and fuelled my investigation all in one. Could these facts explain the death of the last Emperor, could the local Rector have acted in support of making his son the new leader of the town's criminals? Either way, it was clearly important to me at that moment to protect Delyth and so I gave her instructions to walk to Dowlais, I myself escorting her to Pontmorlais to make sure she left the area safely. As I watched Delyth walk away from the town she carried with her a letter of introduction to my own mother who lived in the houses that surrounded the great ironworks that were to be found there.

Friday 16th August 2013

Another day shift greeted Angharad and she knew that the priority for the day was to get a copy of the diaries to Thomas. Something that from her experience of her grandfather would probably not be that difficult as he was likely to pop up in the station at some point, especially if he knew she was working. Angharad had read late into the night as Tim snored next to her following their mutual exertions and she had eventually fallen asleep with the manuscript lying on top of her. The arrival of the morning also meant the arrival of a new clarity of thought and a clearer idea of how to progress the investigation. The knowledge of who the new Emperor of China had been meant that Angharad and Thomas could do their own research to find out who took over the other two pillars, business and politics. She waited until it was a sensible hour and then called Thomas who said that he would start doing the research and would pop into the station later in the day in order to pick up the diaries so that he could read them himself.

Luckily the night before had been quiet in Merthyr and so Angharad kicked all of her team out the door early, the scene watch in the Gurnos having finally been removed. It had been an impressive show of intention by the Major Investigation Unit but the discussion behind the scenes was that they were already on the verge of declaring the murder as unsolved. Angharad understood the thinking well enough to know why, to the investigating officers it was simply a case of "shit on shit" in a world where nobody cared. They made sure that they turned up, appeared to do their bit and then when the world moved on they quietly packed up and left.

As she waited for the opportunity to call Thomas, Angharad took the chance to do her actual job, the one she was officially paid for. She settled in to start reviewing the work load of her officers. Opening the first case, Angharad was only part way through getting a grasp of the basics she sensed someone stood in the doorway. Turning, Angharad found George stood there patiently, not saying anything as he waited for her to focus on him. Seeing that Angharad had finally given him the attention that he clearly craved she noticed that his eyes were burning bright and with his voice reduced to a whisper he spoke, "we need to talk" he said. There was a sense of urgency in his voice that seemed to infect the room, "we've had the fingerprint results". Watching George for a second, Angharad felt the anticipation build within her and she realised that she was desperate to know the answer. Angharad motioned for George to close the door and take a seat and following her request George did so but only after he had checked the corridor outside to make sure that there was nobody in a position to overhear.

While Angharad waited for George to sit down she called Thomas on her mobile phone and placed him onto loud speaker. She was aware that it was still early and that she wanted to call Thomas later anyway but news such as this needed to be shared now. "So, what have you got?" came the tinny voice of Thomas, sounding as if he was a little person hiding within the phone. George hesitated and looked at Angharad before replying, "it's a known criminal" he said, "someone whose involvement is concerning but it explains why we didn't hear anything from him for a couple of days". As he finished his sentence George sat back with a broad, beaming smile on his face clearly happy that he had thrown out a well baited hook. Angharad looked at George for a second, not saying anything but raising her hands in question as to why he had stopped speaking. Then, as if turning on a light bulb she understood why George had stopped speaking and why he was so happy with himself. The realisation of what George was saying dawned across her face, "Simon Lewis", she said, "Simon Lewis was in that building". The tinny voice from the mobile phone spoke again, "Simon Lewis...", clearly Thomas was trying to place the name. "Simon Lewis, isn't he the thug who you were friends with Angharad?" said the tinny voice again, "yes", said Angharad, "we were very good friends once".

The conversation fell to silence as each of the three participants pondered the situation. "What happened with yesterday's investigation?" asked Angharad suddenly remembering that Simon Lewis had been arrested. George smiled, "they still have him in custody having got a Superintendent's extension, he's been a busy boy recently and they are desperate to avoid bailing him" said George. "I'll speak to you later Gramps", said Angharad, ending the call quickly before jumping from her seat and shooting out of the door. "You coming?" she called over her shoulder as she went but there was no need to ask the question, George was already hot on her heels.

They rushed into the custody block which luckily was empty for once and so only attracted the derision of the Custody Sergeant who was sat behind the desk. A middle aged female who Angharad did not know, she stared over the counter at the two excitable people stood in front of her. "Inspectors and Sergeants ought to know how to behave" she said gruffly and George smiled, "Sam, Sam, Sam" he said, "let's not judge too harshly when you are looking at two officers who have just had some exciting and rather urgent news". Sam looked at George over the rim of her glasses, "and what is this exciting and rather urgent news that brings you before me?" she asked, mimicking the Inspectors voice as she spoke. George laughed at that which caught Angharad off guard, technically what Sam had just done was insult a senior officer, "What's happening with Simon Lewis?" he asked and the Sergeant smiled, "what's it to you?". Cursing herself for not picking up on it,

Angharad realised that Sam could get away with her behaviour because she had a strong friendship with George, a friendship that maybe even bordered on a strong liking for each other in a sexual manner.

Angharad didn't want to let them spend hours flirting with each other though and so butted in, "is he here, yes or no, that's all I need to know as I need a chat with him". Sam looked at her computer and then back at Angharad and then over to George who nodded gently, "you better make this up to me" said Sam and Angharad was sure she detected a small wink from George. Sam slipped a set of keys across the desk in the direction of Angharad, "Cell 8" she said, "but you need to be quick as the interviewing team will be back from breakfast soon".

Standing outside Cell 8 Angharad stared at the metal door as she played with the keys in her hand. George stood next to her, "everything alright?" he asked and Angharad took a moment to answer, "he was my first love" she said, "we were friends, I fell in love and he broke my arm in return". Nodding, George made it clear he understood and put a hand on Angharad's shoulder, "well let's see how he feels about you right now" he said. Opening the hatch, Angharad peered inside to see that Simon was lying on the low bed looking completely fed up with the situation he was in. Angharad closed the hatch and unlocked the door, opening it wide so that Simon could see that she was not alone. He stared at her, not saying anything and not moving beyond the small turn of the head that brought her into view. "Simon, I need to know something" she said but he did not respond, "who is your boss Simon?" but again there was no response. The silence seemed to extend out of the cell and engulf the corridor beyond, "Simon" called Angharad again and he slowly stood up before backing away to the far side of the cell. Once there he watched Angharad and George, not speaking and not moving.

"You gave me your disease" he finally said, his voice sounding gruff from a lack of conversation, "you gave me your disease and now, do you know what I wish I had done all those years ago". Shaking her head Angharad replied, "no" and Simon stared at her again, "I should have fucked you hard, used you as a sex toy and then killed you". His words hit her like a train and she unconsciously took a step back away from the open cell door. "All those years ago, when you tried it on with me, I thought it was the most vile thing in the world", continued Simon. "Now? I still think your desires are vile but you gave it to me, I got your disease", Simon paused again, "I wish I had fucked you because that is what I wanted, I just couldn't bring myself to admit it". George looked at Angharad, worry creasing his brow but she waved a hand at him indicating that she didn't need any support. Stepping forward again Angharad raised herself up, finding confidence in herself as she did so, "and what about now Simon, what about me now? What do you think?". Simon looked her up and down, "do you still have it?" he asked, nodding towards her. "Would it make a difference? Would it make a difference to whether you will talk to me?" asked Angharad and Simon shrugged. "I don't know but I need to know if you are the person I still wish I had fucked", said Simon. Angharad nodded and took another step towards Simon, "there is only one way for you to find out isn't there" she said and this time she stepped in close. George watched in shock as Simon and Angharad stood as close to each other as lovers. Simon reached out and touched Angharad, embraced her and groped her and all the while their faces remained calm and emotionless. After a minute or so Angharad stepped away from Simon, "does that answer your question?" she asked and Simon's face creased with a big grin as he nodded "I'll talk to you" he said.

   "I'm a Shop Boy" said Simon "but they are just a tool in the arsenal of Chris Pritchard" he continued. Looking at George, Angharad sought some hint that the name was relevant as it meant nothing to her but George's face was equally blank. "Where can I find Chris Pritchard?" asked Angharad but Simon did not answer, "I like prison", he said, "in fact I love prison, I love the order and I love the fact that I am important in there". "OK" she said, not sure as to how the conversation was relevant but feeling a need to entertain

Simon's thoughts. Simon seemed to slowly construct a sentence in his mind before speaking it, "you're not here for the other things, all the stuff I have been speaking about in interview". He looked Angharad in the eye, "no, I thought you weren't" he said. "So what are you here for?" he enquired before answering his own question, "you want to know what I was doing in the shop don't you?" Simon asked, "you want to know what I know about the death of Marion Davies, after all what reason would I have to kill someone like that?".

That hint of a confession hit Angharad and she couldn't believe her luck, was it really going to be this easy to solve the entire case. Losing control of her emotions for a second, Angharad's reaction flashed across her face and Simon picked up on it. He laughed out loud, "I'm more observant than you thought I would be?" he offered, "that catches many people out, I'm not thick, I just love violence and making people fear me". Not taking her eyes from Simon, Angharad motioned for him to continue his story, "I was asked to make sure Marion died and nobody could tell how. I was given a setup for her death and a way to make it happen and so that's what I did. Marion died, I killed her". Now, Angharad really was taken by surprise, it was not a hint at a confession, instead she had the entire thing in front of her. "So you killed Marion on orders from Chris Pritchard?" she asked and Simon grinned, "I told him that we would get caught and he insisted that it would never happen, so now you know" said Simon. Angharad turned to George and indicated with a nod of her head that the conversation was over, they turned to walk out of the door, "aren't you going to arrest me?" Simon called after them, "I'm a murderer after all" he shouted. Turning back to face him, Angharad held the cell door, "in time, yes and when I do you will make a full confession on tape?" she asked and Simon nodded, "that's what friends are for" he offered. "Right now I need you to be quiet", said Angharad, "you are just a pawn in this game and I need to get the others, understand?". Simon looked into Angharad's eyes, "for you, for all I owe you and for the mistakes I made in driving you away, I will" he said.

After the shift had ended Angharad changed from her uniform and headed straight to Thomas' house. She had spent the afternoon tidying up her team's paperwork and there had been no chance to call him back. The shifts were making it difficult to discuss the finer details of the case with her sidekick and things were moving fast. As she pulled up outside Thomas' house he came out of the front door and waved to her. "So, we have one of our first suspects?" he said as she opened the car door, "we have two suspects" replied Angharad, "Simon has confessed and he has given us the name of the person who instructed him, the man behind the killing of Marion Davies is called Chris Pritchard". Thomas pulled a face, "What do we know about this Chris Pritchard?" he asked but Angharad shook her head, "all we have is a name, we know nothing about who this person is". "Hmmm", said Thomas, "so in reality we are at a dead end?". Angharad had to admit that in that respect Thomas was correct but at the end of the day a name was a name and it was more than they had had at the start. "How do we know we can even trust the account of this Simon Lewis?" asked Thomas. "We used to be best friends and in the last week we have come to a certain understanding", she replied, "he wasn't lying to me".

Thomas cooked food for them which they ate in the dining room of his house, the weather had been hot for a number of days but now seemed to be changing. A cold north wind blew across the reservoir and with the chill from the water it was no longer suitable to sit outside in the evening. Even with a jumper Angharad and Thomas agreed that it was certainly too cold to eat food in the open air. "There has to be a link between the owners of the shop and this Chris Pritchard" said Thomas in between bites of his food. "I think that is the next thing we need to prove or disprove" replied Angharad, "that and whether he has taken over the criminal underworld in Merthyr Tydfil". Thomas nodded as he put each of his thoughts into order, "but I don't see how we prove either that or the relationship" said Angharad, "not without something more than a name".

She pondered the situation, speaking her thoughts out loud, "in the diaries it turned out that the new Emperor was the illegitimate son of the Rector" she said. Thomas interrupted her spoken thoughts, "you're suggesting that maybe this Chris Pritchard is related to William Davies?", he offered. Realising that she had spoken out loud, Angharad confirmed her thoughts, "I don't see why not, everything else seems to have followed the events of 1844". They both ate in silence for a while as they considered how they would progress such enquiries, "we need to speak to Berwyn Davies" said Thomas, "I'll call him after food and see when he is available". They both nodded, satisfied that they had found a way forward.

After food Thomas spoke on the phone to Berwyn Davies, it was only just gone 7pm and he indicated that he was eager to meet sooner rather than later. "We'll be with you very shortly" said Thomas while looking at Angharad for confirmation that this was agreeable and she nodded back. Stepping outside they both got into the Gilbern, "we'll be quicker if I drive" said Thomas and Angharad laughed, "I've done the Police training as well" she said but Thomas brushed her protestations away.

It took Thomas only 10 minutes to negotiate the narrow roads that led out of Pontsticill, passed Trefechan and down to New Church Road in Cefn Coed. Pulling up outside a large house on a junction with a small lane Thomas ushered her towards the front door. Pressing the doorbell, Angharad could hear it echo through the large house beyond and a few moments later the door was opened by Berwyn Davies. He was looking more tired than he had when they had met him just a few days before. Letting them both into the house in silence, Berwyn then closed the door and led them down a long corridor, passing sumptuously decorated rooms. "You're here on your own?" asked Thomas as they walked and Berwyn nodded in the affirmative. As the three of them reached the room at the end Berwyn indicated that to Angharad and Thomas that they should enter. This room contrasted heavily with the others they had seen as they walked passed, it was simply decorated and clearly setup for the watching of television on a small set that sat in the corner.

Berwyn closed the door sealing them all inside and then took a seat in a large wooden rocking chair in the corner opposite the television. As he did so he pointed towards a small poorly maintained sofa "please sit" he said and Angharad and Thomas both caught each other's eyes as they pondered whether the sofa would be able to hold them as they sat on it. As she lowered herself into the seat, Angharad noticed that the sofa creaked unnervingly underneath their combined weight and so she perched herself on the edge just in case.

"What is it that you need to speak to me about so urgently?" asked Berwyn, weariness in his voice in a way that had not been there during their previous meeting. "We need to know more about your third cousin?" said Thomas, "we think he might be important to the story of what happened to your daughter". "Hmmm", said Berwyn, "there is not much I can tell you, his name is William and he owns a number of properties in the area". "Where does he live?" asked Angharad but Berwyn shrugged to indicate that he did not know, "where does he work?" she asked and Berwyn thought for a moment, "I believe he has a business over on the old Cyfarthfa Industrial Estate but that is all I know" he replied. "What about his family, is he married, does he have children?" asked Angharad and Berwyn shrugged again, "he is younger than me, his father is more my age" came the reply and Angharad and Thomas looked at each other.

"His father? What's his father's name?" Angharad asked and Berwyn replied as if expecting them to recognise it immediately "Henry Davies". Angharad looked at Thomas and shrugged her shoulders to indicate that she did not know who that was. Thomas acknowledged Angharad's reaction before turning his attention back to Berwyn. "Henry Davies?" he asked, "the Henry Davies?" and Berwyn nodded in reply. He seemed to have already resigned himself to the fact that his family might have committed a great evil against itself. "I still don't know who this person is" said Angharad, interrupting the conversation with a hint of frustration in her voice. "He's the current Parish Vicar" said Thomas as he shot her a look of concern, "fuck" she mouthed back without saying it out loud.

The conversation with Berwyn was finished, Angharad and Thomas realised that they needed to do a lot more work and a lot more investigating if they were going to bring this case to a sensible conclusion. It was also clear that Berwyn was in the process of breaking down and there was no point in pushing him any further at present. As the three of them headed back towards the front door Angharad remembered the one question that they had not posed and which she needed to ask now, "Berwyn, before we leave, do you know who Chris Pritchard is?" she asked. Berwyn continued to walk as he thought about the question and when they got to the front door, before opening it he turned to Angharad. "Sorry", he replied, "that name means nothing to me".

By the time Angharad made it back to her home it was getting on for 9pm. She parked her car and climbed out of the seat before stopping in the open door. Looking up she imagined what she would be able to see above her head, inside her apartment where Tim would be pacing up and down wondering where she was. Already this evening she had ignored multiple calls from him and she knew that such things could make Tim very angry. Angharad accepted that she was at least in part directly to blame for the situation she was about to walk into. She had failed to tell him that she would be late but then that was the life with Tim that she had been used to in the past. When Tim had been with his wife he would insist on Angharad not contacting him, she had to wait for his call or his visit and never knew when to expect it. This being in a proper relationship thing was something that she was struggling to adjust to having not lived with anybody since the breakdown of her marriage to Susan. "Then again, it's not all my fault, Tim makes the situation worse with his behaviour" she thought to herself and in that moment Angharad knew what she was going to do. Looking down she checked that her light cream, sleeveless top and skinny blue jeans with plain black heels would be acceptable. Pulling her phone from her jeans pocket she threw it onto the seat of the car and headed for the entrance hallway. Rather than face Tim, Angharad was going to go and have some fun and let her hair down, at least metaphorically.

Not completely certain where she was going to go Angharad wandered out into the road and found Ibrahim driving down the street looking for a fare. She flagged him down and instructed him to take her somewhere out of the way, somewhere where she wouldn't be known and a short time later he pulled up outside the Victory in St Fagans. Angharad recognised the pub having been there before for food but she would never have picked it as somewhere to go and have a drink. Walking inside she found it to be surprisingly empty for the time of night, especially given it was a Friday. Looking around she quickly noticed that the handful of customers left were finishing up their food rather than there to have a drink. Taking a stool by the bar Angharad browsed the shelf before ordering a pint and a double whiskey. Drinking the pint quickly, Angharad necked the double whiskey before ordering the same round again. She looked around, from what she could see there was nobody in the pub that she recognised and that anonymity brought a feeling of peace within.

While Angharad drank her mind whirred through everything that had happened over the last week, how she had been kicked out of the Major Investigation Unit only to find herself stuck in the middle of a series of murders that had taken place in her home town. To her, it seemed crazy how events had taken such a turn but there was nothing she could do about it, she just needed to switch her brain off for a bit. As Angharad started her fourth round of drinks she didn't notice the door to the pub open and Rhys step through. He looked over towards the bar and his jaw dropped as he saw Angharad sitting there trying her best to drink herself into a stupor. Approaching carefully he positioned himself further down the bar and caught the attention of the bar keeper. He couldn't stop looking at Angharad but wasn't sure if he should say anything, this was not somewhere he expected her to appear and he thought that maybe he should pretend not to have seen her. Then again, he could feel a strong urge to speak to her, they got on well and he enjoyed her company.

Ordering a pint his voice carried across the bar and he saw Angharad stop mid drink. Slowly, she put the glass back down and then turned her head in his direction, the look on her face was as if she had been caught cheating. Rhys smiled and tried to look as non-judgemental as possible, "do you want a drink?" he asked, making sure to keep the greeting informal. Angharad smiled back on seeing him, "thank you Rhys" she replied, and she watched as the bar man poured another pint for her. By the time he had finished she noticed that Rhys had disappeared and she glanced around the bar wondering if the conversation had been part of her imagination. To her relief it had not been a hallucination, Rhys was sitting at a small table in the corner of the room near to the window.

She spotted him looking in her direction and she quickly glanced away so as not to be caught staring. Dropping her head, Angharad peered into her pint glass as she contemplated the situation. She had come to this pub to have solitude from the rest of the world and now someone known to her had walked into that same place. Worst of all this was not just someone known to her but it was someone she felt a certain connection with both physically and mentally. Looking at her drinks intently Angharad realised that the alcohol was already impairing her judgement and that this fact would only make matters worse.

That thought did not deter her though. Standing, Angharad collected her drinks and then walked over towards Rhys. Unconsciously she pushed back her shoulders back as she did so in order to accentuate her figure. "Do you not want to drink with me?" she asked, almost pleadingly and Rhys smiled back at her. "It's not that", he said, "you just looked like someone who wanted some time to yourself and not me interfering in your life". "Thanks", replied Angharad, "but I think that having some time to lose myself with a friend might be even better". Rising from his seat, Rhys indicated the chair opposite him with his hand, "I would be honoured if you would join me" he said "and I am glad you think of me as a friend". Angharad slipped into the seat, "how come you are here?" she asked, intrigued by his presence in the pub. It was Angharad's understanding that Rhys lived near to Aberdare in the next valley over from Merthyr Tydfil, a pub this close to Cardiff was not a natural place for him to be on his own. "I'm house sitting for my parents" he replied, "they only live around the corner but are away on holiday at the moment". Nodding, Angharad indicated that she understood completely, "I never got a chance to say thank you" she said and Rhys made a face, "you have nothing to thank me for" he replied. "You have been a great support" said Angharad, "since I joined the team" and Rhys grinned at the compliment, "it's not difficult to be supportive to a good Sergeant especially when they are a good person as well". Angharad thought she could detect a glint in Rhys' eyes and felt herself blush as she detected a natural spark in the air between them. Looking at her drink again Angharad grinned to herself, the alcohol was impairing her judgement even more than she thought it would.

Chapter 10

Finally I had a rest day today and after much bartering with the Inspector he gave me permission to leave the station and visit my family. It is a relief to be able to get out and about and not have to be worried about where I am patrolling or what I am doing. The recent warm weather finally broke and a storm washed the streets of Merthyr Tydfil clean of days of grime. Such a heavy downpour made for a long walk to Dowlais and by the time I got there, even with my heavy cloak I was soaked through to the skin. Luckily my mother had the fire going and I was able to dry out in front of it while I caught up on the news from my family.

Delyth already seems a lot happier now that she is safe from her brother though I am sure that her mood was also lifted by the chance to wash and put on clean clothes. It was clearly a wise judgement to send this vulnerable young female to my mother. They clearly get on well and my mother has been treating Delyth almost as if she was her own daughter. From what I can see Delyth has responded well to this and is already assisting my mother in her household chores. I am very grateful to my mother for the assistance she has provided in this matter and I gave her extra money on this visit in order to make sure that she could make ends meet. It would be remiss of me if I was to leave my mother to cover the cost of looking after Delyth herself.

While I warmed myself by the fire I was able to question Delyth further about the events that had led to the murder of James Smith. What Delyth had to tell me has thrown a question mark over everything that I know to do with the murders. Her mother, Sian, had indeed been involved in a plan to rob the young man who was killed last week. In recent times her looks had started to fade and she wasn't raising the money that she had once made from her work as a prostitute. Smith had been supportive, he owed Sian for favours that she had done him in the past and asked her to help out in setting up the robbery in return for a fair share of the money. Sian had been unsure but had eventually agreed to it and only a couple of days later the plan had been carried out. The young man was led by Sian down into the depths of China to a hovel that had been identified to her. As they entered into the darkness beyond the doorway the man was jumped by three of Smith's men. Delyth was sure that once the robbery itself had started Sian had left so as not to be implicated in what happened next. It was these three men who Sian had handed over to the Police following her arrest, after all she had never agreed to take part in a murder.

This was not the whole story though, Delyth had established after the arrest of her mother that there were other people carrying out their dastardly plans on the day that the young man was killed. After being robbed by Smith's men, the victim was left to find his way back out of China, his valuables having been taken and distributed amongst the accomplices. The young man was never to survive this journey though. By the time he was released by Smith it was late at night, the darkness helping to hide where the crime had taken place. As he found his way out though, the men of Iolo Thomas were waiting in the shadows, watching and biding their time in the hope that an opportunity such as this would present itself. Iolo Thomas had killed the man and dumped him into the River Taff that night. The following day his men moved against James Smith, discrediting him by suggesting he was behind the murder and would bring the authorities down onto all the residents of China.

The facts of what happened after that are now well known, James Smith was killed and Iolo Thomas took his place as the Emperor. Delyth, with the death of James Smith then felt vulnerable and so visited her mother in prison, knowing that she had no future in China.

Saturday 17th August 2013

Angharad woke slowly, the feeling of alcohol still flowing through her system left a sensation of grogginess that she hoped would clear soon. Opening her eyes she realised that she was not in her own bed, in fact she was in no bed that she recognised. Lying on her side Angharad looked around the room trying desperately to place where she was but with no success. Glancing down she saw that she was lying under a duvet and on peeling it back discovered that that she was wearing just her knickers and bra. Pulling at the duvet quickly Angharad covered herself back up and attempted to process what had happened the night before. The last memory that she could recall was of her and Rhys in the pub talking and drinking and she let out a groan as she realised that her current situation could only mean one thing that they had spent the night together. Rolling over in the bed Angharad discovered that she was all alone which made her feel even worse. It was logical that Rhys must be somewhere in the house but why had he not slept in the bed? Had he used her and after having his fun gone somewhere else to sleep she wondered. Then an even more horrible thought filled her mind, they had got to the bedroom, Rhys had looked at her without her clothes and found her to repulsive for sex.

That Angharad might not have had sex with Rhys and so remained faithful to Tim did not ease the way she felt about the situation. Thoughts about how attractive she was to the men in her life had always filled Angharad with doubts and there had even been bouts of depressive behaviour brought on by this. That was one of the reasons why Angharad had clung onto Tim, not just because she cared about him and loved him but because he had openly shown a sexual interest in her. So to think that Rhys had rejected her swung Angharad back down into the darkest of feelings. In many ways she would rather have been unfaithful to her boyfriend and found herself attractive to another than the other way around. In the past she had sought help on the subject and it had been explained to her that it was a matter of acceptance and that in time the anxiety would ease.

Angharad slid from under the duvet and rose to her feet. As she stood upright her head spun and she lost her balance, a quickly placed hand being the only thing that stopped her from falling over. Looking around the room Angharad could only find her jeans and she pulled them on and headed for the bedroom door as her head throbbed with the sensation of movement. Opening the door, Angharad found herself on a galleried landing which looked down onto a large living room, a clock on the wall showed that it was gone eleven o'clock. The sound of cooking reached her ears from somewhere downstairs and the smell of bacon filled the air. Slowly, carefully, Angharad went to see what she could discover and on getting to the bottom of the stairs she found that underneath the landing were large double doors. Walking slowly towards the double doors Angharad could see that on the other side was a large kitchen, stood at the end of which was Rhys who was bent over an Aga.

Entering the kitchen, Angharad took a seat at the breakfast table that she could see just inside the door. The sound of the metal chair scraping along the tiled floor echoed through the room and Rhys turned around. "Morning" he said, his mood seemed to be bright and happy and all Angharad could do was murmur a reply, "morning". "I take it you like bacon?" asked Rhys and Angharad grimaced, "yes, though I prefer sausage..." meaning to add "if you have any available" but Rhys was too quick for her this morning, "so I hear" he said with a wicked grin. "Where's my top" asked Angharad as she became aware that she was sitting in front of Rhys in just her bra. He pointed towards the radiator where it was laid out, "I've washed it for you" he said and she picked it up. It was still damp but she slipped it over her head anyway. Slumping back into the chair, Angharad looked at Rhys, "so we did then?" she asked and Rhys looked at her with a blank face, "did what?" he asked. "We fucked?" said Angharad partly hoping that the answer would be yes and so allowing her to feel good about herself again. Rhys remained silent, his only reply being a pair of raised eyebrows before turning away and looking out of the window.

Now Angharad felt really bad, Rhys couldn't even bring himself to admit to her that she was unattractive. She thought about getting up and walking out the door, running even to get away from the embarrassment but a dull thump at the back of her head indicated that such an action would be a mistake. Especially as she didn't even know where she was and Tim would be way too angry to come and pick her up. A couple of minutes later Rhys placed a plate of bacon sarnies in front of Angharad with a clang on the marble top of the table. The noise shook Angharad from her reverie and she watched as Rhys took the seat opposite her with another plate for himself. He looked straight at Angharad, "we didn't" he said, noticing that Angharad's dark mood did not improve at the news. "We almost did but we didn't" he repeated, "why" she asked and he smiled, "because you are in love with another and because you were too drunk to make the decision either way".

Staring at Rhys, Angharad's face was full of questions, "I don't understand" she said and he thought long and hard before giving his reply. "I'll say this once and then we will never discuss last night again" said Rhys and Angharad nodded. "Nothing good ever comes from making decisions about sex while drunk", offered Rhys and Angharad again nodded in acknowledgement. "Would you have been happy if you had found out we had slept with each other?" he asked and inside Angharad realised she was conflicted on that matter but she also knew what the correct answer was, "no, I love my boyfriend" she said. Rhys smiled at that, "that's what you kept saying last night" he said, "that and the fact that you wondered if my love muscle was as big as my other muscles". The comment made Angharad meet Rhys' eyes, "did I really say that?" she asked and Rhys smiled. "God, I was seriously drunk then" Angharad said. They looked at each other, trying to see into the others soul before both breaking out into a burst of laughter. "It was a good night?" asked Angharad and Rhys continued to smile, "it was a good night" he replied. "Friends?" offered Angharad, holding out her right hand towards Rhys who took hold of it in a firm handshake, "friends" he confirmed.

An hour later Rhys dropped Angharad back to her home and she left him with a gentle kiss on the cheek. Angharad's mood had lifted slightly but she was still feeling conflicted about the night before and whether Rhys had really told her the truth. Overall though she was happy with her decision to go out and not say anything to Tim. A lot of things had happened over the last week and while Tim would be angry Angharad felt that she was now stronger and more able to deal with all of the changes. Today was going to be the first day of a more positive attitude to her relationship reasoned Angharad.

Walking into the apartment she found Tim sitting on the sofa and watching the television. "Hi" she said sheepishly but, however angry she had expected him to be, Angharad had completely underestimated it. Tim's anger was beyond anything she had ever experienced before. Standing. Tim strode over to her until they were nose to nose, "I love you" he said, "I love you more than I have ever loved anyone", Angharad doubted that would be the case but she understood the point. Tim snapped, "you fucking whore!" he said and grabbed her by the neck, pushing Angharad back against the door, "you fucking whore!" he said again. "You just can't be content with one cock can you" he continued, his voice and body language became increasingly aggressive as he gave into all of the anger that had built up inside. Angharad tried to answer but at that moment she was struggling to breath and either way she wasn't sure there was anything that could be said to calm him down. Tim dragged Angharad through the living room, out into the hallway and on into the bedroom. "I will make you remember whose whore you are!" he said as they passed through the door and he threw Angharad onto the bed before stripping her clothes off. In that moment Angharad froze, she didn't know what to do, it was her belief that if she ever found herself in a position such as this then she would fight and bite and punch and kick until she was safe but in this exact moment she was unable to do anything.

Two hours later, Angharad still lay in the bed with tears streaming down her face. She had not moved since Tim had taken her without care as to what she wanted. Inside she felt disgusting and at the same time she was angry with herself. Throughout her life she had done some crazy things, she had put herself at risk and she had found herself in situations that she had regretted but this was the first time when she could honestly say to herself that she felt violated. The bedroom door opened and Angharad froze, giving out a slight murmur as she did, fearing what was about to happen again and then Tim was stood over her, he was holding a cup of tea. "Hey" he said in a gentle and smooth voice, "don't cry", he sat down next to her and put the tea on the bedside cabinet. "I was worried about you and it got the better of me" he said, "if you showed me that you were happy for me to be here then things like this wouldn't happen". He gave a smile and put a hand on Angharad's head, "come on, I've made you a cup of tea, you're just hungover, things will feel better after you have had some rest". Tim's voice was so soft and reassuring and while part of Angharad screamed at her she couldn't help but respond. Sitting up in the bed slightly, she wiped the tears from her face, "I'm sorry for letting you down" she said. "Shhh" said Tim, putting an arm around Angharad and pulling her in close to his chest, "shhh".

Angharad showered and as she dried herself she looked in the mirror to see the bruise on her neck and on her upper arms. Tears welled in her eyes again but she pushed them back and then put on the clothes she had been wearing when she got home and walked through into the living room. Tim was in the process of hanging up the phone. "That was your Grandfather" he said to her, "that's the second time he has called today but I'm not sure that the amount of time you are spending together is healthy". Nodding, Angharad acknowledged what Tim had said, "you might well be right, it's just that I've not had the support of someone as understanding as you" she said before adding, "I'm not going into work tonight, I don't feel well". Tim stepped over to her, "I understand completely" he said, "I am sure your hangover is horrendous and you look like you need sleep", he kissed her on the forehead. "I need to go anyway" he said and with that he left for work. For a moment Angharad stood there, unsure what she should do but then she felt her knees buckle underneath her and she sat down on the sofa before she fell over. Taking a moment to compose herself, Angharad picked up the phone and looked at. She searched for Thomas' number and her finger hesitated over the call button but she never pressed it, choosing instead to put the handset back on the coffee table.

Remaining there on the sofa, Angharad's mind swirled and she felt lost in the chaos and confusion of the last week. It had been only a few hours since she thought she had found some clarity but now, the actions of Tim had put her back to square one. As she sat there Angharad felt sleep take over, slowly sweeping through her mind and encouraging her eyelids to close. No matter how hard she fought it her eyelids became heavier and heavier and she found she had no hope of holding them open until a fitful sleep took over.

A ringing sound woke her up with a jump and she realised she was still on the sofa, sleeping at an awkward angle. Reaching forward she picked up the phone spotting the time as she did so, it was gone 5pm, "shit!" she said out loud as she answered it. "How are you feeling?" asked the familiar voice of her Inspector, George Williams, on the other end of the phone. "Don't worry, Tim called me and told me you were not feeling well and that you just needed sleep" he said, a hint of a smirk in his voice. "I've also spoken to Rhys and he confirmed to me that he saw you last night and you were very ill", this time there was no hiding the sarcasm in George's voice. "Rhys will cover for you today, hope you are better tomorrow". All Angharad could manage was a murmured thank you before she heard the other end of the phone go dead.

Now awake Angharad resolved to move to somewhere more sensible to sleep. Rising gently from the sofa she walked over to the bedroom and on entering caught a view of herself in the mirror. On seeing herself the excess alcohol of the night before and the events of the day caught up with her and she immediately felt sick. Running to the bathroom she made it just in time, bringing up the contents of her stomach into the toilet. Having not eaten since being at Rhys's house earlier Angharad realised just how hungry she was. "I need another shower" Angharad said to herself before climbing into it fully clothed and running the water, removing her clothes as she showered.

Half an hour later Angharad climbed out of the shower for the second time that day. Feeling physically better than at any point since she had woken up she looked out of her window to see a grey day outside. Dressing in clean clothes this time, jeans and a light jumper, Angharad popped downstairs to her car and finally picked up her mobile phone. On looking at it she could see that there was just enough charge in it to reveal that she had received a text message from Susan and a voicemail. She started the car engine and plugged in her car charger before reading the message from Susan, "I've finished the translation of the diaries, you need to pick them up" it read and Angharad smiled at the typical curtness of conversation that had become normal conversation between her and Susan these days. Angharad then listened to the voicemail which was from Thomas who wanted her to visit him as he had found someone who knew about the modern Davies family. Immediately, Angharad called Thomas back, "Gramps, sorry I've not been in touch" she said honestly, "I've been ill since last night". This time she lied and hoped that the untruth was convincing enough to deceive a man who was famed for his ability to spot dishonesty. "Ah, Angharad", came Thomas' reply, tone of voice indicating that he was not convinced by her statement. "I have a friend here who will be able to tell us about the Davies family" he said. "How long will they be staying?" she asked and Thomas' tone changed as he became uncomfortable with the answer, "um, quite late" he offered.

The drive to Merthyr Tydfil was quick and Angharad was soon parking up on Queen's Road within sight of her former home. While Susan had left a voicemail there had been no agreement on when Angharad should visit and neither had she called Susan back. Angharad knew that an unannounced visit might well make the situation more difficult but she needed the information in the diaries and wasn't prepared to wait. Marc answered the door and he did not look pleased, "what are you doing here?" he asked seemingly oblivious to Susan's assistance in translating the diaries that had been written by Ephraim. Thinking quickly Angharad realised that if Susan hadn't told Marc then she was keeping the entire thing secret from him. Not surprising really she thought as Marc would probably explode if he discovered that Susan was doing anything for Angharad. She searched for an excuse and realised that there was only one real option open to her and so she took it.

Angharad threw her children into the breach while hoping that Susan and the kids themselves would forgive her, or at the very least understand. "I got a call from Susan to pick up some paperwork for Sion" she said, hoping that Marc was not as good at Thomas in detecting lies. "What paperwork?" asked Marc, "and why didn't you call to let us know you were in the area?". Angharad's mind was racing now as she tried to stay one step ahead of Marc's interrogation. "I just happened to be passing and so thought it was easier just to pop in", Angharad lied still trying to think what paperwork she would need to collect in the middle of summer. Sion, who must have overheard the conversation saved the day as he appeared from the living room. "I'll get it" he said and ran off towards the kitchen while completing his sentence, "I know Mam left it in the kitchen". Marc grunted, clearly not amused and unsure as to whether he was being duped or whether he was simply out of the loop.

Reappearing in the hallway Sion had a carrier bag in his hands, the contents of which stuck out slightly through a hole in the end. From Angharad's position she could clearly see that it was a ream of A4 paper. Approaching in a confident manner, Sion pushed passed Marc and handed everything to Angharad. Marc was clearly ready to challenge Sion and Angharad as to what was going on but Sion showed that he had the same genes as both her and Thomas as he continued his lie. "I've been talking to Mam about trying to get an acting job in Welsh language television and she said that you need to take a look", said Sion, "all of the details are in the bag".

The look from Marc made it clear that he thought something odd was going on but he couldn't quite work out what, "when did you discuss this with your mother?" he asked. Confident in his own deceit Sion turned to Marc, "it's been an ongoing thing", he said, "Mam said not to trouble you with it as you were busy and it wouldn't interest you". "Hmmm" said Marc, he obviously was still suspicious but he had to admit that the one thing he didn't understand with Susan was her obsession with the Welsh language. "You're really sure that this is what you want to do?" asked Angharad who was now taking a lead from Sion, "I thought it was just a flight of fancy?". Sion smiled, "it's something I really want to do Cariad", he said, "I've even been speaking to a couple of agents and I visited the set of Pobol Y Cwm last week". Sion had saved Angharad with his expert deceit, calling on a genuine interest which he had to create the lie and protect all of them, Susan included. "Thanks" said Angharad and nodding goodbye to Marc she walked off, turning at the end of the footpath to look at Sion, "tell your Mam I'll be in touch with an answer next week", Sion grinned in reply and waved.

Getting back to the car Angharad sat in the driver's seat and opened the bag; inside were the diaries that Susan had translated. On top of that was a letter from an agent in Cardiff in relation to Sion seeking permission from his parents to put him forward for a casting call. She looked up at the house and saw Sion and Sioned smiling down out of the window, and a burst of pride filled Angharad as she realised what had happened. Susan, in her typical stuffy, school first wisdom would have told Sion that he could not try acting. That wouldn't have stopped Sion, especially if he had support from Sioned in his endeavours. Taking advantage of Angharad's visit he had made sure the paperwork had reached her in the hope that she would put pressure on Susan. Still looking up at Sion and Sioned, Angharad could not help but laugh out loud. Sion had not just deceived Marc, he had actually pulled the wool over the eyes of all three of his parents. There was definitely the blood of the Jones family coursing through his veins.

A short while later Angharad pulled up outside of Thomas' house and immediately noticed something different, a modern Volkswagen Beetle was parked on the driveway a large flower sticking out of the dashboard instantly giving away that the driver was female. Thomas met Angharad at the front door with a big smile on his face and he gave her a big hug. Stood behind him in the hallway, in just a dressing gown was Julie Williams, the librarian who Angharad had found to be so jealous just a few days before. "You remember Julie don't you?" asked Thomas and Angharad nodded, "hello again" she said offering her hand for Julie to shake. This time Julie seemed to be far more positive in her response, as if she felt that she was the one with the upper hand and that Angharad should be jealous. "Hi Angharad" purred Julie with a look of satisfaction on her face and Angharad smiled back, if only Julie understood how much of a player her grandfather could be Angharad thought to herself.

"Shall we sit" suggested Thomas indicating that they should all move through to the living room. Angharad led the way followed by Julie with Thomas last in the procession. On entering the room she sat in one of the chairs belonging to the leather three piece suite that dominated the centre of the large space. Angharad watched as Thomas sat on the sofa followed by Julie who almost completely curled up alongside him like a cat claiming her territory. "So Gramps, I take it Julie is the person who can help us?" she asked perceptively as Thomas put an arm around Julie, "yes, she goes to Church every Sunday and knows the Davies family quite well". Julie smiled, "I know them well but I wouldn't trust them, in fact, I find Henry Davies to be not very nice at all". The last bit was said as if Julie was a woman whose unquestioning love had been spurned by another, a person who she felt did not appreciate her beauty and loyalty. Clearly, for Julie, there might well be an element of this in which she was seeking revenge. It was not ideal and Angharad would have to take care with the information Julie provided. Then again, she reflected, so much of the information that was passed to the Police came with the tint of revenge plastered over it.

Angharad nodded to Julie, "please, tell me all that you know" she asked and Julie grinned at the thought of being able to supply salacious gossip and information to a person who was so eager to hear it. "Henry Davies has two sons by his wife, William and Jonathan. His wife died giving birth to Jonathan and so he has lived alone as a widower ever since" said Julie. "Being the local vicar of course, having such a secure job in a world dominated by lonely women he has had his fair share of opportunity to avoid being completely lonely", she continued, a hint of pain entering her voice. "The rumour is that he had a third son with a woman from down the valley, one who had fallen into a life of drugs, drink and prostitution", Julie paused there letting the statement sink in. "This woman certainly had a child around the time that Henry", there was an over familiarity in the way she used the name, "was, ahem, helping her". The implication that Julie was making was clear, Henry had publicly helped this woman with her problems but it was obvious that those in the know thought that she had helped him with his as well.

"This child was born to a mother with problems and so adopted by a family from Swansea when he was 4 years old", Julie's smile gave away the fact that she was definitely revelling in being able to educate Angharad. "Anyway he has returned now and is using the name his mother gave him...", Angharad cut her off, "Chris Pritchard" she said watching Julie's ego deflate slightly on having her thunder stolen. Julie frowned and then her face brightened again, "I bet you didn't know that Chris Pritchard was known as Chris Probert when he lived in Swansea?". The question was clearly rhetorical and didn't require an answer, of course Angharad didn't know this but it was a useful piece of information. It may explain why there had been no history for Chris Pritchard when Angharad had looked previously she reflected. Keeping quiet, Angharad decided to let Julie have her new moment of triumph.

"So tell us about the rest of the family" said Thomas and Julie steeled herself for the opportunity to impart more about the Davies family. "Well as I have already mentioned to you, there are two official sons, William who is a very successful local businessman and Jonathan who is a councillor in the Town Ward". "Henry and Jonathan still live together in the Rectory in Merthyr", Julie said, "while William lives with his family on the other side of town. Angharad nodded as she took all of the information in, "Outwardly William is quite normal but Jonathan, he is a bit special" Julie said adding the last bit with a conspiratorial air. Not saying anything, Angharad looked at Julie waiting for her to elaborate on what exactly was meant by the word "special" yet Julie kept quiet clearly wanting to drag out her moment of glory. The point went to Angharad though as Julie eventually gave up on waiting for a response, "he's a bit weak, very much led by Henry in his thoughts but I understand that he is a bit forward when it comes to women" Julie explained at last.

Julie waited while Angharad processed this information. After a moment of silence and contemplation Angharad nodded, "what else?". "William has been in direct competition with his distant cousin Marion for a number of years and at times the rivalry has become very intense" said Julie. "Meanwhile, Jonathan has built up quite a following on the council though he missed out on a chance to be leader of the council a couple of years ago". In Angharad's head things now started to make sense. The four pillars of society, religion, business, politics and crime and one family with interests in all of them, interests that recently had been boosted by the convenient deaths of those who had been in charge. Now though, there were two big questions, what did each individual member of the Davies family know and how to prove the case against them?

Chapter 11

Sunday 18th August 1844
Diary of Sergeant Ephraim Jones

It was a warm Sunday morning, the rain of the day and night before had cleared leaving the ground wet and the air humid as the sun shone down on the town. I was on patrol again my one day off having been enjoyed as much as possible. My patrols took me to the south of the town for the day and this gave me an excuse to travel down to the Caedraw area and watch the parishioners arriving for their Sunday service at St Tydfil's. After watching the congregation enter and listening to the service as it echoed out through the walls I saw Abraham Davies step outside to greet his flock as they left. As I watched he was joined by two men, both of whom looked very similar to him though a number of years younger. One of them I instantly recognised as Solomon Davies who also sat on the local watch committee. It had never occurred to me before that there was a link between Solomon and Abraham but now, watching from my position across the road I could see that there was a clear familial relationship between the two.

As the crowds thinned Abraham Davies walked over to my location, his face welcoming as he basked confidently in his position. "Ah, Sergeant, good to see you" he said and I greeted him back, "I hope that your presence does not indicate that my Church is next to be seen by the local Constabulary as a den of sin comparable with China?". I smiled and acknowledged the rector for his efforts at humour with a gentle laugh. It was not in my interests to have the rector get suspicious and so I created a story in the hope that it would distract him. "I'm having a crisis of confidence in my own belief in the Lord" I told him and since I was passing I was just listening to the singing when the service finished and you all came out. The rector smiled, "let me introduce you to my family" he said and I am sure I saw an evil glint in his eye, in fact I think he was testing whether the Police were suspicious in anyway. That morning I found out that not only was Solomon his son but that the other man who looked like Abraham Davies was his other son, Joseph Davies. A man who had recently returned to the town and was looking to build up a business profile having previously been looking after family investments in London.

I am concerned by my findings, I had my suspicions as to what was happening anyway, especially after I found that Iolo Thomas was an illegitimate son of Abraham Davies but now I find that he has motivation to take care of things for his other two sons as well. Could it really be the case that Abraham Davies has conspired with his three sons to take control of the town by eliminating their rivals?

Sunday 18th August 2013

Tim returned home in the early hours while Angharad was fast asleep in bed. When she finally stirred around ten in the morning she felt healthier and more alert than she had for a few days. Climbing under the duvet and pulling on a dressing gown she took a moment to watch her lover as he slept. As Tim lay there Angharad forgot about the trials of the day before, or at least cast them from her mind and instead thought about how lucky she was to have someone in her life who seemed to be so content with her. To Angharad, Tim looked handsome and she couldn't help but study the shape of his face and the toning of the arm that sat outside the covers as he rested.

Moving out into the living room Angharad took the opportunity to tidy up, she had not had a chance to clean for a few days. Now that there was two of them living in a one bedroom apartment it was becoming a tip very quickly. She found the translation work that Susan had completed, still inside the plastic carrier bag that it had come in. Distracted for a second Angharad wondered where Susan would have got a plastic carrier bag from given that there was a charge for the use of each one. She smiled on realising what was happening, Angharad's relationship with Susan was long over and it was no business of hers what her ex-partner did in their day to day life. Yet, here she was analysing things and even tuning her Police head into looking at how Susan lived. Leafing the pages of the translation Angharad wondered whether now was a good time to sit down and read the contents but instead she settled on the need to exercise instead.

Just over an hour later Angharad returned from her run and found that Tim was still asleep; that didn't surprise her given that he had not got to bed until gone five that morning. She made herself a large drink of water and downed it before opening the patio door onto her small balcony. Removing her top so that she was just wearing a sports bra to protect her modesty, Angharad stepped outside and looked down on the world six floors below her. It was a grey day and a wind stirred across the Bay and as it brushed against her skin, it cooled her body and dried the sweat. Down below she watched people as they moved into the Bay to take advantage of the bars and restaurants that dotted the area while in the distance a ship slowly moved out through the lock that led to the still working parts of the old Cardiff docks.

Feeling suitably chilled, Angharad moved back inside and closed the door over so as to stop the wind from getting into the apartment while still allowing there to be a movement of fresh air. Making herself another drink, a sugary tea this time, she sat down on the sofa and picked up the translated copy of the diaries and started to read. Soon she was lost in the world of 19th Century Merthyr Tydfil with its frontier town feel. That the town felt like that was not surprising to her, the diaries were written in 1844 in a place which had in many ways been at the vanguard of the industrial revolution. Less than 100 years before Merthyr Tydfil had been little more than a hamlet or small village in the Taff valley. Yet by the time it was the home of Sergeant Jones Merthyr Tydfil had four major ironworks including the two largest in the world and it was the largest town in Wales. Such rapid growth had brought a vast and unruly urban working class and unemployed under class with it. Only thirteen years before the time of her ancestor, the Merthyr Uprising of 1831 had threatened to spark a wider rebellion. Order had only been restored after four days during which the army fought battles on the streets with the occupants of the town. In that event people had died and a Socialist martyr, Dic Penderyn, hung for stabbing a soldier, had been created. Out of this world came China, a large slum with a reputation for crime and violence. The place itself had been pulled down in post war Merthyr yet its legend still echoed through the ages such that even Angharad had been raised on stories of its infamy.

A noise behind her made Angharad jump, she had become lost in the diaries and forgotten that she was not alone in the apartment. Turning around she saw a very tired looking Tim walk into the living room, he was naked and she looked him up and down admiringly. "Sorry, did I disturb you?" she asked but all Tim could do was grunt in reply. "Do you want a drink?" she offered as he plopped on the sofa next to her. He put his head on her shoulder and slowly blinked his eyes, "I don't want to be awake" he said and Angharad looked at the clock, "I'm not surprised it isn't even midday yet". Tim leaned forward and picked up the remote control, turning on the TV and scanning the channels. Looking down at the pile of papers she had been reading through Angharad sighed, there was no point in her trying to concentrate in silence anymore.

Just before five o'clock that afternoon Angharad appeared in the briefing room at Merthyr Police Station in full uniform. Rhys was already sat in his usual seat near the front so that he could see everyone as they walked through the door and he looked up and smiled as she entered the room. "Feeling better?" he offered and Angharad blushed in response. Thanks for looking out for me" she said and Rhys nodded with a cheeky grin, "anything for you Sarge".

George Williams walked in behind Angharad and seemed to be in a good mood as well, "ah, Angharad" he said with a hint of sarcasm in his voice, "so good of you to join us". Angharad turned to face him, "afternoon Sir", she said adopting a more formal tone in the presence of other officers, "I'm glad to be back". "Fighting fit?" asked George, the grin on his face confirmed that Rhys had provided full briefing on the events of the day before. "Of course Sir" replied Angharad before looking over her shoulder at Rhys who was smirking to himself. "What did you say?" she mouthed to Rhys but he shrugged his shoulders and feigned innocence.

The briefing was short and as it finished the officers filed out of the room and George leaned over from her seat so that he could whisper to Angharad. "Bad prawns I understand?" he said and Angharad looked at him with a blank expression and so George continued, "I understand from Rhys that you bumped into each other on Friday night and grabbed a bite to eat together and you had the prawns?" he offered. Angharad finally caught on, "oh... yes", she confirmed, "made me really ill almost immediately". George nodded in understanding, "don't worry" he said, "now tell me where you are with your little", he looked around him as if hoping not to be seen or heard before continuing, "investigation".

Angharad told George everything that she had learnt since she had last spoken to him and on hearing the name Chris Probert his ears pricked up. "Probert, Probert, Probert", he mumbled to himself, "oh yes, I remember him, I was working in Swansea before I found my way here and he was one of the little shits who caused the most problems". "What can you tell me about him?" asked Angharad but George shrugged, "I've not heard the name for a few years, I'll give someone a call though, I still have contacts down in that area".

After the discussion with George, Angharad walked through into the report writing room and summoned Rhys who was deep in conversation with Claire. It was clear from the way Claire was looking at Rhys that she was developing a thing for him and Angharad felt a pang of jealousy pass over her. Rhys seemed to be oblivious to the attention he was getting from Claire or at the very least, he was pretending that he didn't see it. Guiding Rhys into a side room, Angharad looked him in the eye, "prawns?" she asked, "I don't even like prawns". Rhys raised his hands in an indication that he wasn't to blame, "I needed to cover for you, I needed to explain what we had been doing, otherwise how would I have known about you being ill and I needed to justify the illness" he said pleadingly. There was nothing she could do but admit that he was right, "well let's not get ourselves into that mess again" she said and made to leave the room.

As Angharad passed by Rhys he caught hold of her arm with his hand and leaned in towards her. Whispering with a naughty glint in his eye Rhys spoke, "I'd be happy to get myself into that mess again". For a moment, Angharad's mind filled with thoughts and confusion about what Rhys was getting at but she pushed them all from her mind as quickly as they had formed. "I don't think that is a good idea do you?" she offered, raising her eyebrows as a hint that he should say no more. "Besides I don't think it is good for a Constable to see his Sergeant in quite such a drunken mess". For a moment he looked almost heartbroken but Angharad put that down to having misread what he was thinking.

Angharad went to open the door to leave the room as her radio rang in her ear. She answered it and heard George's voice in reply, "I've found Chris" he said with a hint of excitement in his voice. "He came out of prison last year and has been on probation ever since, he is living in a guest house in Merthyr". Angharad frowned, how could a man, on probation afford to live in a guest house she thought to herself. George cut in again before she could reply, "I was thinking the same thing" he said as if reading her mind "so I did some digging and guess who owns the same guest house?". This time, Angharad didn't need space to think and pressed the button on the radio to reply "William Davies" she said, there was no need for George to reply.

Clearing the private call Angharad had just had with George she heard the radio crackle into life with reports of a large fight involving at least 30 people. The location was given as the park next to the Rocky Road that ran between Dowlais and Penydarren. Angharad started to run towards the report writing room in order to make sure that officers were turning out for it and as she did so Rhys came barrelling passed her on the way to the car park. "I'll get the transit" he shouted as he turned the corner at the end. Within a couple of minutes Angharad was outside watching as her officers raced out of the gate in a blare of sirens heading for the fight. As Angharad got into the transit van she could hear Rhys revving the engine, they still had to wait for George who quickly appeared in full kit and jumped into the back. "Go!" he shouted as he slammed the sliding door shut and Angharad climbed into the front passenger seat and nodded to Rhys who required no further prompting. Screaming through the town, they headed for Bethesda Street before travelling through Pontmorlais and on to Penydarren High Street. As they travelled Angharad was glad to see that the streets were empty for the time of evening so making their journey easier.

Within a couple of minutes Rhys pulled the van to a stop on the Rocky Road, joining onto the end of the row of parked police cars which had formed opposite the park. Exiting the vehicle, Angharad surveyed the scene and could see that at least two people had serious injuries, one was nursing an arm which was clearly misshapen and the other was lying on the floor with blood pumping from a head wound. The majority of those involved in the fight had dispersed except for two people. One of them was being held down by two officers as they placed him into handcuffs while a second was using a knife to keep another three officers at bay while he backed himself into a corner. Turning to Rhys, Angharad pointed towards the incident with the knife and he understood completely, running over and drawing his Taser as he went. In the initial chaos it had not been possible for anybody to request an Ambulance and Angharad called up on the radio to let the control room know that two were needed.

Resurveying the scene, Angharad could see that one of her team was already dealing with the guy with the head injury, however, there was nobody looking after the one with the broken arm. Angharad walked over to him and took him by the shoulders, he was only young, maybe no more than 16 or 17 years of age and his face looked white with pain. "Sit down" she said but the boy ignored her, "sit down!" she commanded and this time he listened. "What's your name?" asked Angharad but the tears in his eyes and the pain in his face made it clear that he did not exactly want to speak, "what's your name?" she asked again, softly this time and the boy looked into her eyes. "I don't talk to pigs" he said with a venom and anger that made Angharad smile. "Given the level of injury to your arm I suspect you aren't going to have much choice in the matter" said Angharad, "at the end of the day I am not here to judge you". The boy didn't break eye contact with Angharad but neither did the stare he gave her soften, "I ain't talking" he said and he tried to pull himself up to emphasise his determination not to speak to her but the move caused a wave of pain to flow through his body and he bent over the broken arm and screamed. Angharad reached forward and took his chin in one hand and pulled his face up to look into hers, this time the tears in his eyes had become a river on his cheeks and his face had softened into one of someone who was desperate for their mother. Seeing an opening Angharad pulled the boy in close and there, held against her chest he sobbed like a baby.

Shortly afterwards the Ambulance arrived and the boy was taken to Prince Charles Hospital but Angharad avoided leaving his side. She would never have described herself as motherly but in that moment she found herself being one anyway. Waiting with the boy for treatment he finally started to open up about who he was and finally he told Angharad that his name was Craig and that his father was Simon Lewis. Angharad paused, taken off guard by this revelation, "so you're a Shop Boy?" she asked and Craig nodded, "yes", he replied, "I've been told I need to take my father's place while he is in prison". She looked at the boy who sat before her and as she studied him Angharad could see the family resemblance to Simon. There was one thing though that stood out to her, this boy did not have the makings of the hard man that Simon had proven himself to be. "You're not like your father, are you?" she asked and Craig looked up at her and then shook his head, his face looking more miserable at the thought as if he had somehow failed. A soft smile formed on Angharad's face, one that was intended to be warm and reassuring.

"I know your father" she said in a matter of fact way and Craig's face lit up at that knowledge before taking on a more steely look. When he spoke there was an edge of suspicion in his voice, "all coppers know my Dad?" he said rhetorically. Nodding, Angharad had to agree with the boys point but she persisted, "I knew him when he was young, we were friends when we were children". Craig continued to look at her, "I don't believe you" he said, "my Dad wouldn't have had girlfriends, he has never been one for hanging around with girls, he didn't even stay with my mother". Inside, Angharad laughed at what Craig was saying, realising that while he was speaking from a point of innocence his words carried more truth than he realised. "I was never your dad's girlfriend" said Angharad figuring that it was essentially a truthful statement and Craig seemed to just accept the point before becoming taut with pain again.

"Craig?" ventured Angharad when the pain seemed to ease off again. "Would you like to be free of the Shop Boys?" she asked and without making eye contact he nodded slowly. "You know", she said, "the Shop Boys were just a typical street gang that people grew out of when I was a kid but something changed" she said. "Do you know what changed?" she asked and Craig nodded again. Craig took a deep breath and slowly raised his head to look at Angharad, "things changed when the Davies family took over" he said and Angharad kept silent as he spoke, her face betraying nothing. "My father told me that he was running the Shop Boys and they were having fun and then one day he met William Davies and in time his younger brother Jonathan Davies" he continued. "It was William Davies who made the decision to turn them into a proper gang, my Dad said he wanted to be bigger than Stephen Thomas". The use of the name caught Angharad's attention but she did not show it as she continued to listen to Craig, prompting him where it was necessary but never forcing his story.

"What happened to William and Jonathan Davies?" she

asked and Craig thought hard for a long time, "they became respectable, first Jonathan when he became a councillor and later William as his job took off", he said. "To protect themselves they started to run things more at arm's length and left my Dad to get on with it and then they withdrew completely about a year ago". "The family are still there though, their younger brother Chris runs the show now" he said. Making a mental note, Angharad realised that it would be useful to find out how William and Jonathan had managed to fly under the radar, especially Jonathan who now held an elected position. "Is there anything else your father has told you?" she asked tentatively knowing that at this point she may push Craig to far, "yes!", he said "he said that he had overheard them speaking once and they mentioned how they were fulfilling their family destiny". It seemed a strange thing for Simon to have told Craig, strange enough that it meant that he was unlikely to have made it up but Angharad couldn't grasp what was meant by it. Standing, Angharad walked over to Craig and put a hand on his back and tried to comfort him, she had learnt much but she was sure that there was much more to discover.

Chapter 12

Monday 19ᵗʰ August 1844
Diary of Sergeant Ephraim Jones

A family of criminals living in plain sight; that is the only description that I can think of to describe the Davies family. They have these respectable jobs and hold trusted places within society but criminals are definitely what they are. Today the watch committee elected its new chairman and the new holder of such great responsibility is unsurprisingly Solomon Davies. The rumour is that the business community are going to look to Joseph Davies for its leadership in the future as well. His support has been described as unanimous now that Samuel Powell is dead.

I am now confident that this has all been planned by Abraham Davies and his sons. Iolo Thomas as the hidden son has probably been doing a lot of the dirty work and in the process they have grabbed the town by the scruff of the neck. How do I prove it though? All I have is the hearsay of Delyth and she lacks the first-hand knowledge that would allow me to build a case against the four of them. Right now I fear for the future of the town, of my family, of Delyth and of myself. It has come under the control, under the spell even, of a murderous evil family and there is nothing that can be done about it.

Monday 19ᵗʰ August 2013

Angharad had a late finish but with it being a Sunday the day before it could have been far worse. When she had got home she felt guilty about everything that had happened between her and Rhys. Even though Angharad had not slept with him she felt as though it had happened. Tim was already in bed when Angharad got there and so easing her guilt as much as possible, she took the chance to show him how much she cared. Even with the extra distraction that Angharad provided they had both managed to get to sleep before the sun started to rise.

When Angharad finally woke Tim was not there. The night before, he had told her that he had been asked to look after his children that day and so had risen early to go and be a Dad for the day. Tim's early departure left Angharad to have a lazy day; at least that was the plan until she realised that it was important to bring Thomas up to speed. A quick phone call to her grandfather revealed that Thomas wanted to give the car a run and so he was going to come down to Cardiff to get a catch up in person.

A couple of hours later the door entry system rang loud across the apartment and Angharad ran to answer it. The face of Thomas filled the picture that was relayed from the small video camera downstairs. She buzzed him through and opened the front door while she waited for the lift to deliver him to her floor. The sound of the lift lowering and raising met her ears and soon the ping of the doors sounded loud in the corridor giving her the first indication that Thomas had made it to her floor. He exited the lift and walked over to her, giving Angharad a big hug as he got to the door. She stepped aside and Thomas walked in. He had been to her apartment before but it was not a common visit for him to make. As Thomas walked through the apartment he noticed the little things that indicated a man was now living there, the razor in the bathroom, the "World's Best Dad" mug in the kitchen. "Tim's moved in then? Finally left his wife I take it?" he asked, though mentally he corrected himself that more likely Tim's wife had thrown him out.

Thomas knew about Tim but Angharad had not known how to tell him that things had changed over the last week. Typical Gramps, she thought to herself, he never misses a trick. "Yes", said Angharad, "his wife threw him out". Thomas nodded as if he was listening but didn't believe what he had been told and walked through to the window where he opened it and stepped out onto the balcony. After a couple of days of poor weather, Monday had brought a big improvement, the air was not particularly warm as there was a cold wind but the sun was shining strongly. "You softies living down on the coast" said Thomas, "the weather in Merthyr today is what makes men". Angharad guessed what that meant, "windy and wet today then?" she said and Thomas looked at her, "good to see you manage to keep your wits even when you are in Cardiff" he joked.

Angharad and Thomas sat out on the balcony and she made them both tea. They sat and enjoyed the sunshine for a moment before Angharad brought Thomas up to speed on everything that she had heard. "Family destiny?" he said when she had finished, "that would suggest that they feel there is some sort of prophecy" he continued and Angharad nodded in agreement. "I've been speaking to Berwyn Davies" Thomas said, "Gwyn Davies and Thomas were distant cousins as well". Frowning, Angharad thought about what she had read in the diaries before slapping her forehead. "Family destiny!" she said aloud, "of course, why didn't we see it before?". Thomas looked at her with concern written across his face, "are you losing it?" he asked as Angharad jumped to her feet and ran back inside. When she reappeared she bent over Thomas and started rifling through the translated diaries, "see Gramps, family destiny" she said excitedly. "It has happened before" but Thomas was struggling to make sense of what Angharad was on about. "I don't follow" he said and she pulled away and looked at him, "what do we know?" she asked. Shrugging his shoulders, Thomas was clearly still not following what Angharad was trying to tell him. "What do we know?", she asked again, "we know everything, we just can't prove it yet". "Right" said Thomas his face still blank, "you are losing it" he said as he seemed to confirm his earlier question. Realising that she needed to spell it out for her grandfather that is exactly what Angharad did.

When she had finished, Thomas stared out at the Bay and the sea beyond as if in shock. That such a thing could happen once, in 1844, was crazy but that it could happen again with the same family and in 2013 was insanity. "They feel that they are losing control of the pillars" he muttered but Angharad did not reply as she did not need to. "I bet there is something written down somewhere" she said, "I can't imagine this has travelled in oral history alone". Thomas nodded, "probably from eldest son to eldest son from Abraham Davies all the way to Henry Davies" he said. "Now we just need to work out how to prove it" offered Angharad and this time it was Thomas' turn to have a moment of inspiration. He turned to face her, "that's easy" he said with a conspiratorial air to his voice.

Luckily for Angharad, the night shift turned out to be very quiet. After her conversations with Thomas she had a long list of actions, some of which had to be completed with the greatest of discretion. She already knew that she would get very little sleep over the next 48 hours but that it would be worth it if she could deliver the results at the end. Calling a meeting in the early hours of the morning with Rhys and the Inspector, Angharad sat them both down and explained to them in detail what was needed. It was already three hours into the shift and Angharad had already spent those hours gathering the names and addresses of the people that she needed to target. Now it was time to move to the next stage and bring Rhys in on the plan, she needed his support if everything was going to be delivered on time.

Angharad sat before George and Rhys, she knew that one of them would agree with everything that she asked for, the Inspector already having been involved in the case. Rhys, however, was an unknown quantity. They had rapidly developed a trust in each other but now she was asking him to put that and a lot more at risk. Starting with an introduction to the case, Angharad outlined everything that had been discovered so far. As she spoke Rhys' face slowly moved from curiosity to suspicion and then onto shock. "Have you lost your mind?" he asked incredulously, "are you seriously suggesting that the Major Investigation Unit have missed out on taking a family of murderers off of our streets?". Nodding slowly, Angharad waited for him to continue, "and your main belief for this is a series of texts that were written in 1844?", Angharad nodded again. Rhys looked at George and then back at her before turning to George again, "you believe her?" he said pointing towards Angharad and George nodded. "Yes I do", George said, "I have seen enough to convince me that this case is real". "Do you?" asked Rhys, "well I'm starting to worry if I misplaced my trust in my Sergeant, I think she might need some time off".

Feeling hurt at the lack of trust from Rhys, Angharad asked George if he could step outside for a moment which he was only too glad to do. Alone with her officer, Angharad moved her seat so that she could talk with Rhys in a more intimate way. She knew it was important to reassure Rhys as a friend as much as her being his boss. "What's the matter?" she asked, "why are you doubting me like this?". Rhys did not reply, he simply looked up at the window of the office. Outside it was too dark to see anything other than the amber glare of a street light nearby. When he looked back at Angharad his face had changed, "I'm sorry" he said, "but you have to admit that this is a crazy story". Smiling gently Angharad held his gaze, "it's absolutely crazy and absolutely true" she said. Dropping his head, Rhys broke eye contact with Angharad, "if you have got this wrong you will cost me my job". Deep down Angharad knew that what Rhys was saying was true but she also needed his support. "I'm not wrong", she said, "I can deliver this case but there is a lot of work between now and then". There was no change in Rhys demeanour, "I've called you in because I trust you, I believe in you and right now I need you". Rhys nodded, "why didn't you involve me before?" he asked and it was Angharad's turn to look away. "This is a strange case and I am going out on a limb with it, I didn't want to drag anyone else into this until I knew I was onto something". "What about George?" asked Rhys looking towards the door where he knew somewhere outside the Inspector would be lurking, waiting to be invited back in. "That was my grandfather's idea" she said, "we needed something that George could deliver and my grandfather trusted him".

Rhys stood and walked away from Angharad to the far side of the room. He stood there with his back to her, staring at the ceiling. When he turned around his face was set with a determined look. "Fine", he said, "I just hope you are right". Rising from her seat, Angharad took Rhys' change in attitude as an indication that he was ready to continue. Walking to the door she opened it and looked out to find George stood further down the corridor. "Ready?" she asked. George walked up the corridor and entered the room, closing the door as he did. Angharad outlined each of the things that she needed and both agreed with the tasks that she set them. George was to quietly arrange for each member of the team to be available for the following night shift while Rhys was to go to each of the addresses on Angharad's list during the night and work out what would be required if the addresses were to be raided.

At the end of the meeting Angharad felt that there was a clear nervous tension hanging in the air. She looked at George and Rhys in turn and they both stared back with a grim determination. "Thomas will be here for it all as well" she said and the others nodded in understanding. Inside, Angharad realised that she had got to a point where she was about to involve an entire team in an operation that could cost them all their jobs. "Let's hope I'm not as mad as Rhys thinks" she said with a smile on her face and she winked at him. George and Rhys let out a laugh which helped to dispel some of the fear that they all felt about their near futures.

Just before three o'clock, Angharad's mobile phone rung. "You need to go to West Grove, walk in from the bottom and it's the house with the light on" said the voice at the other end. The instructions were whispered though there was no mistaking that it was actually Thomas who was speaking. "Don't come in a marked car" he continued and Angharad gave a curt reply without giving any indication as to who was on the other end of the line, "understood". Her reply given, the phone call was ended by Thomas without even so much as a goodbye. Personally, Angharad was not convinced that there needed to be quite so much secrecy about this particular event. After all, there was no reason to suspect that the Davies family knew anything about what either of them were planning but Thomas had insisted on it. The phone call ended, Angharad paused for a minute as she thought about her grandfather, she was risking her job and so was George but then they were seen as mavericks on the edge of the system. Thomas, on the other hand, was risking a sixty year old reputation as a stand out officer, a legend who was worshipped whenever he stepped near a Police station. In some ways, Angharad thought, he stood to lose the most.

Angharad popped her head round the door to George's office, "Rhys is out doing his thing and I need to pop out for a little while", she winked on saying it and George nodded. "Keep your radio close", he said, "just in case". Smiling, Angharad nodded in confirmation and then disappeared from the doorway leaving the corridor as quietly as she had entered it. She stepped outside and found the unmarked car that she had the keys for, loading the bulky bits of her uniform into the boot. She was wearing a lightweight civilian jacket that she had brought into work with her for the purpose. Onto the front passenger seat of the car she dumped a bag that contained all of the paperwork that had been collated in relation to the case. Checking around to make sure that she was not being watched too closely, Angharad started the car and edged it forward towards the automatic gate at the rear of the station. The gate slid open silently and Angharad pulled forward onto the access road and then onto Swan Street. As she moved further away from the station she picked up speed and soon she was driving up through the town and onto Brecon Road before turning by the Catholic Church onto The Walk. As a child, Angharad had often hung around this area and so she knew exactly where she needed to go.

Bringing the car to a stop on The Walk, just passed the turning to King Edward Villas, Angharad switched off the engine and peered out through the windows into the darkness. The street was empty and there was no movement from any of the houses to suggest that she had disturbed them. She pulled up the hood on her jacket and exited the car, picking up the bag as she did so. Looking around again, Angharad double checked that there was nobody watching as she closed the car door and walked down the street before turning into the junction she had parked next to. At this point the houses ran down only one side of the street and on the other were trees surrounding the grounds of a large house. The trees provided a limited shadow from the street lights and Angharad used this to the best of her ability as she headed for the narrow footpath at the top of the street, which led through to the bottom of West Grove.

As Angharad approached the footpath she looked about herself again. Confirming that she was still all alone she cautiously stepped forward into the dark alleyway. Moving carefully and as quietly as possible so her movement did not echo off the walls to either side, Angharad made her way up the footpath and into the bottom of West Grove. She paused at this point, still just on the edge of the shadow that the lane provided. Leaning forward slightly until her head poked out into the street beyond Angharad looked to her left and right. There was a house on each side with a light on in the doorway and her heart almost stopped as fear gripped her. This was the most delicate point, the point where if someone was onto her it could all be blown before she had a chance to execute the plan. Stepping back again, Angharad ducked into the shadow and leant against the cold brick of the wall on her left. Putting her hand into her trouser pocket, Angharad touched her mobile phone as she considered whether to call Thomas. Poking her head forward again Angharad checked to her left and right a second time but this time there had been a change, she was sure that the door of the house on her left was ajar. Adjusting her position slightly and raising her right hand to try and block out the street lights, Angharad peered through the darkness at the house. She was right, the door was only slightly open but it was clearly ajar and scanning the street one last time she stepped out of the shadow and tip toed over to it.

Getting to the door, Angharad gently pushed it open all the way. The inside was in darkness and she strained her eyes trying to make out what, if anything, she could see. A voice called out to her quietly, the darkness seeming to suppress its volume, "step inside and close the door" it said and Angharad obeyed the instructions. "Walk forward" the voice said again and Angharad carefully moved forward into the hallway. As she took each step she put her hands out in front of her in the vain hope that should she trip over something in the dark she would be able to catch herself. "Stop and turn to your right" said the voice and Angharad did this again, "now walk forward". Stepping forward carefully again, Angharad had only moved about a metre when she heard the voice call out, "stop".

Suddenly, a light in front of her switched on, the strength of it searing into Angharad's eyes and forcing her to raise a hand to shield herself from the sudden change. As her sight adjusted, Angharad blinked and lowered her hand slowly until she was able to look into the well decorated, though old fashioned room beyond. She found that she was stood in the frame of the door that separated the hallway from the brightly lit room. In the middle of the room, leaning on an old wooden walking stick was a very slight, well dressed, elderly woman. Angharad looked her up and down, she had a grey haired perm and a long purple dress with a cream cardigan on her shoulders. On her legs she was wearing opaque black tights and this was finished off with a pair of small black shoes with a slight heel. "Angharad?" said the woman, who spoke with a determination that came from years of experience of being in charge. Nodding in confirmation, Angharad realised that it was this old woman's voice that had guided her into the house. "Good, I understand from Thomas that you want some rather open ended warrants approved?" said the woman and Angharad nodded again. "Hmmm", said the woman, "do you actually have a tongue you can use?". Angharad looked at the woman again before replying, "yes, sorry, just finding all the secrecy a bit odd". The old woman grinned, "well, it was Thomas' idea. He said that we had to be extra careful as certain people would be upset if they were to find out about all of this". "True", answered Angharad, "I apologise for getting you up so early in the morning". The old woman looked up to her left as if studying something on the wall and then looked back at Angharad, "when you get to my age you will find that you never sleep" she said, "this is quite late in the morning for me".

"OK" said Angharad and at that the woman held out her

right hand, "please take a seat" she said and Angharad stepped through the doorway and turned in the direction that the old woman had indicated. In front of her was a large varnished table surrounded by six wooden chairs. Selecting a seat just to the side of the head of the table, Angharad sat down and waited until the old woman had placed herself into another chair; something that seemed to take an age. The woman hobbled forward looking awkward and uncomfortable and struggled with the larger chair with arms at the head of the table. Having finally taken her seat the old woman spoke, "I am Elizabeth Pryce" she said, "long standing and I mean very long standing, Magistrate of this town". Angharad nodded and the old woman smiled, "and you are Angharad Jones, Police Sergeant and granddaughter of the single best Police officer I ever worked with" she said. The praise put a little joy into Angharad's heart, she knew Thomas was worshipped in the Police but to see that he was so respected outside of it as well was a lovely sensation. "You're wondering if Thomas and I ever had a thing?" said Elizabeth, fixing Angharad with a determined look and the old woman grinned. After leaving the question hang in the air, Elizabeth's face filled with sadness, "no, no, we never had a thing, your Thomas and I, he was very much in love with your grandmother and by the time she died, I was too old and ill to be interested in such things" she said. Suddenly, Angharad felt uncomfortable and a need to apologise to the woman for her being unwell. "I'm sorry to hear that" she said and Elizabeth waved away her apology, "it is not your fault, or that of your Thomas that I developed problems with... you know what" she said with an almost wink, "it never stopped me from being a magistrate anyway". Elizabeth smiled at this and her eyes gleamed as if being a magistrate was an achievement that she took a particular pride in. "Shall we get down to business?" she asked making it clear that the small talk was over.

Putting her bag onto her lap, Angharad pulled out all of the paperwork and started to lay out the evidence in front of Elizabeth. As Angharad worked, Elizabeth stared at every document intently before exclaiming, "Henry Davies is it?". Nodding, Angharad continued to lay things out for Elizabeth who continued to talk. "I am a good Catholic girl me", she said, "getting one over on that lot will be a bit of fun". Stopping what she was doing, Angharad looked at Elizabeth and raised an eyebrow, "really?" she asked and Elizabeth smirked, "oh don't worry about me, there isn't any real hatred over such things but I do find him a smug git and one of my best friends goes on and on about how wonderful he is, I can't wait to wave this one in her face". Relaxing on hearing this, Angharad resumed her work as Elizabeth started to sing to herself. The way that this old woman was behaving Angharad started to wonder if she had some form of dementia. Soon everything had been placed in its proper location within the evidence chain and Angharad looked up from the paperwork and made eye contact with Elizabeth. "So" said Angharad in a voice aimed at raising the tension, "let me tell you a story about my ancestor, Sergeant Ephraim Jones of Merthyr Tydfil".

It must have taken Angharad nearly an hour to tell the whole story and throughout the telling Elizabeth said nothing. When Angharad finally stopped she folded her hands in front of her and waited for Elizabeth to reply. Time seemed to crawl as the old woman picked up the various bits of paper and re-read them all, muttering to herself as she did so. In Angharad's mind she envisaged that she could see small rusty cogs inside Elizabeth's head that were whirring away trying to put all of the jigsaw pieces together. Finally, she put down the last piece of paper and looked at Angharad, remaining silent as she did so. As Angharad watched Elizabeth back she realised that the old woman was staring at her rather than looking, seemingly hoping to see into her soul. "It's an interesting story" said Elizabeth, at last breaking the silence that had greeted the end of Angharad's presentation. "You put a convincing case as well" Elizabeth continued and Angharad acknowledged the praise, "thank you". The careful and measured way in which Elizabeth was speaking started to worry Angharad, had she not done enough, had she not won the magistrate over?

"Hmmm", said Elizabeth, "so what is the end game of this?". Taking care to formulate her reply, Angharad presented her solution, "it is clear that for too long the town has been in many ways under the control of a family that will do anything to protect their position". "Very true", said Elizabeth, "but your actions over the next few days may well cut the head off a serpent but I put it to you", the old woman paused for effect, "I put it to you that the serpent has served us well and we must be wary of what will happen in the event that we kill it". Now Angharad was very worried, Elizabeth seemed to be leaning towards the argument of better the devil you know than the devil you don't. Taking a deep breath, Angharad decided to make one last grab for the authority she needed to take on the Davies family, "we do not know what will come next", she said, "but a family with such power, a family of such evil intentions, a family that is so corrupt and which corrupts all that is around it; must bring untold suffering on the thousands of good people who live in this town".

Stopping for effect Angharad fell into silence and waited. She felt that she could do no more, the case was presented and the argument set. It was all down to the old woman now, either she would agree with the premise that something should be done or she would destroy everything that had been worked for over the last week. At least, Angharad thought to herself, if it dies now then nobody need know that she had taken one almighty kick between the legs of authority in the town and the authority of her father himself. After all Mike Browning was, in the eyes of her father, a chosen one.

Knowing she could do no more, Angharad waited for the judgement of Elizabeth. The old woman reached to her neck where, hidden amongst the neckline of her dress she wore a set of rosary beads. She pulled them out and started to play them in her hands, muttering very quietly to herself as she did so while keeping her eyes closed. Elizabeth was clearly seeking the guidance of a power that she believed was greater and wiser than herself. As she watched, Angharad pondered what life must be like for someone with such a strong sense of faith. It was something that she had never had personally, even though her parents had done what they could to raise her as a Christian. Angharad's thoughts were broken as Elizabeth stopped praying and her eyes shot open revealing a hardness that had not been there before. "I will give you your warrants", she said, "but if you are wrong, if you do not get the results that you and Thomas believe in, then God will grant me the strength to make your life hell!". Angharad met the glare of Elizabeth and inside she felt a little bit uplifted with joy, "thank you" she said.

Chapter 13

I received terrible news today, Sergeant Tudur who covers Dowlais died in the night while chasing a thief through the streets. The officer who witnessed his death reported that he tripped on a kerb and smashed his head into the pavement. He lived for a couple of hours afterwards but never recovered enough to speak and died before I awoke. The Inspector has asked me to go to Dowlais and take responsibility for the Policing of the area for the day. He stated that my knowledge of the local community, my family being from Dowlais and all that was a good thing.

On being instructed I made my way straight there and took the opportunity to call in on my mother in the process. It is amazing the change that has taken place in Delyth, when I first met her she was dirty and poor and looked like she had not eaten well for a few weeks but my mother, with help from the money that I have provided, has fed and bathed her and now it is possible to see how fortunate she is with good looks and a kind soul. For a girl who grew up in China, the daughter of a prostitute and who has worked as one herself, she has somehow managed to keep a level of beauty that is rare in this Godforsaken town. Her looks are such that it makes me wonder if she had been blessed by the Lord himself.

During the afternoon, Delyth brought me a lunch that my mother had put together for me and it was gratefully received. We spent time talking and I find her to be most pleasant and enlightening of company when we steer clear of the horrific events of the last week. That said, our conversation did fall to the matter in hand and through it, I was able to establish that there is another person who might be able to help me in my cause. The wife of Abraham Davies who, according to Delyth, spends many an hour helping the poor of Merthyr. Delyth informed me that she has gone to this woman for assistance on more than one occasion, so much so that they have built a mutual trust between them. The wife of Abraham Davies describes the rector as an angry and intimidating man, a very different person to the one who you see in the street and in the pulpit. Now I just need to engineer a meeting with this woman to see if she can provide me with information that I need to benefit my case.

Tuesday 20th August 2013

It was still early in the day when Angharad finally stirred from a heavy and fitful sleep. When she awoke she found Tim lying next to her. Even though she had further to travel at the end of a night shift, she had still reached home before him and when she had gone to sleep he had not been there. Lying in the bed, she propped herself up on her left elbow and watched as Tim slept. She was feeling tense with the events that were ahead of her in the night to come and needed a release that right now could only come from the man lying next to her. A twinge of anger about the events of Saturday filled her mind. In quiet times Angharad knew that her attitude and relationship with sex was unhealthy. She didn't know where such things came from but it was something that she had covered in counselling in the past yet it had never been resolved. Rape was a painful experience and rape by a loved one particularly difficult but Angharad also found it very easy to bury such things down inside; to the outside world it was all too easy to give the appearance that she had moved on. In reality though, Angharad, in quiet moments, knew that such acceptance was wrong. For a brief time this was one of those quiet moments but she couldn't afford for it to be so and the need to relieve the tension within was more important. Reaching out with one hand, Angharad felt for Tim's body under the sheets and when she found him she was relieved to see that he was in prime condition for what she would do next. Angharad dived under the sheets and seconds later, Tim moaned in his sleep.

The release of tension had allowed Angharad to get back to sleep and this time, when she awoke again, she was alone. It was late afternoon and the sound of the television reached her ears from the living room. Crawling out of bed, Angharad pulled on her dressing gown and walked through into the living room where she found Tim stood in the open doorway to the balcony. Stepping up behind him, Angharad put her arms around Tim and clasped her hands together, in response he put a hand on top of hers so that she could not release her grip. "Shall we eat out?" he asked and Angharad mumbled her response while nodding her head against his back.

By the time they left the apartment it was early evening and they strolled down to the waterfront arm in arm. When they got there they selected a pub and took their seats inside. It had been warm earlier in the day but as the night drew in the skies had become overcast and a cold wind now blew across the Bay making sitting outside rather uncomfortable. Angharad and Tim made their choices from the simple menu that was available and both of them tucked into their food with relish when it arrived. Having worked a night shift, Angharad had not eaten since the day before and so found herself to be very hungry. After finishing their food, they faced each other across a small table with arms outreached towards each other. Tim had covered Angharad's hands with his own and they looked at each other without speaking in a rare moment of peace between the two of them. The events of the afternoon had provided Angharad with a strong distraction from what was to come that night and for the time being, the powerful love they felt for each other won through.

"Angharad, I need to ask you something important" said Tim, his voice light and dreamy as he spoke and Angharad nodded, "sure", she said. Tim rose from his seat in response and Angharad stared at him, "what's going on?" she asked suddenly fearing that Tim was going to leave her when, for once, she had a serene sense of peace with him. However, Tim did not walk away, he stepped around the table and stood alongside it, still facing Angharad. Then, out of the blue, he dropped to one knee and took hold of her hands in his, "will you marry me?" he asked. Angharad's jaw dropped open at the suggestion. Freeing up one of his hands, Tim reached behind into a back pocket and pulled out a small box which he held up towards her. He removed his other hand from Angharad's and used this to open the box to reveal a diamond engagement ring inside, it was a simple ring made of yellow gold and with a single large diamond in the middle. "Well?" he asked and her hesitation caused what had been a happy smiling face to fall slightly as his mind filled with doubts. Staring at Tim, on his knee, with the engagement ring on display, Angharad didn't know what to say, she had never thought that someone would want to marry her again. It had taken a long time for her to accept that anyone would claim to love her, never mind marry her and now she was simply lost for words.

"Yes!" screamed Angharad finally finding her voice and her ability to express herself, "yes!" she said again, "of course I'll fucking marry you". She grabbed Tim and pulled him up onto his feet and towards her and they embraced in a passionate kiss. As the kiss ended, Tim pulled himself away and took hold of Angharad's left hand, taking the ring from the box he slid it onto her finger and found that it fitted perfectly. Angharad stared at the ring, her eyes wide with shock at what had just happened. Standing and guiding Tim to stand alongside her she glanced at her watch, "we still have an hour" she said, "take me home". Tim and Angharad kissed again and then he led her back to their apartment.

Less than three hours later, Angharad sat in the briefing room of Merthyr Police Station as her team filed in. She had arrived extra early and sat in her seat, making a point of flashing the new ring at everyone as they entered. As the team all settled down Claire looked at Angharad's hand and smiled, "congratulations" she said and Angharad nodded back, "thank you". Finally the Inspector walked into the room and checking that the corridor was empty outside he quietly closed the door. George looked at Angharad and smiled, "everything is set" he said, "I've sorted some cover for the first three hours but after that you need to start freeing up officers". Angharad nodded and then turned to the team who all looked back, confusion filled the faces of all but Rhys who, having been briefed the day before, had an idea of what was to come.

Carefully and methodically, Angharad laid out the plan for the night ahead. Many of the team looked on in confusion, not sure as to why a team of officers from Merthyr would be involved in what was clearly a large scale operation. From the description, some of them wondered if they were about to be involved in taking down a group that was starting to sound like some form of Welsh Mafia. "Why are we dealing with this?" asked a voice belonging to one of the officers at the back of the room and Angharad rose from her chair to see them. Once standing, she could see that the disembodied voice belonged to Robert James, who was only a year out from retirement. The effect of working shift for his entire career showed in his heavily bearded face, the hair of which was almost as grey as his skin. From day one Angharad had been worried about working with Robert, he had the look of someone who was due to keel over with a heart attack. His massive experience would have been useful, if he had cared enough at this stage in his career to dispense it.

Fixing him with a hard gaze, Angharad replied, "because clearly this town has often been getting short shrift from those in the know". Robert shrugged his shoulders in reply, clearly he didn't care one way or the other, "it's not our place" he said. Glancing around the rest of the room, Angharad caught the eye of George and Rhys, who were clearly supportive and then finally, she settled on Claire. Looking into Claire's face, Angharad could see what she had seen every day of her time on shift in Merthyr, the face of someone who was developing a strong sense of hero worship towards her Sergeant. Claire also brought something else with her, a belief in the greater good. It was a common thing for every new officer to feel but slowly, over time, it so often wore off to become the negative view of the world that Robert was displaying right now. Taking strength from this contrast, Angharad settled on what she needed to do and felt the confidence in her decision grow within her. Returning her gaze to Robert, Angharad knew that it was more important to keep hope in people like Claire than to care about the feelings of an old timer such as him. "We are dealing with this because I say so" she said with an edge to her voice. Robert saw the eyes of the other officers turn to him, his face reddened and he sank back in his seat, there were going to be no more objections from him. Even in his late career, Robert understood that he could not oppose the power of the group.

Briefing over, the officers all filed out of the room and went to organise themselves for the individual tasks that they had been set. Angharad faced George and he nodded, "I've not felt this invigorated for the job in years" he said and Angharad embraced him, "thanks" she whispered. George took hold of Angharad by the shoulders and held her at arm's length, "you have nothing to thank me for" he said, "all the thanks should go to you and Thomas for giving me the chance to take part in a real investigation again". The mention of Thomas made Angharad jump, "I almost forgot to go and greet him" she said and she rushed from the room and headed for the station car park. As she entered the yard, it was alive with officers going about the business that they had been assigned. Her eyes scanned the open space until they settled on the closed rear gate, there leaning against the bonnet of his car, just outside the fence was Thomas. She crossed over to the gate and looked at him through the white metal railings, "are you ready?" he asked and Angharad winked back. "Ready to change the world Gramps?" she said and Thomas raised himself from the bonnet, "you better let me in then".

The sound of the Gilbern entering the car park made everyone look, they were familiar with the driver but he tended not to bring the car in to the secure area at the rear of the station. Many of the officers admired the car as it roared in but a couple of them seemed to go beyond admiration and openly drooled. As Thomas exited the car; Angharad caught his attention and pointed towards the transit van, his face beamed at the sight of the vehicle and he strode over to it. Rhys was stood next to the van and he welcomed Thomas warmly and they quickly engaged in conversation. Angharad looked around the rest of the team and saw that the three officers assigned to the guest house and the four, including Robert, who were going to William Davies's house were ready to go. She called up on the radio, George was waiting for her call to confirm that everyone was ready. Then, Angharad walked over to the van and the conversation between Rhys and Thomas quickly died though not before she picked up the tail end of it. "You seem like a good choice for Angharad" Thomas said and Rhys laughed, "I get the feeling that she knows exactly what she wants" she heard Rhys reply.

They both turned to her and their faces portrayed an image of innocence, clearly whatever Angharad was a good choice for they didn't want to discuss in front of her. "In!" she ordered and pointed at the van before her face broke out into a grin. Angharad was annoyed that they felt that they could talk about her but also flattered. Anyway, this was not the time for two men to be gossiping like fish wives. Rhys jumped into the driver's seat while Angharad moved towards the other side of the vehicle. Thomas stopped her, "after all of this we need to have a personal chat" he said. Screwing her face up in confusion Angharad looked into Thomas' eyes as she tried to read what he was going on about. "About what?" she asked and Thomas smiled, "about this" he said as he raised her left hand up and looked at the ring. As he did so a hint of betrayal crossed his face. Thomas indicated that the conversation was over by standing to the side and waving Angharad passed him. She took the hint and jumped into the front passenger seat amazed again at the observation powers of her grandfather. That had not gone as Angharad had planned, it was her intention to tell him in private when all this was over. Now a part of her felt guilty about the way Thomas had reacted.

Looking over her shoulder Angharad watched as Thomas climbed into the back where Claire was already sitting, her head down and her mind lost in its own thoughts. "Everything OK?"

Angharad asked Claire but there was no response, "Claire!" she called, louder this time, "is everything OK?". Finally Claire snapped out of her thoughts and met Angharad's eyes, "yes Sarge". Claire was trying to present the image of a strong person but her eyes could not lie, inside she was terrified. "We'll be fine" Angharad said, "Rhys and I will look after you" and Claire forced a slight smile onto her face.

Finally, the last member of the team going to the Rectory joined them. George, climbed into the back and slid the door closed. He looked around everyone, his face was completely straight but the way he held himself belied that inside he was buzzing with adrenaline. "Shall we go?" he said with an impatient air as if they had not been waiting for him and it was the others who had held things up. Angharad turned to Rhys and nodded, "you heard the Inspector, what are we waiting for?". On hearing the instruction Rhys laughed, "yes Sarge, sorry for taking so long Sarge" he said with a sarcastic air. From the back of the van, Angharad heard Thomas speak, "George, how do you put up with such a bossy woman in your life?". Someone sniggered but Angharad was not sure who, "I know", said George, "I used to come to work to get away from the wife, now I go home to get away from my Sergeant". Sitting back into her seat to watch the journey Angharad couldn't help but smile. Banter between experienced officers in a situation like this was essential to help dispel the nerves.

The van pulled forward and headed for the gate which slid upon on its approach. As they pulled through the opening, Angharad looked in her wing mirror and felt a buzz from the sight of the other Police vehicles following behind. The guest house was on Courtland Terrace and so not far from where the van was heading while the home of William Davies was at the other end of town. At the end of Swan Street as the van turned left the team going to the guest house followed. Meanwhile, the officers going to William Davies turned right. At the roundabout at the bottom of Twynyrodyn Hill, the van turned right to slowly climb up the steep old road out of Merthyr. As they did so, the officers heading for the guest house continued straight on, the route to their destination finally taking them another way. Rhys guided the van skilfully up the hill before turning onto the back streets of the area of Merthyr called Thomastown. Negotiating through these narrow roads with cramped housing and crammed with parked cars was not easy, especially in such a large vehicle but they made it without incident.

As the van turned into Brynteg Terrace, Rhys slowed down to a crawl in order to keep the sound of the engine to a minimum. The entrance to the Rectory was around a left-right S bend in the road and the rear of the house had a view of the approach that Angharad and her team were using. Unfortunately due to a one way system and the need to avoid parking by the front gate of the house they had no choice but to go this way. Holding her breath as they passed, Angharad stared at the house looking for any indication that the arrival of the van had alerted the occupants. Seconds later they were through the moment of danger and the van was now sheltered by a brick wall which was dwarfed by the dark, barrier of tress that rose far above it. It was a narrow part of the road here and Rhys had to pull the van partly onto the pavement to allow cars to pass. The narrowness of the road meant that it was not an ideal place to park but it did make a perfect hiding spot.

Waiting in the darkness, Angharad and her team listened for the others to call up and confirm that they were in position outside the different locations. Getting the final signal to confirm that everyone was set, she turned to her own small group and even though they were still inside the van, whispered "let's go". They all climbed out and Angharad grabbed the heavy, red coloured, enforcer that was stowed just at the back of her seat. The enforcer was a specially designed metal ram that could be used by one officer but in the Police, it was common to call it the Universal Door Key. Holding it in her right hand, the enforcer hung towards the floor as Angharad carried it round the van until she stood next to Rhys. Behind her, Angharad could hear Claire slowly and as quietly as possible, slide the rear door of the van shut.

Looking around her, Angharad confirmed that all five of

them were now gathered together in the darkness before turning to Rhys. Nodding to him he stepped forward, leading the way as everyone else followed in single file. Angharad was second in the line with Claire behind her and then George, while Thomas brought up the rear. As they approached the gate to the Rectory, Angharad looked behind to check that everyone was still there. She smiled as she looked down the line, at the back Thomas had removed his coat and had put on a balaclava that covered his face so that he looked like a burglar rather than part of a Police operation. Thomas still moved in a graceful, cat like, manner and seeing him suddenly filled her mind with thoughts of the Milk Tray man who had dominated adverts in such a misogynistic way in her childhood. The small gate was opened by Rhys and it squeaked slightly as it moved. Everyone paused and looked at the house but if it had been heard within it was not important enough to raise the alarm. Now was the moment of truth and Angharad felt the butterflies fill her stomach until she pushed them back down.

Creeping forward, she was relieved to find that there was no security light to give away their presence. The large trees blocked out the light from the street outside and left the garden in almost complete darkness. Angharad looked up at the building, it was old and with the trees towering above and the darkness that surrounded it, the setting took on a spooky air. Rhys got to the door and Angharad handed the enforcer to him, glad to be free of its weight after the slow walk to their position. The door was large, black and wooden with a wooden frame and a big brass door knocker. Studying the door Angharad, could see that the handle was on the left and so Rhys stood towards the right hand side. Stepping in tight behind Rhys, Angharad placed her right hand on his shoulder. Opposite her position, hidden from the door on the left hand side stood Claire followed by George and at the rear Thomas.

Angharad pressed the button on her radio three times, making it beep in the ear pieces of everyone else and moments later she heard three beeps in return. Looking outwards towards the darkness of the trees Angharad imagined the view of the town she would receive from this position. In her mind, out there in the night she could see the other officers all in position or moving into position. Another three beeps came across the radio and she now knew that everyone was finally ready. Turning to Rhys, Angharad found him looking at her waiting for the signal. There was so little light that she could not make out his face but she was close enough to see the whites of his eyes and to sense that he was holding the enforcer in two hands. His left arm was tensed slightly against her side and she knew that he was ready and waiting for her.

Raising her left hand, Angharad put it on her radio and counted to three in her head. Then she nodded at Rhys while tapping him on the shoulder with her right hand. At the same time she pressed the button on her radio and spoke "GO! GO! GO!", as the noise of the enforcer making contact with the middle lock of the door echoed in the night. Despite the door looking large and strong it took just three hits to open it up with a loud crack that echoed through the large hallway beyond. As the door itself bounced back towards the frame Rhys dropped the enforcer to the side and rushed into the hallway followed by Angharad who could sense Claire directly behind her. As they entered Angharad dug in her stab vest and pulled out a torch which she used to illuminate the room beyond. The house was in darkness and the only noise she could hear was that of the officers making their way in. In the torch light Rhys and Angharad identified the stair case and ran for it while Claire, George and Thomas fanned out around the downstairs.

By the time Rhys and Angharad had made it to the top of the wide stair case someone had found a light switch and the landing became illuminated. Reaching the galleried landing, the path split both ways and Angharad turned to her right having seen Rhys, who was leading the way, turn to the left. Directly in front of her was a door and she kicked it open, shining a torch light inside but it was the bathroom and it was empty Moving again, she quickly located the next door and opening that found a large bedroom with heavy curtains that blocked all of the outside light and left the room in total darkness. Stood next to the bed was a person though she could only see them in a faint silhouette caused by the light from the landing. There was no time to move the torch around and find out who it was and so Angharad stepped forward and rugby tackled them onto the bed, dropping the torch in the process. "Found one" she screamed as the sound of more doors being opened reached her from behind.

In the dark, Angharad wrestled with the unidentified person as the sound of more people coming up the stairs reached her. Relying on muscle memory and her sense of touch she managed to get the stranger onto their stomach and into handcuffs. The jingling sound of someone wearing Police equipment filled the doorway, "light switch!" exclaimed Claire, "where's the light switch?" she said again but Angharad was too preoccupied with her prisoner to reply. A faint click in the darkness was met with a dim light appearing in the bedroom followed by a shout from Claire, "found it!". The light in the bedroom was not very strong and suddenly seemed to disappear, before returning stronger than before. Angharad looked over from her position lying almost completely on top of the stranger; in the doorway she could see Claire fiddling with a dimmer switch, trying to make the light as bright as possible. Meanwhile the stranger started to shout out, "what the fuck is happening!", the voice said, sounding deep and rough like a man, "I'm a fucking councillor!".

Angharad climbed back to her feet and looked down realising that the stranger, while lying face down was completely naked. She glanced over at Claire again and raised her eyebrows. Claire blushed slightly and then stepped in alongside Angharad, "is it Jonathan?" asked Angharad and the man's voice replied, "of course it's fucking Jonathan, Jonathan Davies, I'm a fucking councillor, now what are you fuckwits up to?". "Well he has a definite sense of entitlement" said Claire making Angharad smirk as she caught a loud laugh that was about to escape from her voice. "Shall we get him up and see how entitled he is?" Claire asked, looking directly at Angharad who looked back at Claire with wide eyes before raising a finger to her lips to demand silence. "Jonathan, it's the Police" said Angharad, "I'm Sergeant Angharad Jones and I'm investigating a series of murders". "Murders!" came the reply from Jonathan who was still face down on the bed, "what the fuck have murders got to do with me?" he asked, "I know the Chief Constable!". The implication from that statement was clear, Jonathan was prepared to make a complaint and, in his mind, make life difficult for any person who was involved in his arrest. Angharad shrugged and rolled her eyes at the threat, "you know the Chief Constable?" she asked and Jonathan screamed, "yes!". "That's good" she said, "I know the Chief Constable as well". Jonathan took a deep breath ready to throw some more abuse at Angharad, "he's my father" she said and he realised there was no point saying anything more.

Angharad and Claire got Jonathan to his feet and soon he found himself stood in the bedroom, facing two female officers, naked from head to toe. He looked at Angharad and Claire and a seductive smile formed on his face. The two female officers looked at each other and raised their eyebrows, Jonathan was rather impressive in the nude. "So do you think we can come to some sort of agreement?" asked Jonathan and he winked at Angharad as she turned her head to look at him. "Agreement?" asked Angharad pretending not to grasp what he was suggesting. "Yeah, you know, let me go and I'll let both of you try it out" he said and he nodded down towards his groin. Fully turning towards Jonathan, Angharad stepped forward until she was inches from him and she could feel the end of his penis touching against her trousers. "I let you go and I can have that?" she asked, repeating Jonathan's nod towards his groin area. He grinned, "yeah, I think I can make it worth your while" he said. Acting as if considering the situation, Angharad could see that Jonathan was getting his hopes up, he genuinely seemed to believe that his tactic was working. "Nah", said Angharad, "we're both dykes" and at that she looked at Claire who followed the lead, "yeah, do you have a sister with big tits?". Jonathan collapsed backwards onto the bed and Angharad could not tell whether it was shock at what was happening or at what had just been said.

Rhys entered the room, "we've..." he said before catching himself on seeing that there was a naked man in the room. He swallowed slowly and recomposed himself, "the Inspector is with Henry Davies, he'd like you to join him" said Rhys. "Thanks", said Angharad, "can you stay with Claire and get Jonathan here into some clothes?". Rhys nodded and Angharad walked out of the room and onto the landing. She looked around her and saw that of the multiple doors upstairs there was a light coming from only one of them. Crossing the landing Angharad headed for that door, as she went she checked inside each of the other doors that she passed. As Angharad had hoped for, Henry and Jonathan were the only two people present. Walking into the other bedroom, an elderly looking man wearing blue check pyjamas sat on the edge of a large bed. This bedroom was far larger than the one in which Jonathan had been found and it was decorated in a more traditional style. Even though he was sitting, Angharad could see that he was quite short and frail with grey hair that had been messed up by a night's sleep so much that it looked like it was windblown. George stood over the man and on Angharad entering the room he turned to her and winked.

"Hello Henry" said Angharad, who was finally facing the person she thought was likely to be the true architect of everything that had happened. "How are you doing?" she asked but Henry did not reply, he simply watched her. Despite being so frail, he was clearly still mentally alert and far wiser than his son. Rather than being angry or threatening he held himself with an air of self-belief and assurance that almost made Angharad doubt herself. Finally he spoke, "what is all this about?" he asked, his voice remaining calm. "I'll give you three names" she replied, "Gwyn Davies, Stephen Thomas and Marion Davies". Henry took a moment to consider the list and then fixed Angharad with an icy glare, "two of them are a great loss to the town" he said, "I'm sure nobody misses the evil that was Stephen Richard though", at this he smiled as if waiting for

Angharad to agree with him. Instead, Angharad, realised just how cold and heartless the man in front of her was. She was starting to get a sense of real evil from him, it seemed to emanate from all of his pores and as she looked into his eyes they seemed dark and soulless.

Stepping forward, Angharad took hold of Henry by the arm and forced him to stand. "Where are you taking me?" he asked and while Angharad continued to look at him she chose to ignore him. Her experience of dealing with people over the years had taught her that people who had not had contact with the Police before invariably became scared and nervous when they did. However, for Henry, there was no reaction at all, his face remained calm and free of any emotion. As she led Henry out onto the landing, Angharad called out to Rhys and Claire and asked them to bring Jonathan. By the time she had got to the top of the stairs they had appeared from the other bedroom, Jonathan now wearing a pair of jeans, though his upper body was still naked. In jeans, Jonathan was far less impressive to look at and it was clear that he had a good sized pot belly that hung over the top of clothing. Tears also streamed down his face and that reassured Angharad that at least one of her prisoners had normal human emotions.

As they descended the stairs, Angharad kept a firm grip on one of Henry's arms even though she had to walk behind him to ensure they both made it down safely. At the bottom of the stairs, just to the right of the door that had been forced open by Rhys only minutes before was a large wooden chair, almost throne like in design. Sitting in the chair with his nose buried in a copy of the Parish Magazine was Thomas. "Hello Thomas", said Henry, "I didn't expect to see you here". Thomas ignored him and turned over another page. "Which way is the living room?" enquired Angharad who from her position could not see into any of the rooms. Henry refused to answer her, choosing simply to look straight ahead but Thomas raised his left arm and pointed at the open doorway to his side. "Move!", said Angharad in a commanding voice and she pushed Henry towards that door by the arm she was holding. As she stepped away from the stairs she glanced backwards to see that Claire was stood halfway down from the landing, holding onto Jonathan and waiting for Angharad to get out of the way. At the top, deep in a quiet conversation were Rhys and George, from the way their hands were moving it looked like they were discussing the layout of the house.

On entering the living room Angharad found it to be a large room with an open fire on the far wall. The room covered the whole depth of the house with a window to the front and to the back of the property. At the rear of the room, directly beneath the window that looked onto the back garden, sat a large, three seater Victorian style sofa in a deep red colour. Angharad guided Henry over to this and sat him on the right hand seat. She then turned to see Claire still stood in the middle of the room and pointed to the left hand side of the sofa. As she watched, Claire guided Jonathan over to this seat and sat him down as well. "If either of you talk I'll rip out your tongue" Angharad said, obviously it was a blind threat and she was confident that Henry would not speak, however, she was worried about Jonathan. While he had been overly confident in a sexual manner when in the bedroom, from everything she had heard Angharad suspected that he would now be feeling weak and eager for support.

Turning, Angharad made to walk out of the room but had to fight the urge to take a backward step with fright as she found Thomas stood directly behind her. He was carrying the Parish Magazine he had been reading when Angharad had last seen him, now rolled up and tucked under his right arm. "It's OK", he said with a hint of naughtiness shining through his eyes, "I'll help Claire". Stepping out of the way, Angharad indicated to where she had been standing, "be my guest" she said. Thomas waltzed passed her and stood in front of Henry and Jonathan for a moment. Then, selecting a large brown leather chair that was positioned along the wall to the right of the sofa Thomas dropped himself into it, putting his feet up onto the foot stool in front of it in the process. As he made himself comfortable, Thomas unrolled the magazine and returned to the place where he had been reading. As Angharad left the room she heard Thomas speak, "so, Henry, tell me where you sit on this gay Bishop thing" he said. Angharad knew what Thomas was doing, he was making idle conversation to distract from the desire to speak about what had actually happened.

When Angharad got back into the hallway she found the house to be silent except for the murmur of Thomas' voice from the living room and a shuffling sound that came from down the side of the stair case. There was no sign of George or Rhys so she guessed that the sound came from them. Taking the opportunity presented to her, Angharad checked in with the other officers who had taking part in their own small raids. Everything was a success, Chris Pritchard had already been arrested for his involvement in the murder of Marion Davies and while two officers took him to the station, the third was searching the small room in which he lived. Meanwhile William had been secured in his house and three of the officers were busy searching it in conjunction with the warrant. Luckily for Angharad, it had turned out that William's family were visiting his wife's parents who lived in Newport and so they were not expected back until the morning.

Secure in the knowledge that so far everything was going according to plan, Angharad headed down the hallway to find George and Rhys. They had located an office which looked like it had been decorated a long time ago. Inside the room, all of the walls were lined with wood in a Victorian style. The whole of the left hand side of the room was a floor to ceiling book case which held hundreds of leather bound books. In front of the window, which looked out of the office over the side garden, was a huge oak desk with a large leather swivel chair. The room was large enough that even with George and Rhys in there it was still possible for Angharad to comfortably fit in. George was slowly working his way along the books, spine by spine, reading each of the titles while Rhys was on his knees just to the right of the desk, looking through a metal filing cabinet. Given the age and styling of the rest of the room the filing cabinet, especially with its chipped paint showing how tattered it was, looked out of place. "Anything?" asked Angharad but there was no response from either George or Rhys. Angharad realised that they were completely engrossed in their work and oblivious to her presence.

Raising her right hand to her mouth, Angharad made a fist with her fingers and thumb. Covering her mouth like this Angharad issued a short, sharp cough. George and Rhys both jumped and turned to face her, clearly surprised to see her stood in the room with them. "Anything?" asked Angharad again and George stopped working long enough to shake his head without taking his eyes from the bookshelf. Rhys's voice cut through the silence of the room and George at last took his eyes away from his work. "Maybe" Rhys said and he reached down to his left and picked up a folder, "you might find this of interest". Rhys offered the folder towards Angharad who crossed the room and took hold of it. It was a plain blue cardboard folder, the type that holds a handful of A4 pages when a ring binder is too excessive, written on the front in ink was "Items of Note". "Where was it?" asked Angharad and Rhys pointed to the drawer that he was searching through, "in there". Looking around the room, Angharad realised that the desk was tidy with no paperwork lying about on it and she stepped over, pushing the chair out of the way in the process. She laid the folder down on the desk and looked at the front again before glancing at Rhys who had returned to being nose down in his search. "Items of note?" she said to herself and her mind raced with why she thought Rhys would find it of interest to the case.

Slowly, almost delicately, she turned the cover over to reveal the first page and in that moment her heart skipped a beat and she gave out a soft "oh!". There, looking up at her was a news article, a very old news article from the Merthyr Guardian which had been placed inside a poly pocket. She looked at the date Thursday 15th August 1844 and then she looked at the headlines, "Four Dead in Weekend of Death". Reading the rest of what was clearly the front page of the newspaper, it reported on the death of four people that had taken place in the town in the intervening week. She turned the page again and with each leaf it revealed more cataloguing of what had happened all those years ago, sometimes in Welsh and sometimes in English, dependent upon the newspaper or journal involved. There were obituaries of those who had died and a recording of the elections to replace the previously deceased town leaders. Then, written as a side article, in a newspaper published some six months later, in the early Spring of 1845, was mention of a Sergeant Ephraim Jones.

Suddenly hungry for information on her family, Angharad read the article, it was clearly about her own ancestor. The story told how Ephraim Jones had been moved to Dowlais, where there was a problem with theft from the ironworks following the death of Sergeant Tudur. It praised Sergeant Jones for his diligent work in catching the offenders and bringing them to justice and then, at the end, was some personal information. It revealed that Ephraim had recently, with permission from his Inspector, married his sweetheart Delyth. Tears welled up in Angharad's eyes as she realised what she was reading. Delyth Bwthyn Bach, so weak, so poor and so unfortunate when she first appeared in the diaries. Yet, she was the one, she was the woman who stood as a legend over the family, a legend for which no diary was needed. The woman who married a Sergeant in Merthyr and drove him to the rank of Superintendent, the woman whose son became a Chief Constable of the Glamorgan Police. Delyth Bwthyn Bach was the woman to whom all the generations of Jones' in the Police owed everything and she was the legend that Angharad had always wanted to be.

For a moment, Angharad forgot what she was doing there and she ran from the room with the folder in her hands. She got to the living room door and paused just in time, stopping herself from rushing in and giving away what had been found. Leaning round the door frame she called out, "Gramps?" she said and he turned to face her. Angharad nodded with her head, slightly to the side and away from Thomas and he immediately understood what was being asked of him. He walked over to her and stood in the doorway and Angharad smiled. "We are the children of Delyth" she said in a whisper and Thomas looked at her confused. "Look" she said and taking care to keep the folder on her side of the door she held it up for Thomas to read. As he finished reading the article he smiled gently and looked into Angharad's face before wrapping her up in a big hug. Putting her free hand around Thomas they held each other for what seemed and eternity before naturally releasing. They smiled at each other one last time and then parted, Angharad returning to the office and Thomas to his seat.

By the time Angharad got back to the office, another two blue folders which on the outside looked identical to the first, had appeared. Rhys had moved up the filing cabinet to the next drawer and was obviously having great success in his search. These folders were more modern in content. One of them contained up to date cuttings from the Western Mail about the most recent murders but the other; that was a surprise. In that folder was coverage of another series of deaths, another almost identical series of deaths which had taken place in the summer of 1929. Angharad couldn't believe what she had found in this one and called over George and Rhys. "Nine murders" she said, "nine murders involving the same people in society and all circulating around one family".

Rhys studied the pages intently while George looked at Angharad. "What? What are you saying?" he asked and Angharad pointed again at the folders. "The first time they took control, then in 1929 they consolidated" she said, "now they have consolidated again". Turning his attention back to the folders George swore under his breath, "shit!". His eyes settled on a quote in a newspaper article from 1929, a quote from the Rector of the Parish of Merthyr Tydfil, a man by the name of Josiah Davies, who spoke as his family's representative after they had been struck by two unfortunate deaths in the same weekend. "I wonder if this Josiah Davies was as cold as our Henry Davies is?" asked Rhys, not really aiming the question at anyone. Feeling relief that she was not the only person to have spotted it, Angharad replied, "Probably, you would need to be completely cold and heartless to do what he has done especially knowing that he was killing off his own".

Returning to the search, George and Rhys left Angharad to contemplate the content of the various news articles that had been recovered. Putting the three folders together in a pile on the table, Angharad happened to look down and realised that there was a small gap at the front of the desk. She studied this gap, it looked out of place and didn't make sense to her. Stepping back, she looked directly at the desk and realised that it could not be seen from any position other than standing over it. Angharad leant in closer and hooking her fingers into the gap she pulled. Slowly, a hidden drawer, which had not been properly closed, revealed itself and her mind raced with thoughts of what would be inside. George slammed a large book down on the desk. The bang from the book made Angharad, who had been stood with her back to him, jump "what the..." she exclaimed as she stepped away from the desk. Feeling reassured that she had support, Angharad sensed Rhys move quickly to her side in a defensive reaction to the noise. Lying on the desk, open wide, was the book that George had just thrown down with a very detailed family tree clearly visible on its pages. Pointing at the open book, George beckoned Angharad and Rhys to follow his finger, "Henry Davies is the only son of his father, who was also a vicar, though not here in Merthyr Tydfil". Everyone nodded in understanding as Angharad's eyes raced ahead trying to catch up and even overtake George's thinking, "and he is the first born son of Josiah Davies" she said, "who was Rector of Merthyr Tydfil in 1929". "What about Abraham Davies?" asked Angharad noticing that he was not mentioned on that page. George turned a page to show the family tree further back, "Henry Davies is first born son of first born son all the way back to Abraham Davis" he said.

The book joined the pile of exhibits along with the three folders as in her mind Angharad started to put together all of the evidence in front of her. Though in reality it was still all just circumstantial, she needed something more concrete. Then she remembered that she was about to search that hidden drawer in the desk. Returning her attention to it, Angharad finished opening the drawer and looked inside. As she searched the documents contained within she noticed that one of them was a diary, a large 2013 diary. Opening it up Angharad found that its contents were written in Welsh. Her knowledge of the language was limited but even Angharad understood enough to recognise that 15 Awst meant the 15th August. She turned the pages that followed that date and looked at the text, the names of the people who had died, Gwyn Davies, Marion Davies and Stephen Thomas leapt out at her and she gasped. This diary might well be the hard proof that I need she thought to herself.

"Has anyone found any more diaries?" she asked of George and Rhys and they both shook their heads and looked at her in expectation. "I've found one", said Angharad, "a current one" and she held it up. Remaining silent, George and Rhys watched Angharad hoping that she would reveal the big secret to them and she held that feeling for a moment. "It's in Welsh" she said and the other two sighed in disappointment. "I could just about manage one language" said Rhys with a grin on his face. George shrugged his shoulders, "I'm from Monmouth originally" he said and Angharad got his meaning, "so you're English then?" she joked. Fixing Angharad with a hurt look that he couldn't keep for long, he burst into a grin "never!".

There was only one way forward concluded Angharad. She contacted the officers who were with William Davies and updated them accordingly. "Come with me" she said to Rhys and she walked back towards the living room. As Angharad entered, everyone in the room looked towards her. Her face was set with a determined look and on seeing it Thomas knew exactly what was about to happen. Standing in front of Jonathan and Henry, Angharad looked at each of them in turn and then at Claire who was standing on her left. Angharad looked Claire in the eye and smile gently, then she nodded and stepped to her right so that she was stood next to Thomas.

Stepping forward from her position, Claire stood in front of Jonathan and Henry so that they could both see her clearly, "You are both under arrest for the murders of Gwyn Davies, Stephen Thomas and Marion Davies" said Claire in a matter of fact way. Jonathan jumped up, his mouth open and his face set in shock, he was going to shout and protest but Claire was quicker and pushed him back down onto the sofa. Angharad nodded at the reaction of Claire, her heart filled with pride as she saw the young officer come into her own. Not missing a beat, Claire carried on "you do not have to say anything but it may harm your defence if you do not mention when questioned something which you later rely on in court, anything you do say may be given in evidence". Watching Jonathan and Henry, Angharad noticed how while Jonathan still seemed to be in shock, there was no outward expression from Henry, no movement to protest, no reaction of disbelief. Angharad signalled to Rhys who moved forward to assist Claire in taking both of her prisoners from the house. "Once they are booked in come back here" she said and Rhys nodded in confirmation that he understood.

The room, although large, felt far emptier without Claire, Jonathan and Henry in it. Angharad and Thomas stood in silence, neither breaking eye contact with the other. In the quiet, the sounds of George continuing to search the office reached their ears. Thomas smiled and then he stepped forward, he was tempted to embrace her but with all the equipment that Angharad was carrying he opted for putting his hands on her shoulders. Thomas seemed to have an ability to always read how Angharad was feeling and know what he should say and when he should say it. Deep inside she knew that there had been no going back once she had arranged the warrants, but that feeling had returned when she had raided the house. Now that she had arrested everybody she couldn't stop thinking again that maybe this last bit had been a step too far if she could not prove the offence.

"Angharad!", the voice of George rang out across the house seconds before he appeared in the doorway. Turning towards him, Angharad found that George's face was a picture of shock as he realised that Jonathan and Henry were no longer present. Showing his experience, he quickly recovered, "so you've done it then?" he asked and Angharad replied, "yes". Nodding, George moved the conversation on quickly, "good, good, I've found these" he said, lifting up two books, "diaries from the 1840's". Angharad stared at them and felt hope fill her heart as she considered all of the evidence that had been found. "I think we've found everything that we are were going to find" said George and Angharad and Thomas agreed.

The three of them searched the rest of the house while they waited for Rhys and Claire to return. By the time that they did, the three of them were all sat in the living room with the exhibits piled up on the floor. Angharad, George and Thomas were locked in a conversation about rugby, in particular the British and Irish Lions tour that had finished the month before. As a group, they had picked rugby as a topic as it meant that none of them would, for once in their lives, be talking about the case that they were dealing with. As all five of them left the house, Rhys looked at the door and Angharad was relieved to find that it was possible to secure it with a few minutes of tinkering. The actual damage caused had been minimal in the end.

At the request of Angharad, Rhys drove straight to Queen's Road, straight to the home of Susan. George and Thomas remained inside the van while Rhys and Claire walked with Angharad up to the front door. It was still night time and the sun would not rise for another hour; amber street lights provided the only illumination and every house was in darkness. Knocking loudly on the door, Angharad waited as Claire stood to her side and Rhys remained at the entrance to the garden. After the third attempt, a light sprang to life inside and shone through the glass of the front door. Getting the response that she wanted, Angharad stopped knocking and waited as the silhouette of someone approached from the other side.

Watching through the glass Angharad could see and hear the person on the other side fiddling with the lock and to her relief, at this closeness, despite the glass being patterned, she could see that it was Susan. The door opened on a chain and Susan peered out through the gap. "What do you want?" she asked in a whisper, her voice tinged with anger, "it's stupid o'clock in the morning". Angharad looked back through the gap in the door, she could see enough in the limited light to see that Susan clearly had bed hair and that she was wearing a very short pink dressing gown. In that moment Angharad thought back to when she had lived with Susan, a time when she got a thrill from such things. "Seriously Angharad, what the fuck do you want?" Susan asked again and Angharad paused, was she really doing the right thing in being here? Angharad looked around at Claire, at Rhys and back at the van where George and Thomas waited in the dark, it wasn't just her job on the line now she concluded.

Lifting up the two exhibit bags in her hand, Angharad allowed the limited light to cast on the bags to reveal the two diaries held inside. "I need these translated urgently", she said with a hint of desperation in her voice, "we've seized them and they are in Welsh, the one covers 1844, the other today". Susan stared at the bags, "now?" she asked, "really! Now? Why couldn't this wait until the morning?". "Yes, now", said Angharad, "because I only have 24 hours". Dropping her head, Susan sighed deeply and then closed the door and then the sound of the chain being removed emanated from within. A moment later the door was reopened completely and Susan looked at Angharad and Claire, "you better come in" she said. Angharad nodded her thanks and stepped into the doorway. A sound came from behind Susan and Marc appeared wearing just a pair of boxer shorts. He was a short man but incredibly well built from hours spent in the gym and on the rugby field, "what the fuck is going on here? What the fuck are you doing here? Why the fuck are you letting this fucking prick in?" he shouted stepping, forward to block Angharad's route into the house. Turning quickly, Susan put a hand on his chest and tried to hold him back, "Marc" she begged, "Marc, this is important and they need my help". However, Marc could not be placated and he took hold of Susan by the wrist and started to peel her hand away.

"You left this idiot years ago", said Marc "and yet when it comes running you can't help yourself!". Trying to placate Marc again, Susan put her hand back on his chest and this time stepped more in front of them. She looked into his eyes and moved in very close, "Marc, I need your help in this, the kids will need your help in this!". Slowly, Susan attempted to push Marc backwards, away from the door and further into the hallway.

Following behind, Angharad stepped into the hallway, she knew that she should not interfere and that she had to let Susan deal with the situation. At the back of her mind though, something told Angharad that she couldn't take the risk of letting Susan deal with it completely alone. Putting the exhibit bags down, Angharad continued to follow Susan and Marc. In his younger days Marc had been known for having a bit of a temper on the rugby and football pitches of South Wales and had been in many a fight. Seeing what Angharad was doing Marc exploded; he grabbed Susan by the arms and threw her to the side, crashing into the wall. As she hit the wall, Susan immediately grabbed the back of her head. Angharad responded to this action, moving forward to meet Marc who was now rushing at her. In the tight confines of the hallway though there was very little that Angharad could do to protect either Susan or herself.

The fight would come down to one of pure strength and in that Angharad lost quickly, Marc grabbed hold of her by the shoulders before pulling her forward and then turning at the hip and leveraging with his legs he slammed her into the wall. The force of the slam winded Angharad and she struggled for breath as Marc pulled back with his right hand and swung with it catching her in the face. For a moment, Angharad felt as if she had blacked out from the force of the punch and as she raised her head back up she could see Claire step in to help. Claire pulled out her pepper spray but in the closeness of the situation, Marc reached out and pushed with his left hand sending Claire sprawling onto the floor. Angharad looked to get a purchase on Marc, on his arms, on his body but she was struggling to think, her mind cloudy, as she saw him prepare to punch her again. Angharad closed her eyes and braced for the impact.

Whatever impact Angharad was expecting never came, instead Marc released his grip and Angharad felt him being pulled away, leaving her to slump to the ground. Sounds of a fight reached her ears and she opened her eyes and looked further into the hallway, following the noise. There, kneeling over Marc was Rhys, he had placed Marc face down on the floor and was holding an arm up behind his back. "Don't fucking move, don't even fucking think about pissing me off anymore" said Rhys as Marc tried to struggle against the grip that he was held in. As Angharad watched, Susan climbed down beside her husband and tried to sooth him. Angharad rose to her feet and walked over, producing her handcuffs in the process. A short while later Marc was secured and then with help from Rhys, he was brought back up to his feet. Guided by a strong grip from Rhys, Marc was walked into the living room and made to sit down in the middle of the sofa. Rhys was taller than Marc anyway but now that the latter was sitting, Rhys towered over him with his face full of anger. Putting a hand onto Rhys's shoulder, Angharad whispered her thanks, she could see that he was just looking for an excuse for Marc to do something. The touch from Angharad seemed to relax Rhys a bit and she started to feel more comfortable about leaving the two of them alone, "I'll be back in a minute" she said.

Walking out of the living room, Angharad found Susan still stood in the hallway with Claire. They were checking each other for injuries as tears streamed down the face of Susan. Angharad guided Susan into the kitchen and Claire followed, "this is your fault Angharad" Susan said, "why did you have to come here?". The way Susan spoke made it clear that the earlier conversation had now been forgotten. Angharad put her arms round Susan and hugged her, there was no attempt to fight her off. For a moment, Angharad thought back to what life had been like in an earlier time, a life that seemed to have belonged to someone else. Time passed as Susan cried on Angharad's shoulder, neither saying anything until eventually Susan appeared to have got all of her emotion out. Pulling away from Angharad, Susan became strong once more. "You are not going to arrest him" said Susan and Angharad nodded, "I don't want to" she said, "I have more than enough on my plate without another prisoner".

Susan seemed buoyed by this reply, "after all this, I might as well help you out" she said, "what do you need?". Angharad looked around, suddenly realising that she no longer had the diaries in her possession and for a moment panicking that she had lost them. Claire, who was stood in the kitchen doorway held them up with a smile on her face and Angharad felt relief on seeing the two books as they were placed onto the island. "This is Claire she will take a statement from you" said Angharad, "in that statement you need to tell us what the English translation of the Welsh written in these two diaries is". Susan nodded as Angharad explained, "of particular interest is the last week in the 2013 diary". "Fine", said Susan, "where did they come from?". "From the office of the Reverend Henry Davies" Angharad replied and Susan grimaced. "He's the killer?" asked Susan and Angharad nodded, "looks like it". "When I was young, when I believed, I used to attend his monthly Welsh language sermon" said Susan, "he seemed such a nice man back then". Watching Susan carefully, Angharad could appreciate that Susan might feel sorry for man, "I think it was an act, there is nothing nice or caring about the man we arrested tonight" Angharad said and Susan's face fell. Clearly she still trusted Angharad's opinion on such matters. "I think it might be an idea if we do this back at the station?" interrupted Claire and Angharad watched as Susan nodded in agreement, "I'll go get changed" she said.

Leaving the kitchen Susan headed upstairs while Angharad returned to the living room. Marc was sat on the sofa his arms still held behind his back by the handcuffs, "we'll be leaving soon" said Angharad "and Susan is coming with us". Turning his head sharply, Marc shot a look up at Angharad and she could see that his eyes were filled with tears. "Don't worry" said Angharad, "she is helping us and will be back later. When we leave we'll get you out of those things". "I don't want anything from you" said Marc with anger still in his voice, "I don't need your help". Angharad couldn't help but smile, "you've got no choice in the matter" she said, "because otherwise I'll have you arrested for assault on Police". At the mention of arrest, Marc let his shoulders slump and his head fell lower between his legs. "He's not coming out of those things until we leave" Angharad said, looking at Rhys who grinned back, "there's no chance of that".

By the time Angharad had left the living room, Susan was back downstairs and dressed in a pair of tracksuit bottoms and a t-shirt. "The kids want to see you" said Susan and Angharad nodded before heading upstairs. At the top of the stairs she found Sion and Sioned looking visibly upset, Angharad grabbed them both in her arms and hugged them. "Everything is going to be fine" she said, "your mother is just helping me for a few hours and then she will be home, Marc will look after you". Sion sobbed into the crook of Angharad's neck while Sioned, always the tougher one spoke for both of them, "we love you Cariad" she said, "look after our Mam". Angharad hugged them again, "of course I will", she kissed them both gently and with that they parted.

Half an hour later Angharad walked down the corridor in the custody block. She opened the hatch in the cell door for each of the people who had been arrested and looked at them. Henry Davies was sat there as calm and self-assured as he had been at the house while William Davies seemed to follow the same pattern, showing the stoicism of his father. He had clearly inherited his father's personality, confident in his own ability and comfortable that he would get away with this crime in the same way his ancestors had. When she opened the hatch to Jonathan Davies, Angharad saw a very different person though. This man was nervous, he was scared, in fact, Angharad would go so far as to describe him as petrified and that was what she wanted. A man who didn't have confidence in his own position, someone who was used to being propped up by those around him, those who had stronger personalities. Then finally, she looked at Chris Pritchard, the last of the gang who were responsible for everything that had happened over the last week. This man was different to the others. He paced around the small cell, clenching and unclenching his fists as he went. Here was a man who was angry at the world and the cards that it had dealt him. Not being raised by Henry had obviously had left him different, he clearly hated the world.

As Angharad walked out of the custody block she found Rhys waiting for her, "you said that you had one more task for me?" he said and she nodded. "I need you to go to Cardiff" she said and Rhys looked at her, his face full of questions. "You need to get Simon Lewis and bring him back, he'll be expecting it" she said. "Why?" asked Rhys, "what can he give us in relation to this case?". Angharad smiled, she had held this bit back from all the previous briefings but now it was time to tell. "Because he will confess his involvement in the case and who gave him the orders". Rhys nodded, "is the prison expecting us?" he asked. "Thomas has sorted all of that. Unsurprisingly it is one of those little jobs where who you know is more important than what you know" she said, "make sure you take someone with you but don't take Claire, I need her". Nodding again, Rhys turned and was gone. Angharad walked up to George's office and sat down, "what now?" he asked and Angharad smiled, "now we wait".

Chapter 14

Wednesday 21st August 1844
Diary of Sergeant Ephraim Jones

I met with Mrs Davies today, a well-dressed and very well spoken English woman who married Abraham Davies because her family felt it would be a good match. We met after she had hosted a morning for the women of the town who were interested in helping with poor relief. To my surprise, she was very open and up front about her relationship with Abraham Davies. It did not take much effort to get her to provide all of the information that she held. It is clear to me that what she said about Mr Davies is right. The woman is very unhappy in her life and uses her charitable work as a distraction from the misery of her home life. She confessed to me that she knows about Iolo Thomas and she knows that Abraham has had other lovers as well. In fact according to her there is not a single prostitute in China who hasn't been visited at least once by her husband.

It turns out that Mrs Davies knows pretty much everything that has happened. She knows that there have been three murders and she knows that her husband is behind them with the help of Iolo. She described her husband as Satan, a monster filled with greed and ambition, one who knows what he wants and is prepared to do anything to get it. Her children, Solomon and Joseph, despite her best efforts have followed in their father's footsteps becoming just as focused and just as controlling as he is. I asked Mrs Davies how she knew that her husband was behind everything and she said that he does not hide it, he does not pretend with her. Sadly, it became very clear that she is terrified of her husband and she knows that she shouldn't argue or challenge him.

For a moment, I thought I would get her to agree to provide the evidence I need. A woman such as this, in the witness box would damn her husband to the gallows but she refused. Mrs

Davies is a woman raised on the importance of public impression, raised on the essential fact that one thing she should never do is bring shame on her family. To give evidence against her husband would bring shame on her family and make her an outcast not just from her sons but also from the parents who brought her into the world. Such an outcome would leave her destitute and alone in a world where without money and family, a good woman such as Mrs Davies cannot survive on her own. For her it is better to live with a killer, a controlling, dangerous man than to risk being cast out for her betrayal. She looked at me, she pleaded and there, in that moment I could see one other thing, something that went unsaid. Her children may have followed their father but she cannot help but love them.

That was a touching and emotional visit to Mrs Davies, as I left she begged me to leave it, leave this case and not to investigate it again. As she spoke tears filled her eyes and she said that she would pray for me to find the strength to do as she asked. It was such a heartfelt request from a devastated woman. I have no evidence without her testimony and while I feel sympathy for her position, I am also angry at the fact that she will not put justice and the greater good above her own needs. On that day, I fumed at what had happened and what had been said so I did the only thing that I could.

That night, I waited in the dark, waited for a killer. Abraham Davies was at St Tydfil's until late and then, confident in his own control of the world, he walked home. As he walked I followed in the shadows, watching and waiting. He entered a dark street, an empty street and I struck, knocking him to the ground. I beat that man until he was sore. I needed him to know that this was not an accident and so there, in the dark, as he whimpered and begged for his life, I leaned in close. "You do not have control of this town" I said to him and then I kicked him one more time for good. He begged to be saved, begged me to let him live and in that I found some solace. It will not be possible to bring Abraham Davies to justice but it has been possible to stop him from feeling completely comfortable in his position. He will live the rest of his life knowing that someone out there does not fear him.

Wednesday 21st August 2013

It was a hot and humid forest and Angharad was struggling through it, running from some hidden beast that followed her constantly. She was climbing over fallen trees and pulling away from vines that seemed to grasp at her. In the distance she could hear the beast getting close, giving out a strange guttural snort with every few breaths. Then it grabbed her right arm, pulling on it and twisting it in pain, Angharad fought desperately against it even though its features remained hidden from her. She twisted left and right but it held on invisibly and would not let go, jerking one last time, Angharad tried desperately to pull away from it.

Her body jumped and with that movement Angharad's eyes opened. For a moment she was disorientated, Angharad was no longer in the forest but her arm hurt. Looking down she realised that she had been resting on it and that it was now riddled with pins and needles from being trapped and the blood flow restricted. There was a movement to her right and she twisted in the seat within which she had fallen asleep and saw Rhys stood in the doorway. "Sorry", he said, "I didn't mean to scare you". Rising from the chair, Angharad tried to straighten herself out and looked at the clock on the wall. She must have been asleep around an hour she thought. She was still in George's office but the last thing that Angharad recalled was sitting in the chair passing time, waiting for Rhys to return with Simon Lewis. Blinking, her senses came back to her a bit more, "you didn't scare me" she said. Though it felt like a lie right now, she was not in the mood to discuss her dreams with another person. "I take it Simon is back?" she asked and Rhys nodded. "Do you know where Claire is?" she asked and Rhys shook his head, "I've only just got back, I think everyone else is in the canteen but I don't know for certain". Nodding, Angharad looked at Rhys, "thank you for everything, now go get some downtime".

Rhys and Angharad walked into the canteen; there were no kitchen staff these days but the room had kept its name. The smell of bacon filled the air and Angharad realised that Thomas was stood in a smoke filled kitchen along with George. Claire saw Angharad as she entered and smiled, "Your Grandfather and the Inspector are making everyone breakfast" she said and Angharad realised just how hungry she had become. Walking around the table, Angharad took the time to thank everyone for their work and then she turned to Claire and asked if she would join her on the other side of the room. As Angharad and Claire took their seats Thomas and George appeared with plates full of bacon, sausages and eggs covered in baked beans and fried bread. Serving a plate to Angharad, Thomas put a hand on her shoulder without saying anything, Angharad said nothing back but she understood what the hand meant, reassurance and complete support.

Eating in silence, Angharad and Claire cleared their plates and took a minute to drink cups of strong tea that had also been served with the breakfasts. "I want you to help me" said Angharad and she could see that Claire looked confused, "with the interviews". Claire remained silent, her body language showing that she was deep in thought about the situation, "I'm not a trained specialist interviewer" she said at last. "That's fine" said Angharad, "there is always a first time to learn and besides, I think you have the makings of a detective". Claire thought about it for a bit longer and then nodded, "OK", she said, "if you believe in me Sarge then so do I".

Angharad and Claire took their seats in the interview room, opposite them sat Simon Lewis. Prior to entering the room Angharad had confirmed with Claire that she wanted her to lead, she was confident that Simon would give a full confession to his knowledge of the crime that had taken place. "Tell us about the Shop boys?" asked Claire and Simon thought carefully about his answer, phrasing it in a way that he hoped would help him. "We were a gang of boys, hard boys, and we loved the way people were scared of us" he replied. Remaining quiet Angharad could tell that

Simon wanted to tell everything, "go on" prompted Claire. "Then along came William Davies, he had a different way of doing things and he led us astray with dreams of money and influence", Simon stopped and thought again, "we were stupid enough to go along with it".

Glancing at Angharad, Claire looked for confirmation that the interview was going as planned and she saw Angharad give a slight nod of her head. "What happened?" asked Claire and this time, Simon screwed up his face in anger. "By the time I realised what was going on, it was too late, we were fully into it all", Simon was clearly getting exercised by this point, "we became involved in drugs, prostitution, the full lot and when we got caught, William would buy our silence". "It was never linked back to him?", "never, he walked through it all completely above it, no fucker knew, not even the Police". Claire nodded and checked her notes but Simon was fully into it now, "then, out of nowhere, William withdrew one day, said his position outside was becoming too important and he couldn't risk getting found out... that day he introduced us to Chris Pritchard". Falling silent, Simon looked down at his hands and he studied his finger nails before raising his head again. "Chris was the worst, he ruled with an iron fist and I couldn't control it, couldn't stop it, when I challenged him he threatened to see me dead", Angharad raised her eyebrows. "When boys got things wrong, Chris would make sure they regretted it". "I can't imagine anyone would have ever been able to intimidate you?" said Angharad and Simon shot her a look, "he somehow knew about my tastes". Simon looked Angharad up and down, "he would have used that against me, made sure that the boys would have tortured me and then killed me".

The interview room became silent as Angharad contemplated what Simon was telling her. Confused and ashamed at being gay, he had built a reputation for himself and had been petrified that it would all come down around him. "So what happened?" asked Angharad and Simon blinked, "I was made to help him out with special jobs". Simon stopped but Angharad knew the answer to the next bit. "To kill Marion Davies?" she asked and he nodded slowly, "yes". Over the next fifteen minutes Simon laid out what had happened, Chris had provided the key that allowed him into the old shop next door. Then, in the darkness of the night before Marion's death he had gone down into the cellar and knocked through the wall. Setting up a small camp in the old office upstairs, Simon had watched and waited for the following night. That night, once he knew that Marion was alone in her office Simon crept into the cellar and moving carefully, he was able to make it up into the ground floor without disturbing her. Then, placed the rug onto the electric fire and waited until it was smoking heavily before he headed for the staircase.

Chris had told Simon that he needed to burn the rug but then it was an obvious thing to do, it covered the cellar hatch and so there was no way to put it back when he made his escape. Climbing the stairs, Simon got to the doorway just as the first wisps of smoke reached the room that Marion was inside. By now, the smoke was starting to affect Simon and so he struggled with her when he should have been able to simply overpower Marion before finally he managed to throw her down the stairs. After making sure that Marion was dead Simon left the office just as the firefighters arrived to put out the fire. Back in the cellar of the shop next door he quietly bricked up the wall and then waited for the Police to leave.

"What is the relationship between Chris and William?" asked Claire and Simon shrugged. "I think they are brothers but I don't know for certain, I have seen them together a few times. On hearing that last bit, Angharad perked up and took control of the interview, "when?" she asked, "when have you seen them together?". Simon thought about it, "the last time was the day I killed Stephen Thomas" he said and Angharad felt a jolt as she realised what he had said. "You didn't mention that the other day" offered Angharad, "I didn't think it was relevant" he replied. Claire, who was growing in confidence spoke again, "tell us about that?". Slowly and moment by moment, Simon recalled the events that led up to the shooting of Stephen Thomas. "Chris picked me up late at night, we drove to a house over near Heolgerrig and I was sent to the door". "Go on" said Claire, "William answered and he handed me a gun, wrapped up in a small cloth" he said. Sitting on the edge of her seat, Angharad did not want to say anything in case she spoiled the flow of the situation. "Then I was taken by Chris up to the Gurnos, I approached number 13 and when Stephen appeared I shot him". Unable to believe her luck, Angharad looked at Simon, "what did William say when he gave you the gun?" she asked and she could see that he was thinking deeply. "He told me to make sure that I got the job right", "so he knew you were going to kill someone" Angharad prompted and Simon nodded his head, "I am sure he did". "Afterwards?" asked Claire, "what happened afterwards?". "I threw the gun in the Upper Neuadd reservoir" replied Simon.

Thinking the interview was finally at an end, Claire motioned to start wrapping it up when Angharad interrupted her. "You killed Gwyn Davies as well didn't you?". Simon looked at her, "who's is that?" he asked and Angharad was surprised to see that he didn't know. "Old boy who fell from Cefn viaduct", thinking slowly a smile crept across his face, "oh yeah, him, yeah that was me. I grabbed him from the street stuck him in the back of a van that Chris drove and then we took him out to the viaduct". He fell silent as if he did not feel a need to say anymore. "What happened there?" asked Angharad and Simon smiled, "he squealed like a girl as he wrote a note that Chris told him to write and then I threw him off".

This time it was the end of the interview, Claire ended it and stood up in silence while Angharad stood next to her with tears in her eyes. "Where did it all go wrong?" said Angharad to Simon, watching his face for a reaction, "the day our friendship ended" he replied before letting Claire lead him from the room. Walking outside into the rest of the custody block, Angharad found George and Thomas waiting. She told them what had happened during the interview, "so you're interviewing Chris next?" asked George and

Angharad nodded, "yes, it would seem wrong to interview anyone else".

Ten minutes later Angharad and Claire sat down with Chris Pritchard. This time, Angharad took the lead as now it would need a bit more experience. In his face she could see that he was still angry about being arrested. "Tell me what you know about Gwyn Davies, Stephen Thomas and Marion Davies", said Angharad, hoping to unsettle Chris with the matter of fact delivery but knowing that he was likely to hold his tongue. "I know nothing about any of that" he said, "I'm just trying to go straight after being banged up". "So you know nothing about any of those three, nothing about where they lived or worked?", "I know nothing" said Chris again. Nodding, Angharad smiled at Chris and he met her smile with a grimace. "What the fuck do you think you are smiling at?" he asked. "Who are the shop boys?" asked Angharad and again Chris shrugged his shoulders, "dunno" he said. "Do you know who Simon Lewis is?" Angharad asked and Chris refused to bite, "nope, never heard of him". "Oh, he knows of you" said Angharad almost in passing, "have you had a sexual relationship with him?", Angharad knew that was not the case but she was interested in seeing how Chris would react. Anger clouded Chris's face even more than previously, "is that what that fucking poofter has told you?" he shouted, "has he said that me and him like to play hide the sausage? I'll fucking kill the cunt! People like him rape children!". Angharad kept her face completely calm as Chris raged, even taking time to cast a glance at Claire who seemed to be shocked by the outrage and vitriol that was pouring out.

After letting out all of his anger Chris fell silent again though Angharad could see that he was still seething. "I thought you said you didn't know Simon Lewis", asked Angharad and Chris shot her a look. "Why don't you tell me about how he killed Marion Davies for you?". This time Chris shrunk in his seat for a moment and Angharad knew that she had him on the ropes, "why don't you tell us all about it?". Chris wouldn't bite, "no comment" he said. "How about you tell us about how he killed Gwyn Davies or Stephen

Thomas for you instead?" she asked and again Chris replied, "no comment".

It was a good situation for Angharad, she had caught Chris in a lie about everything that was going on and now he was refusing to correct the situation. Despite being given the chance he was not providing any defence to the allegations that were being made. Angharad was happy with the fact that Chris had chosen to go no comment, he had already demonstrated that he had lied about Simon Lewis. It would be easy to draw the necessary inferences from his lack of an account. "I've changed my mind, I want a Solicitor" said Chris and Angharad knew that she had broken him.

The need to get a solicitor meant that the interview would have be interrupted while one was arranged. Angharad used this opportunity to get Jonathan into the interview room, this was the one who she believed would be best placed to tell everything. Jonathan still seemed to be snivelling while he took his seat and Angharad looked at him. "You're not as tough as the rest of your family are you?" she asked but Jonathan did not reply. "Jonathan?" called Angharad and he raised his head slowly to look at her. "Did you really want to be part of all of this?" she asked and Jonathan shook his head, "why don't you tell me what you know then?". Rather than reply, Jonathan just continued to sit in silence, "how about I help you?" asked Angharad but Jonathan said nothing. She laid out the paperwork and the exhibits in front of Jonathan and went through them one by one. "I know that you are one of three brothers" she said, "William, you and your half-brother Chris". There was a slight flinch as Angharad said the name Chris and she jumped on it. "You don't like Chris do you?" and Jonathan shook his head while Angharad made a mental note of that.

"So you have a father called Henry and he raised you all in the legends of your family" said Angharad and Jonathan nodded slightly. "A legend that you have kept a grip on this town by any means possible for the last 160 years", this time Jonathan looked up to the ceiling. "I always said it was a mistake" he said, "I always said that one day it would all get found out". "What would get found out?" asked Angharad but Jonathan returned to looking down into his lap and refusing all eye contact. Turning to the modern diary, Angharad opened it up and showed Jonathan the Welsh version and he shrugged his shoulders, "I can't read Welsh" he said. "That's understandable" said Angharad, "luckily for you I know a professor of Welsh who has done me a little statement, this statement says that in the diary it records your family planning the deaths of Gwyn Davies, Stephen Thomas and Marion Davies" she said. "Do you know what else is interesting, that matches the way your distant ancestor Abraham Davies also killed three people back in 1844". "I always said that one day it would all get found out" said Jonathan again. Angharad paused and waited, "how about you tell me what would get found out?" she said and Jonathan slumped into his seat.

"This is supposed to be my time running the council and controlling this town" said Jonathan, "my time". Lowering her head to try and catch Jonathan's eye, Angharad spoke very slowly, "Jonathan?", she spoke softly, "Jonathan?" she said again, "you are a gentle person Jonathan, I suspect much more like your mother than like your father". At this, Jonathan raised his head slowly, "William and Chris are like your father aren't they?" she continued, "William is calm like your father can be but Chris is an embodiment of his uncontrolled violence, his desire to kill". Jonathan shuddered at the description but raised his head a bit more. "How do I end this?" he asked, tears filling his eyes and streaming down his cheek, "I never wanted this but I was told it was my family duty". Looking into his eyes, keeping her face as soft as possible, Angharad tried to look more like a gentle mother than a hardened Police officer. "Why don't you tell me everything about your family and their story?" asked Angharad and in that moment of weakness, Jonathan did.

After finishing the interview with Jonathan, it was time to move on to William, Angharad had made the decision at the very start to finish the process with Henry. The interview with William was quick, he was the only one who opted to have a solicitor from the start and throughout, he refused to answer any of the questions that were put to him. When asked about his involvement with the shop boys he refused to confirm or deny that he even knew who they were, never mind who was involved. When they moved on to the discussion of the gun; the same happened, William refused again to confirm or deny anything. Angharad did try to push William on the matter but the Solicitor intervened, "how about you produce this gun and the forensic evidence that my client has touched it?" he asked. There was nothing Angharad could do, not that it mattered. She had pages of evidence and confessions from two of the group to their involvement in the crimes. Now, Angharad was conducting the interviews more out of courtesy and appropriate process rather than because she wanted William to admit it, she had been certain throughout that he never would. For Angharad, she was now eager to move onto the last interview, the man who had controlled it all from the start, Henry Davies.

Interviewing Henry was a different experience, the true, cold blooded killer. Seeing Henry in the flesh immediately after William, it was possible for Angharad to spot that the son was living in the shadow of the father. Henry was clearly a true psychopath, his primary purpose and existence was all about self-protection. Declining a solicitor with a dismissive, "I don't need one", it was clear that he thought that even now he could out think those who opposed him. "Henry", said Angharad, "I'll be honest with you, Jonathan has confessed, and Simon has confessed to their involvements in the death of Gwyn Davies, Stephen Thomas and Marion Davies". "On top of that, Chris, in his anger, broke enough to show that he has lied" she said, "why don't you tell me all about the murders and how you orchestrated them?".

Staying absolutely still, Henry looked at Angharad, his eyes studying her every feature. "Jonathan always was weak" he said, "he is clearly not my son. If I had known my wife had slept around...", he cut himself off before he incriminated himself. "What has Jonathan been weak about?" asked Angharad and Henry turned his attention to Claire before returning to look at her again. "William led him astray" he said, taking Angharad by surprise, "I admit I am not a perfect person, I have sinned but my crimes were of the flesh". Letting him talk, Angharad stayed quiet, "when I was young I had a child with another woman, it was an accident but my wife was dead and that woman needed help and in her lay the devil and for a moment I was seduced", he said, "that is where Chris came from".

Henry thought carefully before continuing, "I tried to do my best for Chris, I gave him guidance and help even after he was adopted but eventually he came to Merthyr and he hit it off with William". It was not clear to Angharad what Henry was hoping to use as a defence and so she continued to let him talk, "William knew about the legend of my family and together with Chris, they discussed with me the possibility of reclaiming our position". Feigning disgust, Henry continued, "but I was horrified and forbid such talk". Holding his arms out palm up, Henry looked upwards as if looking to the heavens, "forgive me Lord for I did not raise my children correctly". Then he looked back at Angharad, "when I found out that my relatives Gwyn and Marion had died and that Stephen Thomas was dead as well, I tried to persuade myself that it was a coincidence but here we are and you think I am guilty" he offered. "That doesn't answer what Jonathan was weak about?" asked Angharad and Henry smiled gently, "Jonathan was always easily influenced by William, I was so glad when William moved out but it would have been William who would have told Jonathan to make a confession". Watching Henry closely and hiding her feelings within, Angharad could not believe what Henry was doing in order to protect himself. He was throwing all three of his children onto the fire, claiming that it was them responsible for everything and that he, the man of God, had attempted to prevent it and was only now realising that he had failed.

"What about the diary you kept?" asked Angharad and Henry looked at her, surprise on his face, "diary?", he asked. "Diary" said Angharad again, "tell me about your diary?" and Henry smiled, "I keep a diary of my appointments" he said, "I keep no other diary". "What about the diary in the secret drawer in your desk?"

asked Angharad and Henry shook his head, "I know nothing about a secret drawer in my desk?". "Oh?" said Angharad and she put the diary in front of Henry. "So you are denying that this is written by you?" she asked and Henry agreed, "of course", he said, "I don't speak Welsh". Now Angharad knew that she had Henry in a difficult spot, "but you do speak Welsh" she offered and Henry shook his head, "no, no I don't, William is the only Welsh speaker in my family". "Oh but you do" said Angharad, "you see a number of years ago you used to give a sermon in Welsh". "You must be mistaken" said Henry. "I wish I was, but I have a statement from a Susan Rogers here who says that she attended them". Henry looked deflated at that and Angharad saw that she was starting to turn the tables.

"Let's say I can speak Welsh?" he suggested, "how does that prove that I wrote the diary?". Angharad smiled at that, "you're right, it doesn't" she said but alongside that modern diary was an old one written in 1844. Henry shrugged his shoulders, "I don't see why that is relevant?" he offered. Putting this older book in front of Henry she pointed at it, "I see that it was kept by an Abraham Davies, he was your five time great grandfather?" Angharad said and Henry nodded, "something like that". "Have you read the story?" asked Angharad and Henry nodded. "Yes, it is sad that my ancestor appears to have been quite an evil man" he said, "yet I still fail to see what that has to do with me?". Letting the sides of her mouth form a slight smile, Angharad looked into the eyes of Henry, the psychopath. "He didn't get all his own way though did he?" asked Angharad and Henry shook his head, "no, he was opposed by a Police officer, a Sergeant Ephraim Jones who I believe finally rose to the rank of Superintendent". "Now you find yourself opposed by Sergeant Angharad Jones". Thinking for a moment, Henry's face fell, "you're his descendent?" he asked. "Yes", she said, "oh and that diary you claimed not to write, maybe you shouldn't have wrote in it that on the Sunday just gone you gave a teaching in church on the subject of Judas". As Henry slumped into his seat, the slouch in his body showing that he had been defeated, Angharad knew that she had won.

The interviews had been over for a couple of hours and Angharad was locked away in consultation with the Crown Prosecution Service. Thomas somehow proving his stamina, sat in George's office and read the newspaper while the Inspector slept in his chair. Sitting in the corner on the floor Claire and Rhys slept, their heads resting on each other as all of them waited. A sudden rush of wind swept through the room as the door was pushed open and in stepped Mike Browning, his face dark and angry as he looked around the room. "Where is that fucking whore?" he asked, "where the fuck is she?". Thomas rose to his feet as everyone else slowly roused from their slumber, alerted by the actions of the angry Superintendent. "My granddaughter is not a whore and anyway she is not here" Thomas said, meeting the aggression of Mike with a calmness that seemed almost out of place in front of such a whirlwind. Mike chose to ignore Thomas and turned to face George, "hey fuckwit" he said, "where is that stupid Sergeant of yours?". Stepping forward to meet Mike face on, Thomas challenged him more clearly, "you don't get to come in here with that attitude". Mike turned to face Thomas, "this is none of your fucking business, like it was none of your fucking business ten years ago" he said. "This is Police business and you were not a Police officer then and you are not a Police officer now". Thomas flexed his hands and stood his ground. "Leave the room now" he commanded but Mike was having none of it. "You don't get to tell me to back off" said Mike, "you're just the demented old father of our beloved Chief Constable and as I have already said, this is none of your damn business".

A cough came from behind Mike and he spun on his heels, just as a female voice spoke, "you're right, it's not his business but it is mine". Mike visibly pushed down his anger quickly as he found himself staring into the face of Deputy Chief Constable Mandy Hughes. "Out of my way" she commanded and Mike stepped to the side as Mandy walked into the room. Seeing Thomas as she entered she turned to face him, "hello, you must be Thomas?" she said shaking his hand. Rhys, Claire and George all rushed to get to their feet and Mandy raised her hands, and signalled for everyone to sit back down. "There's no need to rush to your feet" she said, "I know you have all been working hard overnight". Mike still fumed as the others looked on, still surprised at the sudden appearance of such a senior officer.

"I'm here for the same reason the monkey is" Mandy said and she waved a casual hand in the direction of Mike. "So where is Sergeant Jones?" she asked and turned to face George, "Inspector? Do you know?". As George looked at her he noted that her face was blank and impossible to read. "I... I... I... believe she is talking to the CPS" blurted out George after much hesitation. The presence of Mike seemed to be bringing his worst fears out of him again. Mandy nodded, "well we may as well all wait together then, Mike, why don't you find me a chair, you can get yourself one while you are there?". Mike bristled at being asked, as a Superintendent, to do a job that he felt was below him but he couldn't refuse given who was making the request. A couple of minutes later, as the room remained silent he returned with two extra chairs, wheeling one before him and one behind. Making a point of positioning a chair for Mandy correctly, he then took his own seat. "Thank you Mike" said Mandy before taking her seat and pulling out her mobile phone. "I need to check emails" she said, "I hope you don't all mind?". The hint was clear, Mandy was demanding silence from all in the room and given who she was nobody found it appropriate to argue.

Another hour or so had passed before Angharad finally returned to the office. She walked in, her face drawn and pale looking but with a hint of happiness still somehow burning in her eyes. As she entered, she noticed Mike sitting in his chair and then looking at the other occupants she realised that even he was being outranked. "Ma'am?" she said, addressing the most senior rank in the room. Mandy rose to her feet, putting her phone away. "Sergeant Jones" said Mandy, "I have been hearing some interesting stories about you", the delivery was matter of fact but

Angharad knew that she would need to be completely open in her reply. "Yes Ma'am?" said Angharad, trying to avoid giving away anything until she had a clearer idea as to what the Deputy Chief Constable was doing there.

Mandy turned to Rhys and Claire, "you can go now" she commanded and both of them nodded quickly before making themselves scarce, closing the door as they went. "So", said Mandy, "you've gone behind the backs of the Major Investigation Unit, investigated three deaths, two of which they have already declared as not being suspicious and one of which they said was a murder within the organised crime community, for which they had no suspects". "Yes Ma'am" replied Angharad. "Now, Detective Superintendent Mike Browning is here ready to rip you apart because you have gone out and arrested four people for involvement in all three deaths?". Angharad kept her eyes on the Deputy Chief Constable, only briefly looking towards Mike as his name was mentioned. "Yes Ma'am" Angharad replied again, "so Sergeant Jones, why should I stop Mike Browning from kicking your backside out of the job?".

Angharad fought to keep calm and pulled herself upright, pushing her shoulders back and looking as confident as she could possibly manage, "because I just charged all four of them with three counts of conspiracy to murder, Ma'am". A smile broke across her face at the last bit and she couldn't resist a wink in the direction of Thomas. "You've charged all four with conspiracy to murder?" asked Mandy, "well this is interesting". Turning her attention to Mike, Mandy continued to speak in a matter of fact way, "what do you have to say about this, Superintendent Browning? In fact, what do you have to say that would stop me from letting Sergeant Jones kick your backside out of this station?". His face was full of rage and he appeared to be even angrier than when he had first walked into the room, "what the fuck is this jumped up officer doing interfering in my work?". "Quite", said Mandy, "though I wouldn't call it interfering with results like that, still the point is valid, why did you not just provide the information directly to the Major Investigation

Unit?".

Scanning the room, Angharad took the time to think about her answer, "I tried to raise my first concerns with the attending officer, DC Di Marco but he ignored me". Mandy nodded, "continue" she said, "and when I started identifying things, with the help of my grandfather, I had a chance to speak to Superintendent Browning but rather than listening he acted more like a cunt!". "Hmmm", said Mandy, "how do you feel about this Mike?", the change in title was obviously an attempt to give him a chance to dig himself out of a hole, "how about you give Sergeant Jones a part in your team? She obviously spotted things that you missed". "She used to work in my team, she's a waste of space, that's why I sent her up here to Merthyr, where such an incompetent officer couldn't do any damage" he said, his anger not backing down.

Mandy slowly surveyed Angharad and Mike, looking at each of them in turn before speaking again, "Mike, you're a big mate of Angharad's father Gareth" she said, "but you're as clueless as him at times". Mike moved to open his mouth and protest the situation but Mandy raised her hand, "Mike, leave this room now before I have Angharad throw you out". At that Mandy looked at Mike, keeping silent as she waited for him to turn and leave. Mike clearly thought about protesting but realised that it would be pointless and he turned and walked out the door. The Detective Superintendent gone, Mandy spoke again, "Angharad, can you close the door please, the idiot must have been born in a barn". Angharad did as she was instructed and then sat down in the chair that was offered to her by Mandy, "let's talk shall we?".

"I've never liked Mike", said Mandy, "I've never trusted him and I don't think he is up to the job but he is a mate of your father's so I have to tolerate him". Angharad nodded as Mandy looked towards Thomas, "no offence intended to either of you" she said. Thomas bowed his head to show that he had not taken any. "As you know", continued Mandy, "it is my job to oversee all of the major crime investigations across the whole of the force" and the group indicated that they understood. "For a while now I have felt that the Major Investigation Unit have not been up to it, especially when it comes to looking after the valleys". Mandy waited for her words to sink in, "so I have a suggestion, I want to create a separate team to specifically handle this area and today's developments have given me that opportunity, what do you think?".

Angharad looked at the others in the room and realised that she was the only one prepared to speak. "It sounds like a good idea" said Angharad, "but where are you going to find the necessary people from?". "I'm looking at them aren't I?" Mandy posed the question and let it hang in the air. "What do you think Detective Chief Inspector Williams? I am right in thinking that you are a qualified detective?" the question was aimed at George who cleared his throat before giving a response, "yes Ma'am, qualified Detective and more than happy to help". "Good", said Mandy, "and how about having Inspector Jones here to run your investigations?". George stared at Mandy for a moment as he mulled the situation over, "that would be perfect Ma'am". "What do you think, Inspector Jones?", Angharad shifted in her seat as Mandy stared at her waiting for an answer. Looking first to Thomas who sat quietly with pride in his face and then to George who sat impassively, Angharad turned her attention back to the Deputy Chief Constable. "When do I start Ma'am" she asked. Mandy smiled, "I think Monday morning sounds good, after you've all had a chance to sleep".

Authors Observations

While the above is a product of my own over active imagination I have South Wales and the town of Merthyr Tydfil in particular as my template. As such every place mentioned within that town exists or has existed in some form. Where suitable I have changed the names of locations or called upon places that no longer exist. Any link between the real locations and the events in this story are purely my invention and no connection should be drawn or inferred. The same applies to the people who appear in this book, all of the characters have their own story and bare no resemblance to any person either living or dead. Having said all of that as Andrea Camilleri said at the end of The Dance of the Seagulls "when one writes, even pure fiction, isn't one's reference always the real world?".

I have attempted to be geographically and historically accurate in the telling of this story but at the end of the day I am only human and I make mistakes. Any mistakes that do appear in this book are my own and belong only to me. If you wish to discuss these facts in a sensible and intelligent way then you can always find me on the following:

Blog: **theghostsofmerthyr.wordpress.com**
Facebook: **www.facebook.com/theghostsofmerthyr**
Twitter: **www.twitter.com/ghostsofmerthyr**

Acknowledgements

In the writing of this book I have called on the assistance of a small number of people to help. Sometimes that has been done just to gain confidence that what I was doing made sense but at other times I called on people to provide fresh eyes and a fresh perspective on what I had written. I would like to thank each and every one of them for their assistance and I would not have finished it without their help. In particular I would like to thank my wife Laura Lewis, my parents David and Elaine Lewis and my mother in law Maureen Sinclair. Further, I would like to thank, in no particular order; The Burdens (both of them), Vicky England, Donna Messenger and the Redingensians Coach Potatoes.

27399938R00129

Printed in Great Britain
by Amazon